The MOBSTER'S DAUGHTER

MIMI FRANCIS

Massachusetts Mafia 2

The MOBSTER'S DAUGHTER

MIMI FRANCIS

4 Horsemen
Publications, Inc.

Dedication

For everybody who thought I couldn't.
Guess what? I did.

Irish Words

Amico–Italian for male friend

Сука–Russian for bitch

Мудак–Russian for asshole

Leascheannasaí–Irish for second-in-command

Forneart–Irish for enforcer

Contents

Chapter 1
Caitlin

"Caitlin!"

She swung around, her long blonde hair hitting her face as the wind caught it. Her boyfriend, Bobby, jogged toward her; his dark brown hair fell over his face, and his T-shirt looked like it had shrunk four sizes. Thanks to the chill fall air, his nipples noticeably poked against the thin fabric. He smirked at her, a look she once found attractive, but now it filled her with dread. If she could have faded into the background and disappeared, she would have done it. Caitlin didn't have the energy for him at the moment.

He slid to a stop in front of her and leaned down for a kiss. Caitlin turned her head at the last second, so Bobby's lips grazed her cheek. He huffed and grabbed her chin, forcing her to look at him. He kissed her again, his lips pressing hard against hers. It didn't even feel like a kiss; it was a declaration of ownership.

"Let's go out to dinner tonight," he said.

She tried to pull back, but his grip on her chin tightened. "I can't. I have a crap ton of homework to do, so I need to stay in and get it done."

Bobby laughed. "You can do it later."

Caitlin pushed his hand away, breaking his hold on her, and shook her head. "My father isn't paying for me to fail law school. We can go out another night."

"Your father is an ass, and you know it," Bobby muttered. "Besides, he's fucking loaded. He can afford to pay your tuition to law school several times over. If you fail, just do it again."

Caitlin's skin bristled. While it was true she had a contentious relationship with her father, she didn't like it when her asshole boyfriend talked shit about him. He didn't understand what it was like living with someone like Sean O'Reilly.

"I don't want to argue—"

Bobby cut her off. "Then don't. I'll pick you up at seven." He didn't give her a chance to protest; he just turned around and left without saying goodbye.

For the hundredth time in the last week, Caitlin wondered why she was still dating Bobby. He exhausted her, was an asshole, and wasn't worth the trouble anymore. At first, being with him had helped keep her mind off the man she really wanted in her life. A man she could never have. And her father never would have approved. But sometime during the last six months, she'd grown tired of fighting with him and denying her feelings for the other man.

Her cell phone vibrated in her back pocket. She took it out, and a smile spread across her face. Speak of the devil. Caitlin smirked.

"Hello?" she answered, purposely cheerful.

"I dealt with the problem with your car."

"Well, hello to you, too, Grady."

"I don't have time for your shit, princess," her father's second-in-command snapped. "Your car is in the shop. You can pick it up on Friday. Try not to fuck it up again."

"The accident wasn't my fault this time—"

"It's never your fault," he muttered. "Nothing is ever your fault."

The low growl in Grady's voice turned Caitlin's stomach inside out. What she wouldn't give to hear that sound while he was inside her, fucking her brains out. She closed her eyes, and the image invaded her head.

"Caitlin?"

"Uh, yeah?"

"Did you hear what I said?"

She giggled. "No, sorry. My mind drifted for a second there."

"Your father wants to know when you're coming home to visit," Grady asked.

"I don't know," she mumbled. "Look, I have to go. I have class." She disconnected the call.

Why did the one man she wanted more than anything in the world have to be not only her father's best friend, but his second-in-command, completely off-limits, and twenty-one years older than her? It wasn't fair.

"*Life isn't fair*," her father's voice echoed in her head. "*The sooner you figure that out, the better off you'll be.*"

After arriving home to her small apartment, Caitlin dropped her purse and backpack on the kitchen table. It was a one bedroom close to NYU, with a kitchen and living room combination, a small bedroom, and a bathroom. The apartment was tiny, but cozy. She had decorated it herself, picking out furniture she liked and making it feel like home. Just as she kicked off her boots, someone knocked on the door. She sighed and looked through the peephole. The person standing in the hallway didn't look familiar.

"May I help you?" she asked in a raised voice.

"Is, uh, Bobby here?" the man yelled.

"No. He doesn't live here," Caitlin replied.

"Can I come in and wait for him?" He shifted from foot to foot, repeatedly scratched his arm and peered into the peephole, so close Caitlin could see flecks of dandruff in his eyebrows.

She quietly flipped the deadbolt and pushed the button on the doorknob so the door was locked. "I told you Bobby doesn't live here."

The man slammed his first against the flimsy wooden door. Caitlin jumped and stumbled back. Her knees hit the couch, and she fell onto the cushions. She stared at the door until she heard footsteps retreating down the hall.

"Fuck," she muttered under her breath.

Caitlin had long suspected Bobby was involved in less-than-legitimate activities and while she was definitely not one to judge, she hated he had brought something like that into her life. Moving to New York was Caitlin's escape from the mafia world, and now Bobby had dragged her back into it.

If her suspicions were correct, he worked for Aldo Moretti, an Italian mobster with a frightening reputation. The O'Reilly family had dealt with the Morettis on and off for years, and recently, the O'Reillys had been involved in some kind of negotiations with them, though she didn't know exactly what they were. After certain promises made by her father fell through, Sean O'Reilly had been reluctant to let Caitlin move to New York for school, worrying about her safety. She assured him everything was fine. Her father would go insane if he found out she was dating someone involved with the Morettis.

Yet another reason to break up with Bobby. Caitlin waited a few minutes before she got up to grab her phone. She pulled up Bobby's number to text him, but before she could, his name popped up and a message appeared on her screen.

[Bobby: I'm on my way up.]

"Shit," she mumbled under her breath. She perched on the edge of the couch to wait for him.

Bobby came through the door a few minutes later, using his key to get in. He sat down beside her, grabbed her arm, pulled her against his body, and pressed another one of those hard kisses to her lips.

Caitlin put her hands on his chest and pushed him away.

"What's wrong?" he asked.

"Nothing," she mumbled, staring at her feet.

"Then stop pouting," he said. "Let's go grab some food."

"I told you I have homework. I have a paper due for my ethics class."

Bobby laughed and shook his head. "Are you joking? You're writing a paper on ethics? Are you planning to mention that your father is paying for your education with money he earned illegally?"

Caitlin frowned. If what she suspected was true, he didn't have room to talk. "Knock it off. I'm not in the mood for your shit."

He propped his feet on her coffee table. "You just don't like it when I point out the obvious. What are you going to do with your fancy law degree, anyway? Are you going to work for the family, keeping thugs out of jail? Or maybe you can help your father figure out how to wash all that dirty money he earns. You have so many options."

"I'm going into environmental law," she retorted. "You know that."

"Yeah, until your daddy wants you to help keep his people out of jail. You'll cave. You don't have the guts to stand up to him."

Caitlin got up and went to the kitchen. She took a glass out of the cupboard and filled it with water from the sink. Her hands shook as she raised it to her lips.

God, she wished she'd never confided in him about her family and where her money came from. That had been at the beginning of their relationship, when everything was brand new and she hoped she might fall in love with him. Caitlin usually kept those things private, but when they first started dating, Bobby swept her off her feet, and she thought she wanted to share her life with him.

"You don't have any room to talk," she said. "Haven't you been working for Aldo Moretti?"

Bobby shot off the couch and stalked across the room. He grabbed her upper arm and squeezed. "How the hell do you know that?"

Caitlin slapped his hand away. "Don't touch me."

He clenched his fists and glared at her. "I asked you how you know I'm working for Aldo Moretti."

She snorted, dumped the water in the sink, and put the glass on the counter. "How do you think? I listen. And it's not like you're quiet when you're on the phone. You sure the hell aren't trying to keep it a secret. What have you been doing for him? Selling drugs? I know the

Morettis are deep in the drug trade, so it makes sense he'd use you to do that."

"Forget everything you've heard, sweetheart," Bobby said. "Aldo Moretti isn't a man you want to mess with."

Caitlin laughed. "Neither is my father." She crossed her arms over her chest. "I think you should go."

He took a step closer and raised his upper lip in a snarl. "I'm not leaving."

She stood her ground. "I'm not asking you. I'm telling you. We're done. I don't want to see you anymore. Get out of my apartment. Now."

Bobby grunted something incomprehensible, spun on his heel, and walked away. He stopped at the door, looked at Caitlin, pulled back his fist, and punched the wall, putting a hole in the drywall.

Caitlin stumbled back a step, fear wrapping its cold fingers around her heart.

"This isn't over." He yanked open the door and left.

Ethics papers and alcohol did not mix. Caitlin sat back and rubbed her forehead, angry with herself for giving into the urge to drink after the fight with Bobby. She knew better than to let stuff like that get to her.

Two hours and half a bottle of wine after her now ex-boyfriend stormed out, she remembered he had a key to her apartment. Caitlin kept expecting him to walk through the door, uninvited. If she was at home, she could have called her father, and he would have sent someone over immediately to change the locks. It was the first time in months she missed being in Boston.

Caitlin picked up her phone, opened her contacts, then put it down again. She couldn't call him. She didn't *need* to call him. Grady McCarthy didn't answer to her.

Grady had been around since she was a teenager and friends with her father longer than she had been alive. She hadn't paid attention to him when she was younger; he was always there, but he ignored her, and she did the same to him. It wasn't until Caitlin started causing problems—rebelling—when she went away to college that he became a staple in her life. That had been shortly after her sister Olivia disappeared to avoid marrying a man she didn't love.

Unable to deal with his daughter himself, Caitlin's father instructed Grady to watch over her. If Caitlin got in trouble or needed help—which she frequently did—Sean O'Reilly told her to contact Grady. Her first phone call was always supposed to be to him.

She didn't know when or why he became her father's *leascheannasaí*—second-in-command—though she remembered it had happened after her father was injured in an attack at J. Foley's Café.

Caitlin would never say it out loud to anyone, but Grady was Caitlin's fantasy man, the older man she longed to be with, even if it was only for one night. The only older man she'd ever found attractive. For years, he was at every family gathering, hanging around their house all the time, and he went everywhere the family went. Caitlin couldn't get rid of him if she wanted to.

Not that she did. He was easy on the eyes and damn attractive with his salt-and-pepper hair, neatly trimmed beard, and hazel eyes. He was well built, too. Huge biceps, one of which had a tattoo rumored to be the McCarthy family crest, though no one knew for sure. Then there was the six-pack abdomen and the chest ready to burst from the too-tight T-shirts he favored. He also had an ass you could bounce a quarter off. The man was a walking GQ ad, and he didn't even know it.

The only thing marring his perfect looks was the perpetual scowl on his face. Caitlin never saw him smile. He was all business and insanely devoted to her father. Grady McCarthy's only mission in life was to do as Sean O'Reilly commanded.

Caitlin wasn't sure when she first realized she was attracted to Grady; it certainly didn't come out of nowhere. More like a gradual thing happening over time. One day he was the annoying asshole who tried to keep her in line; the next he was mildly annoying, and she didn't mind when he showed up to fix her messes. Eventually, Caitlin caused problems so Grady *would* come around and bail her out of whatever trouble she got herself into. She daydreamed about him, imagining scenarios she knew would never come to fruition. Her mild crush on him had become an obsession.

Caitlin knew nothing would ever come of her feelings for him. The man was twenty-one years older than her and worked for her father. He couldn't possibly be more out of her reach, so any relationship between them had to remain platonic. Anything else would be a scandal, taboo, and irresponsible. However, that didn't stop her from fantasizing about him every chance she got.

Dating Bobby had been an attempt to flush her system of Grady. He made it easy to forget about her unattainable crush. During the last two or three months, things changed, and she discovered Bobby wasn't the man she thought he was. He was an egotistical jerk who took advantage of her and treated her like a possession.

Caitlin should tell Grady about Bobby. If something happened because she broke up with him and she didn't give Grady a heads up, he would be pissed. She picked up her phone and set it down again. Maybe she would wait until morning. No sense bothering him this late.

Homework was a bust for the night. Forget the paper; she would finish it before class. She shoved her books and laptop in her backpack, laid down on the couch, and turned on the TV. Hopefully, losing herself in some mindless show would help her stop thinking about her pain-in-the-ass ex-boyfriend.

Chapter 2
Caitlin

"I think I had too much to drink," Caitlin muttered under her breath three hours later. She stumbled to the kitchen, turned on the water, and stuck her head under the faucet. The water ran into her mouth and dribbled down her cheeks. She cupped her hands under the flow and splashed some on her face. Praying she wouldn't puke, she hung over the sink and blindly reached for the faucet to turn it off. She shouldn't have finished the bottle of wine, especially on an empty stomach.

A loud meow caught her attention. Sitting on her fire escape and looking in her window was a small gray-and-white cat. Caitlin had been feeding him for almost two weeks and didn't know where he came from or if he belonged to someone. He showed up most nights, she fed him, and he disappeared. He meowed again, louder this time.

"I'm coming, kitty," she mumbled. Caitlin opened the cupboard next to the fridge and took out a can of cat food. If she didn't feed him, she wasn't sure who would. Caitlin dumped the food in a purple plastic dish, pulled on her NYU sweatshirt, and then pushed the living room window open and climbed onto the fire escape. She closed the window, leaving it open about an inch; otherwise, the cat would go inside, and it would take her hours to get him out.

Caitlin sat down with her back against the wall and set the food between her feet. The cat weaved his way around her legs and bumped his head against her hand until she scratched between his ears. After a few minutes of petting, he ate.

Bobby hated the cat, calling him stupid and bitching every time she fed the poor thing. Another reason to be glad he was gone. His attitude annoyed her. *He* annoyed her. She'd wasted too much time on him, time she could have been spent on better things. Caitlin had tried for six months to convince herself that Bobby Corelli was the man she wanted, but she'd lied to herself.

He didn't come close to being the man she wanted—Caitlin wanted somebody mature, older, a man who could satisfy her. Bobby was a distraction, meant to take her mind off Grady. It hadn't worked; she thought about Grady constantly. The man was always on her mind. She had imagined him in more scenarios than she could count, and most of them were not safe for work.

Sitting out here in the dark, thinking about how badly she wanted Grady, and how good it could be with him, had her clenching her thighs together and biting her lip. God, what she wouldn't give for one night in bed with that man.

Her heart nearly stopped when she heard her apartment door slam shut, pulling her from her musings about Grady. A second later, Bobby screamed her name.

"Caitlin! Caitlin, where the *fuck* are you?"
Shit!

She didn't move. Jesus Christ, it sounded like he was drunk or maybe high. There was no way she was going to let him know where she was, especially after what he'd done to her wall earlier; that could have been her face. She had a feeling he wanted it to be her face. Slowly, she got to her feet and inched toward the window.

Bobby was still screaming her name as he moved around her apartment. He probably saw her backpack on the floor, so he knew she was home. It was only a matter of time before he remembered the cat and checked outside.

A loud cracking noise, like wood breaking, echoed through the apartment. Then she heard voices she didn't recognize. Bobby shouted something incomprehensible and grunted, which was followed by the sound of furniture crashing to the floor.

Caitlin hugged herself, stepped over the cat, and flattened herself against the wall, peeking around the edge of the window. Two men stood in the middle of her small living room with their backs to the window. Bobby was on the floor, next to her overturned coffee table, with a hand pressed to his nose and blood seeping through his fingers.

"Where's your girlfriend, Bobby boy?" the large, bald man asked. "She in the bathroom? The bedroom?"

"Joey, listen—"

"Where is she?" the guy named Joey asked again.

Bobby shook his head. "I don't know where she is. I … I let myself in. I have a key."

Joey glanced at the other man. "Gino?"

"I checked the whole place," the other guy said. "It's empty. The girl isn't here."

Joey sighed dramatically. "Well, shit. That makes this a lot harder."

While Caitlin watched, Gino took a gun from his pocket—*her* gun, the one Grady gave her, the gun she kept in the bottom drawer of her dresser. He pointed it at Bobby's head.

"Jesus Christ, Gino!" Bobby screeched, his hand in front of his face. "What the hell do you think you're doing? Do you want me to tell my father you pointed a gun at my fucking head? He will kill you."

"Yeah, he's gonna be pissed." Joey laughed. "But not at us."

Bobby inched back, his hand still blocking his face. "What are you talking about?"

"Do you know where the girl is?" Joey asked again.

"I told you I don't." A strangled sob left Bobby's mouth. "We got in a fight. She broke up with me, kicked me out. I got a little drunk and came back to talk to her. But she's not here."

Joey nodded at Bobby. "Get it over with, Gino. We need to find the girl."

Gino stepped closer to Bobby and put the gun to the center of his forehead. Caitlin jumped back, flattened herself against the wall, and covered her mouth to stifle her scream when the gun went off. Tears leaked from her eyes.

Oh my God. Oh my God.

Caitlin stayed where she was, pressed against the wall. She couldn't hear anything over the sound of her heart pounding in her ears. The urge to move overwhelmed her. She counted to three, then to ten, then she took a chance, crept to the window, and peered in.

Her living room looked like a slaughterhouse. Blood covered every surface—floor, couch, coffee table, the wall, even the ceiling. Her blue-and-white rug, a gift from her mother, was splattered with chunks of brain matter. Caitlin groaned quietly as her stomach turned. She gnawed on her lower lip and prayed she wouldn't vomit.

"What now?" Gino asked, startling her as he came out of her bedroom with Joey. She jumped and leaned against the wall, out of sight.

"We do exactly what he said," Joey replied. "Make it look like the girl did it. We'll watch the place and when she comes back, we follow her up and take care of her. They'll find her dead in an apartment with a dead guy. Murder-suicide. Case closed. Wipe down the gun and leave it on the floor. If we're lucky, she'll pick it up when she comes in. If not, we'll put it in her hand after we do her."

Caitlin pressed her cheek against the bricks. What the hell were they talking about? They wanted to blame Bobby's death on her? Murder-suicide? What was happening? Her head spun.

The cat brushed against her arm as he leaped onto the railing beside her. Spooked, she jumped, and a loud gasp escaped her.

"Did you hear that?" one of the men said.

Caitlin stepped back, her eyes darting around, her hand on her mouth.

Fuck.

The cat jumped down, twisted in and out of her legs, then sauntered down the fire escape. Caitlin looked over the edge, then back at the window. She heard the men moving through her apartment, headed her way. Staying here would get her killed. Decision made, she grabbed the railing, swung her leg over the side, and climbed down the ladder. Just as she got to the floor below hers, she heard the men shouting above her. She moved faster, tears streaming down her face, stumbling when her feet hit the ground. She spun around and bolted.

Caitlin sprinted through the streets of Greenwich Village, jumping at every shadow, fear forcing her to move as quickly as possible. After twenty blocks, her legs felt like rubber and her lungs burned, so she slowed to a stop. She turned in a circle, trying to get her bearings. On the corner across the street, she saw Katz's Delicatessen, so she crossed against the light and ducked inside.

She stood off to one side, gasping for breath. The person in front of her gave her a weird look and inched away from her. Caitlin tried to smile, but it must have looked like a grimace or something, because the person cleared their throat and edged closer to the counter. Caitlin took a step away from them, crossed her arms, and stared at the floor.

The irritated young man behind the counter got her a large coffee, then Caitlin found a table facing the door. She eased into her seat and took her phone from her back pocket. Her hands shook so hard she couldn't read the screen. She set it down, folded her hands in front of her, and closed her eyes.

Caitlin didn't know if she should call the police or call her father. The police might blame her for Bobby's death, which was apparently what those men wanted. Running made her look guilty. And it was her gun that had been used to shoot Bobby in the head. How the hell was she supposed to explain that? Her head spun, and her stomach hurt. If she called the police, as soon as she said her name, they would know who her father was. It wouldn't help her situation; people assumed the daughter of a criminal was a criminal, too.

What if Bobby had been killed because of some slight against Aldo Moretti? If he died at the hands of the Morettis and they knew she was an O'Reilly, it might explain everything. According to her father, the Boston and New York families had no respect for each other, and there was a definite inability to communicate. Sean O'Reilly's decision to call off a business transaction that would have fostered a major truce between the families might be the reason someone wanted to frame her for murder.

Leverage. Or revenge. Whatever it was, Caitlin was once again pulled involuntarily into the family business.

Despite her reservations, she knew there was only one person she could call.

Her hand shook even harder as she picked up her phone and dialed his number. She exhaled slowly and hit the send button.

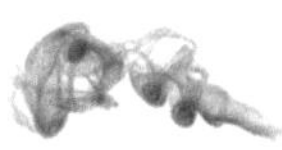

Three hours; Caitlin didn't know if she could wait that long. Thank God she had Apple Pay on her phone, since she ran out of the apartment with nothing. If she kept ordering coffee, she could stay in the deli until Grady arrived. After she finished the first cup, she returned to the counter, grabbed two magazines, and ordered more coffee and a sandwich. The guy behind the counter didn't even look at her as he rang her up and handed Caitlin her food.

Thank God Grady answered when she called, which Caitlin knew he would. Her father would not be happy if he found out Grady ignored a call from one of the O'Reilly daughters.

Not that her sister, Liv, would call him for help; she had her husband, Declan. He would protect Caitlin's sister with his life. He'd more than proven that.

Caitlin shifted in the uncomfortable deli chair to keep her ass from falling asleep. Her mind wouldn't stop replaying the sound of the bullet tearing through Bobby's forehead and the loud *thunk* his body made when it hit the floor. The chunks of his brain were all over her rug. Just thinking about it made her want to puke.

Exhaustion washed over her. What she wouldn't give for a soft bed to crawl into and forget the world existed. Caitlin rested her head on the wall behind her and closed her eyes. She tried to calm her racing heart and overactive brain by taking deep, cleansing breaths.

It must have worked because the next thing she knew, the bell over the delicatessen door jingled, and Grady McCarthy strode through. He surveyed the restaurant, turning slowly until his eyes landed on Caitlin. Before he said anything, she shot out of her seat and threw herself into his arms.

Caitlin buried her face against the side of his neck and inhaled the clean, manly scent that was all Grady—soap, Old Spice deodorant, leather, and cologne. She wanted to stay there forever, but he grabbed her and held her at arm's length.

"What the hell is going on, Caitlin?" he asked. "Explain to me why I had to drive three hours to rescue you. And it better be good."

"It's not good, Grady. It's bad. Really, *really* bad."

Chapter 3
Grady

"What's the word out of New York?" Sean asked. "Is Moretti still pissed?"

"Right now, they're staying quiet," Declan replied. "Maybe they've decided causing problems isn't worth the risk."

Grady cleared his throat. Everyone turned to look at him. He kept his arms crossed over his chest and reminded himself not to fidget. He hated being the center of attention and would have preferred to have this conversation with Sean privately, but it looked like that would not happen.

Long gone were the days when it was just him and his boss, shooting the shit and figuring things out. Now the room was full—Declan, Sean's son-in-law; his nephew Finn; and Declan's second, Conor. In the corner, sequestered behind a computer, was Sean's new assistant, Angus, brought in as their IT guy. Technology moved too fast for the old guys to keep up. God, he missed how it used to be.

"Grady? Do you have something to say?" Sean asked.

"Yeah." He took a deep breath and stepped out of the shadows beside the ornate fireplace. "They're up to something, but I have no clue what. There's been a lot of chatter that the Morettis are scheming, and it will be a big deal. Word is it could cause a rift in our family and take us down."

"Who told you that?" Declan inquired.

"A couple of my guys have friends in the Moretti family," Grady explained. "They said they've heard rumblings of trouble that could extend to us."

Despite being O'Reilly's *leascheannasaí*, he maintained a solid relationship with the men and women who worked beneath him. They talked to him, and he listened.

If he had listened ten years ago, things would be different.

"Grady?"

His head snapped up. "Sorry, boss. What did you say?"

"Do we have somebody inside?" Sean repeated. "Anybody who can get us some information?"

Grady shook his head. "Nobody deep enough to filter information to me. I'm working on it."

"I might be able to help with that," Finn interjected. "I went to school with a couple of guys who are familiar with the Moretti family. One of them is especially close to a high-level player. Let me see what I can do."

Grady nodded his approval; it was one less thing he had to worry about.

They discussed a few other minor issues, then Finn, Declan, and Conor excused themselves. Angus stayed behind until Sean told him to go. Grady poured himself a drink and sat down across from his boss after everyone left.

"Did you take care of Caitlin's car?" Sean asked.

He nodded. Caitlin had wrecked her car for the third time in as many years. She claimed it wasn't her fault, but Grady didn't believe her; it was always her fault.

"Thank you." Sean cleared his throat. "I'm sorry that I keep sending you to deal with my daughter's issues."

"It's my job," Grady replied.

"But it isn't," Sean said. "Jesus, I run one of the most feared crime families on the East Coast, but I can't talk to my twenty-five-year-old daughter." He chuckled and shook his head. "She wasn't always like this."

"You mean she wasn't always a brat?"

Sean snorted. "I didn't say that. Did she, by any chance, mention when she was coming home?"

Grady glanced at his boss out of the corner of his eye. "She said she didn't know. School keeps her busy."

Sean sighed. "You don't have to be nice for my sake. If she said she has no plans to come home, I can handle it. I am well aware of how badly I destroyed my relationship with both of my daughters. It's not easy rebuilding them."

"She didn't say she *wasn't* coming back to Boston," Grady reiterated. "She said she didn't know *when* she would come home."

"Fair enough." Sean scrubbed a hand over his face. "I've got work to do. Let me know if you hear anything else about the Morettis, will you?"

That was his cue to leave. Grady downed the rest of his drink, nodded at his boss, and left.

As he walked through the halls of the O'Reilly mansion, a place as familiar to him as his own home, his mind wandered, refusing to let go of the past. The ten-year anniversary of the incident at Foley's Diner was approaching, and he got nostalgic every year at this time. He hated it. Nostalgia wasn't really his *thing*, but he couldn't seem to stop it from happening. Memories of Oona bombarded him day and night, memories he didn't want. Oona had almost cost him his life, yet he still couldn't stop thinking about her. Love did that to a person; it fucked them up and left them to die. That was why he'd sworn off love. Never again would a woman control him.

Grady glanced at his watch and saw the time. He'd worked enough for one day. He took his phone from his pocket, checked the time, then called The Velvet Lounge to reserve his table. If he hurried, he could be there before the first dancer took the stage.

He tossed his keys to the valet and took the ticket as he walked past him, all without missing a step. The doorman held open the door for him.

"Good evening, Mr. McCarthy," he said.

"Phil," he replied.

The Velvet Lounge was a high-end gentlemen's club, one that required a membership to even walk through the front door. Exorbitant fees deterred most men from joining, keeping the clientele exclusive. The club exuded luxury and exclusivity, noticeable the moment one approached its discreet entrance. The building was tucked away on a quiet, out of the way street, only a small bronze plaque to indicate where the driveway was. Phil—the doorman—wore a tailored suit, and the two valets had on black dress shirts, pants, and vests, so they would fade into the background when they weren't helping clients.

Inside, the club was opulently decorated with rich mahogany wood paneling, soft leather seats, and dim, but warm, gold lighting that bathed the room in an intimate glow. The smell of expensive cigars, high-end liquor, and polished wood filled the room. Bottles of rare scotch, bourbon, and whiskey, along with the finest champagne, were artfully displayed on the gleaming marble bar. The staff were dressed like the valets in all black, professional and efficient.

Booths separated by velvet curtains provided privacy for the clientele—businessmen, politicians, celebrities, and men in Grady's line of work. Countless deals had been struck at the Velvet Lounge over glasses of scotch while the girls danced onstage. More velvet drapes hung at one end of the room, where the dancers entered the stage. It was a twenty-five-foot-long raised platform, four feet off the ground, lined with lights and gold-colored poles every five feet.

The manager met Grady at the bar and escorted him to his usual table. He had been a member for almost ten years and because of his position in the O'Reilly family, he was afforded every luxury the club could offer. At his table, he found a glass of water and a scotch and soda waiting for him. He picked up the scotch and downed it in three swallows. Less than five minutes later, a young, attractive waitress put another one in front of him. He nodded her direction but didn't make eye contact; instead, he stared straight ahead at the empty stage.

The music started, the volume slowly increasing until it was at deafening levels. The dancer, a woman in a pink-and-green outfit, stepped through the curtain onto the stage and began to move, her eyes dancing over the fifteen to twenty men in the audience as she swirled around each pole as she passed it.

Grady sipped the scotch from his glass. He sat alone, watching the dancer in front of him without expression. He might as well have been sitting in church listening to a priest. Even when she sidled up to the edge of the stage and stuck her ass in his face, he didn't blink.

The music stopped, and the girl left. Grady caught the attention of his waitress and held up his glass. She nodded and smiled.

He pinched the bridge of his nose and closed his eyes. The alcohol, loud music, and flashing lights probably weren't the ideal remedy for a pounding headache, but he didn't want to go back to his empty apartment. If he stayed long enough, he was guaranteed to find someone to take home with him. Any of the girls in the club would gladly walk out of here on his arm. After all, he was Grady McCarthy; in this part of town, his name got him everything he wanted, including sex.

The waitress put a drink on the table in front of him. "Here's your drink, Mr. McCarthy."

He smiled at her. He didn't recognize her, so she must be new. She was young, no older than twenty-six, maybe twenty-seven, attractive, and flirty, with short black hair and dark eyes. As long as she wasn't a blonde. Grady never took home a blonde; it was too easy to imagine it was—

"Can I get you anything else?" the girl said, interrupting his musings.

"What time do you get off?" he asked.

"Ten," she said. "On the nose." She winked at him.

He chuckled. "Great. Meet me out front when you're done. I'll be waiting."

She nodded. "I can't wait." She turned to go, but he grabbed her hand.

"What's your name, sweetheart?"

"Marjorie," she said.

He released her. "I'll see you at ten."

The music came on, swelling to a crescendo and making any further conversation impossible. Grady picked up his drink and turned his focus to the woman on the stage. The girl—Marjorie—walked away, the smile on her face bright enough to light up the room.

She was surprisingly confident around him. Most people didn't know what to say to him or how to talk to him. Caitlin said it was the vibe he gave off, but he didn't know what that meant. Grady assumed it was because he appeared perpetually angry, pissed off at the world. It wasn't his fault; people were stupid, and dealing with stupidity was not his strong suit.

At 9:55 p.m., Grady dropped some money on the table, more than enough to cover his drinks, along with a substantial tip, then walked out of the bar. As soon as the valet saw him, he grabbed Grady's keys and jogged across the lot to where his Bronco was parked. The valet pulled it up front and handed the keys to Grady, who gave him a tip before he climbed in the SUV to wait.

Marjorie walked out the door at 10:02 p.m. and looked around. Grady leaned over and pushed open the passenger side door so she could get in. She sat down, turned, and put her hand on his arm.

"Where are we going?" she asked.

"I have a place nearby," he replied. "We'll go there."

Grady didn't take women to his home in Waltham; he didn't take *anybody* to his home in Waltham. In fact, no one even knew where the place was, except his boss. He kept an apartment in Boston for nights like tonight, nights when he needed an escape so he could forget the world existed.

After they parked, Grady led Marjorie inside and upstairs to his one-bedroom apartment. It was sparsely furnished, with only a couch, coffee table, and television in the living and dining room, and a bed with matching end tables in the bedroom; that was all he needed.

Marjorie walked through the kitchen and into the living room. She dropped her bag on the couch and crossed the room to look out the window.

"What a gorgeous view," she murmured. She looked around the room. "You need some furniture, though. It's kind of bare in here."

Grady shrugged. "I like it the way it is."

She turned around and crossed her arms. "You don't spend a lot of time here, do you?"

He shook his head and took a step toward her. "I didn't bring you here to make small talk."

Marjorie nodded and strolled back across the room. She stopped in front of him, tipped her head back, and looked at him. She was short, the top of her head barely coming to his chin. He stared at her.

She pulled her T-shirt off and let it fall to the floor. She kicked off her high heels—making her even shorter—and shimmied out of the tight jeans she wore. Once she was naked, she dropped to her knees in front of him.

Marjorie stared into his eyes as she unbuttoned his jeans and tugged them down past his hips. Grady didn't move. Marjorie didn't break eye contact, even as she removed his cock from his pants and took him in her mouth.

He closed his eyes and imagined the woman on her knees in front of him was someone else, a tall, athletic blonde with dark blue eyes. The one woman in this world he could never have.

Chapter 4

Grady

Grady shoved the naked girl away from him and reached for his ringing phone. Swearing, he watched it tumble off the table and fall to the floor. He threw the blankets off, dropped to his knees, and snatched the phone from under the bed. He turned around and sat on the floor, naked, rested his head on the mattress behind him, and answered the phone.

"Yeah," he muttered.

"Grady? Is that you?"

"Caitlin?" If she was calling this late, something was wrong. If he had to guess, she was in trouble and needed him to bail her out. Again.

"Yes, it's me." The girl on the other end dragged in a shaky breath. "I … I need your help."

He pushed himself to his feet, sat on the bed, and checked his watch. "Fuck, Caitlin, do you know what time it is? What happened?"

Knowing Sean's daughter, the possibilities were endless: drunk, high, another car accident, boy problems, or maybe she ended up in Canada again.

"I'm in trouble." Her voice dropped to a whisper. "Grady, I'm in big trouble, and I'm scared. I need your help."

"Wait a minute. Did you say you're scared?"

"Mm-hm," was her response.

"What happened?" he asked.

"I … I don't think I should talk about it on the phone." Caitlin sniffled and dragged in a shaky breath. "Will you come? Please?"

If she needed him, he would go without hesitation, no questions asked. Part of his responsibilities as Sean's second-in-command were to take care of the family. All of them. Even if they drove him crazy like Caitlin did.

He held his phone between his shoulder and ear, snatched his pants off the floor, and put them on, no underwear in sight. They were probably in the living room by the couch. "Tell me where you are."

"I'm at Katz's Delicatessen near NYU," she whispered.

His patience was wearing thin; he hated it when she was vague. "Go home. I'll meet you at your apartment. You can tell me what happened when I get there."

"I … I can't go home." Caitlin's voice caught, and a sob escaped her. "It's not safe."

"What the fuck, Caitlin? I don't understand why your apartment isn't safe. What did you do?"

"Please, Grady. I didn't *do* anything, but I can't explain over the phone. You'll have to see it; otherwise, you won't believe me. Will you come?"

He snatched his T-shirt and jacket from the chair and looked around the room for his shoes. "Okay. No apartment. You need to listen to me, Caitlin. Stay where you are. If anything happens, call me. I'll get there as soon as I can. Do you understand me?"

"Y-yes," she stammered.

Grady ended the call and shoved his phone in his front pocket. It was a three-hour drive to New York. He could take the jet, but by the time he got it fueled and filed the flight plans, he could've driven the whole way.

"Hey." He patted Majorie on the ass. "Get up. Time to go."

She rolled over and squinted at him. "What?" she asked. "What time is it?"

"Time for you to go. I gotta leave. Get out." Once he had his dark gray T-shirt on, he tucked his holstered gun into the waistband of his pants. "Now."

Marjorie climbed out of the bed with a huff and pulled on her clothes. She couldn't have been more than a year or two older than Caitlin. He liked them young and, despite his age, they liked him.

After she dressed, Grady ushered her through the apartment to the front door.

She paused and took something from her purse. "Call me." She smiled and pushed a business card into his hand. "We'll get drinks."

He nodded. "Yeah, maybe." He opened the door and shoved her out, shutting it firmly behind her. The card went in the trash. He might see her again at the strip club, but he wouldn't be sleeping with her again. He was a one-and-done kind of guy.

Once he had his car keys and his wallet, Grady locked up the apartment and took the elevator down to the parking garage. He debated whether he should call Sean and tell him about Caitlin, but he quickly rejected the idea. If she called him before her father, there was a reason. He would find out what happened and fill his boss in later.

Inside his gray Bronco, Grady plugged in his phone, turned on some AC/DC, and pulled out of the garage a few minutes after 1:00 a.m. Traffic was light as he drove through Boston to the freeway. Once he was on the I-90

East, he got in the left lane and set the cruise control to ninety. With any luck, he'd be in New York in less than three hours.

 A few hours later, Grady found a parking spot in front of the deli; no surprise at four in the morning. Inside, he stopped by the front counter and looked around, spotting Caitlin right away. It was hard to miss the tall blonde with the athletic build and blue eyes the color of the ocean on a clear day. When she saw him, she jumped to her feet, raced across the room, and threw herself into his arms.

Caitlin pressed her face against his neck, and her hair tickled his cheek. She was tall enough to look him in the eye. He resisted the urge to hug her close and kiss her temple.

What the fuck? This is Sean's daughter, for Christ's sake. Get a grip, McCarthy.

He grabbed her upper arms and pushed her away, rougher than he intended, but he needed her to understand this was business. Keeping it professional with Caitlin was the only way he maintained his sanity.

"What the hell is going on? Explain to me why I had to drive for three hours to rescue you. And it better be good."

Caitlin looked at him with tears in the corner of her eyes. "It's not good, Grady. It's bad. Really, really bad."

He sighed. What the hell did she do now?

Caitlin must have known what he was thinking, because she immediately shook her head. "This is worse than anything I've ever done, Grady, and I didn't *do* anything. I swear to you, I didn't do anything."

Caitlin O'Reilly never cried. Not when her sister disappeared for three years, or when her father got shot up at Foley's Café. The girl kept her emotions in check all the time. Her go-to emotion was sarcasm, if you could call that an emotion. Something—or someone—had scared her.

Grady released her, took her hand, and guided her back to the table she was sitting at. He helped her into the chair, then sat down beside her.

"What happened?" he asked. "Tell me everything."

Caitlin swallowed and looked around the restaurant. She inched closer to him, leaned in, lowered her voice, and, without looking at him, explained in detail what had happened at her apartment. By the time she was done, Grady had his hands clenched in front of him and his head pounded.

He rubbed the center of his forehead. "Jesus Christ, Cait. Are you sure? Are you one hundred percent positive that's what you heard them say?"

"Yes," she whispered. "They wanted to blame me for Bobby's death. They talked about making it look like it was me and … and something about suicide. I don't know." A tear slipped down her cheek. "They killed him. Right in front of me." Caitlin caught her lip between her teeth and pressed the heels of her hands against her eyes.

Grady stood up. "We need to go to your place."

She shook her head. "I don't want to."

"You can wait in the car while I check out the apartment," he explained. "Let's go."

She obediently got up and followed him out of the deli. Caitlin didn't utter a word during the drive to her apartment, which was unlike her. Normally, she talked his ear off, spouting off about topics he didn't give a shit about. Grady wasn't sure how he felt about this quiet, reserved version of Caitlin.

"You have your phone, right?" Grady asked, after he parked down the street from her building.

She nodded but didn't speak; she wouldn't look at him either.

"I'm going inside," he said. "Call me if you see anything strange."

She stared straight ahead, not speaking.

"Damn it, Caitlin. Will you look at me?"

"What?" she snapped. She then rolled her dark blue eyes, flipped her hair off her shoulder, and crossed her arms.

There she was. That was the Caitlin he knew—pissed off at the world and everyone in it, especially anyone who worked for her father. Especially him.

Grady grabbed the door handle. "I will be right back. I'm going to check your apartment."

She sighed. "The door is locked, and my keys are inside. You can't get in."

"How did the guys who shot Bobby get in?" he asked.

Her jaw clenched, and her fingers curled in her lap. She hated it when he questioned her; she said it made her feel like a child. "I … I think they broke the door."

"So, it's probably open?"

"I don't know," she snapped. "I guess so."

He reached past her, brushing her leg with his hand as he opened the glove compartment and pulled out a key on a small green key ring. He shook it in her face.

"Not to worry," Grady said. "If they didn't break it, I can still get in."

Her eyes narrowed. "Why do you have a key to my apartment?"

Now it was Grady's turn to roll his eyes. "Your father gave it to me. In case I needed it."

Caitlin snorted, crossed her arms, and stared out the passenger window.

He cursed under his breath, shoved open the door, and headed for her building. She was already getting on his nerves. He would never understand how a beautiful, confident woman like Caitlin could act so childish sometimes. Why the fuck did it turn him on when she got that petulant look on her face, and she pushed back? It made him want to punish her in ways he didn't dare admit to anyone. Shit, he could barely admit it to himself. She was his boss's daughter and therefore off-limits. She was one twenty-something he wouldn't be taking to bed.

At the apartment building, Grady unlocked the building's front door with his key and stepped inside. No elevator because Caitlin insisted on living close to campus in a no-frills apartment. She didn't flaunt her family's wealth because she didn't want anyone to know she was a mobster's daughter.

Caitlin lived on the fourth floor. Her place was at the end of a long hallway, the last one on the left. As he approached, he noticed the door was ajar and the wood cracked. He slipped his hand under the edge of his jacket and rested it on his gun, looking over his shoulder before pushing open the broken door.

The coppery smell of blood assaulted him as soon as he stepped inside. From his position just inside the apartment, he saw the body, pools of blood congealing beneath it. Grady took his gun from his waistband and stepped further into the apartment, shoving the broken door closed behind him. It was dead quiet. He checked all the rooms, but no one was there.

He returned to the body; on the floor next to Bobby was a handgun, a Sig Sauer P365. He recognized it immediately as belonging to Caitlin. Grady had given it to her after she broke up with a kid who refused to take no for an answer. He bent over and rolled Bobby onto his side, then used two fingers to remove the kid's wallet from the back pocket of his jeans, opened it, and took out his driver's license.

Roberto Corelli.

Shit. Oh shit.

Grady darted into the kitchen, snatched a towel off the counter, dropped it on the gun, and picked it up. He wrapped it up and shoved it in Caitlin's backpack on the table, along with her laptop and purse. Then he tucked his gun back into the holster in his waistband, put the backpack over his shoulder, and sprinted out of the apartment and down the stairs.

He ran down the sidewalk, sticking to the shadows, grateful that the sun wasn't up all the way. Less than fifty feet from where he'd parked the SUV, he noticed the coffee shop. Two men sat inside with paper cups and uneaten pastries in front of them. Neither of them looked like they belonged in a neighborhood filled with college students.

As he got closer, Grady realized he knew the guys sitting at the table. Gaetano "Joey" LaGuardia and Gino Russo both worked for Aldo Moretti as *forneart*—enforcers.

Somehow, they knew. They knew Moretti's son—his illegitimate son, Roberto Corelli—was dead. And if they were here, outside Caitlin's apartment, they thought she had something to do with it.

Everything changed at that moment; this was bigger than anything Grady could handle. The New York mob was an entity he couldn't take on alone. If Moretti thought Caitlin killed his son, he would do everything in his power to get to her.

Fuck. Fuck. Fuck.

This would start a war between the Boston and New York families. They had been at peace for the last fifty years, but when Donovan Muldoon gave control of his family to Sean O'Reilly's new son-in-law, things had changed. Aldo Moretti saw the merging of the Muldoons and the O'Reillys as a threat to his existence. The situation had been unstable for months, and this escalated those problems into the stratosphere. Moretti would be out for revenge.

Caitlin O'Reilly had a target on her back and only Grady to protect her.

Chapter 5
Caitlin

While waiting in the car, Caitlin glanced over her shoulder out the back window, but she didn't see Grady anywhere. Her throat felt like it was stuffed with cotton. She checked the backseat, but of course there wasn't any bottled water. Her eyes were drawn to the coffee shop; it would only take a few minutes to grab water and get back in the Bronco. No harm, no foul.

She eased open the door, looked at her building one more time, then surveyed the surrounding area. Nothing seemed out of the ordinary, and she didn't see anyone who looked out of place or was watching her. There was no way those guys who killed Bobby were still around. After another quick look at her surroundings, she hurried inside and got in line.

It took longer than she thought to get the water. If Grady returned to the Bronco before she did, he would chew her out and most likely talk to her in that condescending tone he used whenever she was in his general vicinity. When she finally made it to the front of the line, Caitlin tapped her phone on the card reader, snatched the bottle out of the barista's hand, and hurried outside, opening it as she walked.

Caitlin spotted Grady as soon as she stepped out the café door. He had that perpetual scowl on his face, but instead of making him unattractive, it made him more desirable. Everything about him was desirable. She wished he would see her for what she was, instead of the mob boss's daughter.

She raised her hand and yelled, "Grady!"

His eyes widened. He looked at her, then over her shoulder at something behind her. He broke into a run.

"Caitlin! Get in the car!" he screamed.

She froze, unable to move. What the hell was his problem?

A loud clatter came from the outdoor tables behind her. She spun around and saw the men who had shot Bobby. They shoved tables and chairs out of the way as they stalked toward her. The water bottle fell from her hand, and she stumbled back.

"Shit," she muttered.

"Caitlin!" Grady bellowed.

She took another step away from the men descending on her, hit a planter with her foot, and fell on her ass with a loud, "Oomph." She pushed herself backward, her feet sliding on the concrete, as the large, bald guy who ordered Bobby's death stalked toward her, shoving unsuspecting college students and mothers in yoga pants out of his way. The guy Bobby called Joey.

He grabbed her arm and dragged her upright. "You must be Caitlin O'Reilly. It's a pleasure to finally meet you."

Caitlin swallowed back a scream as he shoved his gun against her ribs.

Grady slid to a stop right beside them, his hand in his jacket on the butt of his gun. "Let her go, Joey," he muttered.

The guy holding her arm snarled. "Grady McCarthy. What the fuck are you doin' here?"

"I said let her go," Grady repeated. "Let's not cause a scene."

"Then get out of my way," Joey snarled.

Grady stood his ground. "You don't want to get on the wrong side of the O'Reillys."

Joey snorted. "I'm more afraid of my boss than yours." He looked over his shoulder at the man behind him. "Gino, bring the car around front."

Caitlin sucked in a deep breath, shifted her weight to her back foot, and elbowed Joey as hard as she could in the sternum. He grunted and took a step back, his grip on her arm loosening. She turned at the same time as he moved, brought her leg up, and kneed him in the groin. He immediately dropped to the ground.

Grady grabbed her hand before Caitlin could fall too. He pushed her behind him and drew his gun.

"Get your ass in the car, now!" he ordered. "Move!"

Caitlin didn't hesitate. She spun around, raced to the Bronco, yanked open the door, and dove inside. As she pulled the door closed, she locked eyes with Joey, less than ten feet away from her. He raised his gun and aimed it at her head. Screams erupted around them as people realized a man with a gun stood on the sidewalk in front of the shop.

Grady hauled open the driver's side door, tossed her backpack at her, and yelled, "Get down!"

Caitlin dropped to the floor in front of the passenger seat and put her hands over her head.

Grady climbed in, set his gun between his legs, and started the Bronco. Horns honked and tires squealed as he whipped the wheel to the left and made a U-turn across three lanes of traffic. He hit the accelerator, weaving through traffic as she curled herself into a ball on the floor.

"You can get up now," Grady said after a few minutes of driving.

She pulled herself onto the passenger seat and wrapped her arms around herself. "You know those guys?" she whispered. "The guys who killed Bobby?"

"What did you say?"

"How do you know them? The guys who killed Bobby?" she repeated.

"They … they're the ones who shot your boyfriend?"

Caitlin hugged herself tighter and prayed the trembling would stop. "Yes."

"They work for Aldo Moretti," Grady explained. "He runs New York. I'm not sure if you're aware of this, but he and your father have had some… problems in the past." He scrubbed a hand over his face. "Jesus Christ, this doesn't make any sense. Those guys are Moretti's men. They would never kill his son."

"His son? What the hell are you talking about?"

"Bobby's full name is Roberto Corelli. He's the illegitimate son of Aldo Moretti, born to one of his mistresses. Those men are going to tell Moretti *you* killed Bobby. Not only is he dead in your apartment, but your gun was on the floor next to him."

"Jesus Christ," she muttered. "Why is this happening?" She put her head in her hands.

Grady glanced at her out of the corner of his eye. "They must know you're Sean O'Reilly's daughter. If I didn't know better, I'd think they were trying to start a war."

"I don't understand," she whispered.

"Neither do I. What I do know is that Aldo Moretti will do everything in his power to find you," Grady said.

"If he kills you, not only does he get revenge for the death of his son, but he gets to your father as well."

Caitlin scowled. "Fuck. Why is everything in my life always about my father? Sometimes, I *hate* being an O'Reilly."

She strongly believed every problem in her life was directly linked to her father and his *business*. Growing up, her and her sister's freedom had been restricted out of fear that her father's rivals might harm them or use them as leverage against her father. She'd been lonely and isolated her entire childhood. The only friend she ever had was her sister, Olivia.

Her father's reputation made it difficult for her to get into a college close to home. Most of the universities in the Boston area were reluctant to associate with her; it was one reason Caitlin had gone to New York for school.

Romantic relationships were damn near impossible once people discovered her father was *the* Sean O'Reilly. Dating and boyfriends in high school were nonexistent. Once they found out she was a mobster's daughter, men avoided her like the plague.

"Caitlin?" Grady said.

"What?" she snapped.

"Are you listening to me? You're in trouble," he said. "This is about more than your father and Declan merging the O'Reilly and Muldoon families. There is something far more nefarious going on here. I need to hide you somewhere while I sort this out."

"P-pull over," Caitlin stammered.

"What?"

"I said pull over!" she screamed.

Grady made an abrupt right turn and pulled into the parking lot of an automotive shop. He drove around the back of the building and slammed the Bronco into park.

Caitlin got out of the SUV and stumbled up the alley, Grady right behind her. Her legs buckled under her, exhaustion and fear weighing her down. Her mind raced with the realization that a powerful mob boss wanted her dead. Her breaths came in ragged gasps as the tears broke free and streamed down her cheeks.

She sank to the grimy pavement below and hugged her knees to her chest. "I can't do this, Grady," she cried, her voice breaking. "I didn't kill Bobby. I didn't. I didn't." She shook her head, her blonde hair flying around her face. "Why are they doing this?"

Grady reached for her, but she slapped his hand away.

"Don't touch me," she snapped. A choked sob escaped her.

He crouched in front of her, grabbed her chin, and held it tight, forcing her to look at him. "You need to keep it together. We don't have time for your theatrics."

"Fuck you," she muttered. Why couldn't he be understanding just once?

"Stop being a brat," he ordered. "I'm not putting up with the spoiled princess shit. You will stand up and get in the truck. You'll also do as I say, and you won't argue with me. Do you understand?"

Shocked, all she could do was stare into his hazel eyes. "What?"

Anger rolled off him in waves. He glared at her, and his grip tightened on her chin. "Get your ass off the ground and get in the truck now. I'm not asking you again. Understood?"

Shocked, all Caitlin could think to do was follow his instructions. "O-okay," she stammered.

Grady released her, took her arm, and pulled her to her feet, then led her to the Bronco. He didn't look at her as they got in, just put the SUV in gear and drove out of the parking lot.

Caitlin clutched her hands in her lap and stared out the window. Fuck, that wasn't supposed to be so hot. She should be pissed that Grady dared put his hands on her, like she'd been angry at Bobby when he'd done it, but all she could think about was the way her stomach clenched with need when he squeezed her chin between his strong fingers and how she had to keep herself from moaning as he gave her an order.

She closed her eyes, and an image of Grady pulling her over his lap and spanking her bare ass filled her head. She bit her lower lip to keep herself quiet as she let her imagination run wild.

"Yes, sir," Grady said.

Caitlin sat up and rubbed her eyes. She peered out the window, but nothing looked familiar.

"Understood."

Caitlin turned to look at Grady. There was only one person he spoke to like that, with that amount of deference.

Her father.

She stared at Grady, curious if Sean O'Reilly would want to speak to her. Their relationship was difficult, something they were both working on, but they were a long way from things being good. Part of her had hoped

Grady wouldn't call her father, though she wasn't surprised he had. He probably didn't take a shit without Sean O'Reilly's permission.

Grady held the phone out to her and muttered, "Take it."

Caitlin plucked it from his hand. "Hey, Daddy," she said nonchalantly.

"Are you okay?" he asked.

"Yes," she replied. "I'm fine."

"Why didn't you call me?"

"I don't know," she mumbled. "I'm sorry."

Her father sighed loudly. "You do what Grady says," he ordered. "He'll keep you safe. Do you understand?"

"Yes," Caitlin said.

The call ended, so she dropped the phone in the cup holder between the seats and glared at Grady.

"I cannot *believe* you called my father."

"Don't start with me, princess," he snapped. "I had no choice. He called me when I didn't show up for our scheduled meeting, and I ignored it. I called him back as soon as we got out of the city."

"Why?" she asked.

Grady shook his head. "Really? You have to ask?"

"Fine. What did he say?"

"We'll talk about it later." He slowed down as they entered a small town, nothing more than a gas station, a diner, and several houses on a wide spot in the road. To her surprise, he pulled into the gas station. He didn't park in front of a gas pump, though; instead, he parked under a tree at the back of the lot and shut off the vehicle.

He pinched the bridge of his nose and sighed, then held out his hand. "Give me your phone."

"What?" She clutched the pink iPhone in both hands and held it against her chest. "No. I'm not giving you my phone."

"Now, Caitlin," Grady demanded. "I won't ask again."

She scowled at him, but she didn't argue. She didn't dare.

"Fine." She tossed it to him, and he caught it with one hand.

He took the case off, pulled a knife from his front pocket, and used it to pop open the small compartment on the side. He removed the SIM card, broke it in half, and threw it out the Bronco's window. Then he did the same with his phone.

"How are we supposed to get a hold of anybody?" she asked.

"I've got burner phones in the back," he replied. "Come on, we're going inside to pick up supplies."

"I'll wait here," Caitlin said.

"No, you're coming in with me." Grady got out of the Bronco and slammed the door closed.

She stayed put, having no desire to go into some convenience store in the middle of nowhere for supplies. Why the hell did they need to buy a bunch of stuff, anyway? Caitlin was tired, she wanted a shower, and more than anything else, she wanted to lock herself in a room alone and take a minute to process everything.

The passenger door opened, startling her. Grady grabbed her arm and dragged her out of the Bronco. She tried to pull away, but his grip on her was too tight.

Caitlin dug her heels in and tried not to move, like a toddler having a tantrum in the middle of the grocery store. "I said I wanted to wait in the car."

Grady kicked the door shut and shoved her against the vehicle. He stepped close, so close she felt his chest rising and falling and the warmth of his body seeping into hers. She struggled to catch her breath.

Grady's upper lip rose in an irritated snarl. "You will do as I say, princess. You go where I go, you stay where I can see you at all times, and you follow *every* direction I give you. You are my shadow. Do you understand me?"

"Yes," Caitlin whispered.

"Yes, what?"

"Yes, sir," she muttered with a hint of sarcasm.

He raised an eyebrow and smiled. "Good girl." Her heart skipped a beat as he took her hand and led her inside.

Jesus Christ, why did Grady calling her a good girl make her break out in goosebumps?

You're out of your mind, Caitlin.

Maybe she was, but that didn't stop desire from pooling in her stomach like a snake about to strike.

The store attached to the gas station seemed to be a one-stop shop. Not surprising since it was obviously the only place to get necessities in the small town. Grady grabbed a small basket as they entered and handed it to her. She followed behind him as he picked items off the shelves and tossed them into the basket—soup, ramen, bread, lunchmeat, cheese, cereal, fruit, milk, eggs, and snacks. When the basket was full, he set it on the counter in front of the cashier, then took Caitlin to the other side of the store, where a variety of clothing hung from rows of racks.

Grady grabbed several T-shirts, two flannels, a package of underwear, and a package of socks. When he noticed she wasn't doing the same, he scowled at her.

"You're going to need some clothes," he said. "Grab them now or spend the next few days in what you have on."

Caitlin wrinkled her nose, but the thought of not having clean clothes made her want to vomit, so she searched the racks, grabbing a few T-shirts, two sweatshirts, a pair of okay-looking jeans, a skirt, socks, and underwear. She also grabbed some cheap slip-on shoes, as well as sweatpants and an oversized shirt to sleep in.

Once they'd made their selections, they dropped everything on the counter.

"Lose your luggage?" the cashier asked.

"Something like that," Grady mumbled.

When the cashier gave him the total, he yanked a wad of cash from his pocket and handed it to her.

"You gave me too much," the cashier said after she counted it. She held out a hundred-dollar bill.

He shook his head. "Keep it. For your trouble. And for helping us out."

The woman raised an eyebrow. "Helping you how?"

"If somebody comes in here asking if you saw us, you say no. Can you do that?"

The woman nodded, shoved the money in her pocket, then quickly bagged up their things. Grady scooped them up with one hand and thanked her as they left. He grabbed Caitlin's arm and kept hold of it as they walked back to the Bronco, as if he thought she would try to run away. While she'd considered it, she knew she had to stay with him because he would protect her.

Besides, she couldn't help but wonder where they were going and if it would still be just the two of them. Because there was nothing more in this world she wanted than time alone with Grady McCarthy.

Chapter 6
Grady

His boss was pissed and if there was one thing nobody wanted to see—or hear—it was an angry Sean O'Reilly.

Grady dreaded making the call, but he knew he had no choice. He intentionally waited until Caitlin dozed off; he couldn't handle her bratty attitude and deal with her father at the same time. Even after she fell asleep, he put off calling Sean as long as he could. When he called for the fifth time in less than fifteen minutes, Grady knew it was time to tell him about the situation with his daughter. He picked up his phone and reluctantly told Siri to call Sean.

The head of Massachusetts' largest crime family initially seemed worried about his leascheannasaí. Grady had never missed a meeting or ignored a phone call from his boss; for Christ's sake, he'd never even been late. He appreciated the concern, but as soon as Grady said he had gone to help Caitlin, Sean went dead silent for almost a full minute.

"What did my daughter do now?" Sean finally asked.

He listened in silence while Grady explained what had happened and where they were. He didn't speak until Grady was done.

"Take her to the cabin in Connecticut."

"In Sharon?" Grady asked.

"Yes. It's close and safe." Sean cleared his throat.

"You don't want me to bring her home?"

"Absolutely not," his boss replied. "Moretti's crew will assume you're bringing her home. She needs to go somewhere else. That's why I want you to take her to Sharon. And Grady?"

"Yes, sir."

"You keep her safe. Do you understand?"

"Understood."

"Where are we going?" Caitlin interrupted his replay of the conversation with her father. "Aren't we going back to Boston?"

"No," he replied. "We're going to Sharon, Connecticut."

Caitlin's face twisted like she'd bit into a sour lemon. "Where the hell is Sharon, Connecticut?"

"It's in the middle of nowhere," Grady said. "There's a cabin there that only a few people in the family know about; it's sort of like a safe house. We'll stay there as long as we can."

He checked the GPS. They were less than twenty minutes from the place in Sharon. He'd only been there once, shortly after Sean bought the place. It was truly a cabin—one small bedroom, a bathroom, and a great room encompassing the kitchen and the living room. Nothing fancy. It was a safe house and had never been used. Until now.

Caitlin sat up straight and looked out the window, still scowling. "It's nothing but trees. Boring."

"We're not on vacation, princess. We're here because you've got a price on your head." The GPS directed him to turn left in 500 feet. If he remembered correctly, the turn was difficult to see and easily missed. He slowed to twenty miles an hour and stared intently at the thick forest passing by, watching for the sliver of road.

"There it is," he mumbled to himself. He hit the brake and slowly turned onto a dirt road hidden among the trees.

The narrow road wound through thick clusters of pines and oaks. Caitlin clung to the door handle as the SUV bounced down the road, muttering words he couldn't understand under her breath until the vehicle emerged in a clearing surrounded by towering oak and pine trees. They cast long shadows over the clearing, making it feel more isolated than it actually was.

The small, rustic cabin sat in the center. The wooden siding showed signs of weathering and age, but it was solidly built.

Grady drove around the back and parked under a ten-foot awning. As soon as he shut the engine off, Caitlin jumped out of the Bronco and darted up the steps. When she realized the door wasn't unlocked, she huffed, crossed her arms over her chest, leaned against the wall, and glared at him.

He sighed. She grated on his nerves on a good day, and this was not a good day. He was tired and pissed, in no mood for Caitlin O'Reilly and her bratty attitude. He understood the trauma she'd been through, but there was no time for hysterics or drama. While he felt bad about calling her a brat earlier, it had to be done. She couldn't lose her shit, not when they were on the run. To his surprise, she'd pulled herself together. Unfortunately, it appeared the princess attitude was back.

Caitlin hadn't always been like this. When she was a teenager, she had been sweet and carefree. After her father sent her sister Olivia off to marry the future leader of the Muldoon family, she had changed. She'd grown sullen and moody; it had only gotten worse after Olivia disappeared.

That was about the time Caitlin started causing problems. Grady lost track of how many times she ditched her bodyguard, but then called him to retrieve her from some club or frat party because she'd been drinking and couldn't drive herself home; or the guy she was with left her stranded or turned out to be an asshole. He thought after she went to college he'd get some kind of reprieve, but she hadn't improved. Wrecked cars, drinking, partying, you name it, Caitlin did it. It was a wonder she maintained her good grades, acting the way she did. When she screwed up, Sean O'Reilly sent his second-in-command to clean up her messes. He didn't trust anyone else to be discreet.

"Grady!" Caitlin shouted. Apparently, the princess was impatient.

He climbed out of the SUV and grabbed the bags out of the back. When he got to the top of the stairs, he shoved them into Caitlin's hands and punched in the code into the keypad on the door. When he heard a click, he pushed it open and ushered her inside.

"Thank God," she muttered. She dumped the bags on the table and dug through them until she found the clothing they'd bought for her. She put everything in her backpack, picked it up and slung it over her shoulder, then walked further into the room.

The cabin's layout was open and dominated by one large room. In one corner was a small, old-fashioned wood-burning stove, flanked by inlaid bookshelves crammed with a variety of books. A flat-screen TV sat in the other corner. A worn leather couch and a recliner faced the television, along with a large coffee table and matching end table. An expensive area rug covered the floor. To Grady's right, the small kitchen held a stove, several cabinets, a refrigerator, and a thick wooden table with mismatched chairs.

On his left were two doors leading to the bedroom and the bathroom. If memory served him correctly, the bedroom had a full-size bed, and the bathroom was barely big enough for a shower, toilet, and sink. There were two doors to the outside, at the front of the house and the one in the back they'd come through, as well as minimal windows. As safe houses went, this one wasn't too bad.

Caitlin stood between the living room and kitchen. "Where's the bathroom?" she asked. "I need a shower."

Grady pointed to the other side of the living room. "Bathroom is right there. Bedroom is next to it. You can put your things in there."

"Great." She spun around without so much as a thanks and disappeared into the bathroom.

He put the food away, noting that the cupboards were stocked with plenty of canned and dry goods. He took the clothing he'd bought for himself and hung it in a small closet in the living room. From that same closet, he grabbed clean linens, put a set in the bedroom and the other he dropped on the coffee table. After he finished, he checked the windows to make sure they were locked, then he closed the drapes and blinds.

Back in the living room, Grady checked the front door to make sure it was also locked. Once he'd done that, he pushed the couch in front of the door. Not only did it give them extra security by blocking it, but he could see the entire cabin from the couch.

After he finished, he sat on the couch and rested his head against the back. Grady exhaled and closed his eyes.

Exhaustion settled over him like a warm blanket. He'd only gotten a couple hours of sleep before Caitlin called, and he'd been running on pure adrenaline ever since. God, he was tired.

The bathroom door opened and through his half-lidded eyes, he saw Caitlin emerge. Her hair was on top of her head in what she called a "messy bun," and her face was scrubbed clean of makeup. She turned left and tossed her clothes in the bedroom before she joined him in the living room. She perched on the edge of the chair with her hands folded in her lap and her lower lip caught between her teeth.

Grady recognized that look; it was the one she got any time she was trying to hold back tears. He'd seen it a lot over the last few years. He sat forward, rested his elbows on his knees, and cleared his throat.

"Are you okay?" he asked.

"What makes you think I'm not?" she snapped.

He bit his tongue and reminded himself that she had been through hell, including witnessing the murder of her boyfriend less than twelve hours ago. He'd already scolded her once; he didn't want to do it again. Now that they were out of danger—for the time being—she could have a meltdown if she wanted.

He exhaled slowly. "You know, it's okay to cry," he said.

Caitlin scowled. "What makes you think I want to cry?"

Grady sighed. "I know you, Cait. Better than most people. In case you've forgotten, I'm the one who comes behind you and cleans up your messes—"

"How could I forget?" she interjected. "You're con-stantly reminding me."

He shook his head. "I don't want to fight with you. All I'm saying is that it's okay to mourn the death of your boyfriend. You don't have to put on a brave face for me."

Caitlin stared at her hands. "He … he wasn't my boyfriend. I broke up with him," she whispered in a shaky voice. "A couple of hours before he was … was murdered, we got into a fight. Bobby is—I mean was—an asshole. He grabbed me once or twice, hard enough to hurt, and I knew he was dealing drugs. If that relationship had continued, he probably would have hit me. The night he died, we fought. He punched the wall and left."

"Jesus, why didn't you tell me?" Grady murmured.

She shook her head and shrugged. "I don't know. It was just one more thing I screwed up." She scrubbed at the tears on her cheek with the back of her hand. "I forgot to get his key. I figured he'd come around again, so I was gonna get the lock changed. I didn't think he would show up so soon. Now, he's dead, his brains splattered all over my apartment, and I know I'm supposed to feel bad, but he was a jerk. A total asshole. I should feel awful that Bobby died, but all I can think about is how glad I am I got away." An odd chortle came out of her, and she slapped her hand over her mouth. "I'm a terrible person."

"No, you're not terrible," Grady said. "You're human. You didn't know he was going to die."

A choked sob came out of her and the next thing he knew, Caitlin was in his arms, her face pressed against the side of his neck. He hugged her closely, though guilt washed over him as soon as he did it. This was his boss's daughter, *his best friend's* daughter. She was off-limits.

Knock it off. You're consoling a grieving woman.

A sweet, young, beautiful woman. A woman who was the same age as other women he'd recently taken into his bed. Not that any of them compared to her. She was soft, warm, and gorgeous.

Something stirred inside of him, something forbidden yet so appealing he couldn't stop himself from imagining how good it could be. An image of Caitlin naked and lying beneath him suddenly appeared in his head, an image so visceral, so goddamn real that his cock immediately hardened.

For a brief second, his hands clamped down on Caitlin's waist, and he considered yanking her close, tipping her head back, and kissing her. Instead, Grady pushed her away and jumped to his feet.

"You should try to get some sleep. It's been a long night," he muttered.

He darted into the bathroom and slammed the door so hard, the sound echoed through the small cabin. He turned on the sink and splashed cold water on his face and the back of his neck until his heart stopped pounding and his breathing slowed.

He stood up and stared at himself in the mirror. "She's off-limits," he whispered.

Tell that to my dick.

That part of his body didn't seem to give a shit that Caitlin was his boss's daughter and twenty-one years younger than him. It wanted her, and it wanted her badly.

Grady bent over and splashed more water on his face. This was ridiculous. He was tired—exhausted—and struggling to keep it together while he figured out what to do about Caitlin's situation. He was *not* attracted to her; it was a reaction to having a beautiful, young woman in his arms and pressed against his body. It was an inappropriate response, an involuntary response. There was nothing he could do about it. What he could do was forget it ever happened, get his head on straight, and do his job.

Grady dried off his face and opened the bathroom door. The living room was empty, and the bedroom door was closed.

"Thank God," he mumbled to himself.

He listened for a minute, but when he didn't hear anything coming from the bedroom, he made his way to the kitchen to look for alcohol. He needed a drink to dull this sudden need for sex, and he needed it fast.

Chapter 7
Caitlin

Caitlin sat on the couch where Grady had dumped her, staring at the bathroom door. She waited a few minutes, but when he didn't come out, she got to her feet, went into the bedroom, and quietly closed the door. The room was half the size of the living room and boring as hell. Obviously, no thought had gone into decorating it. The head of the four-poster, full-sized bed was shoved up against one wall with matching end tables on either side. The room's walls were white, the carpet was an ugly beige, and the lamps were black with cream-colored shades. Sage green curtains covered the one window in the room.

On the bed were clean bed sheets and a pile of blankets. Caitlin quickly made it, crawled in, laid on her back, and pulled the blankets up to her chin. Maybe she could fall asleep and stop thinking about what happened in her apartment.

That didn't happen. As soon as her eyes slipped shut, the sound of a gunshot echoed in her ears, and she saw the blood splattered all over the floor, the furniture, the carpet, and Bobby's empty eyes staring at the ceiling, with blood pooled under him. The coppery scent still filled her head.

Caitlin sat up, pressed the blanket against her mouth to muffle her sobs, and let the tears fall. Aside from her breakdown in the alley, she'd done her best to hold them back. Now she let loose, crying until her chest and head hurt, and her nose was so plugged with snot she couldn't breathe.

Once the tears tapered off, she closed her eyes, hoping she could sleep. She tossed and turned, still fighting the horrific images in her head. After a few minutes, she gave up, sat up, and ran her hand through her hair. Sleep wasn't happening anytime soon, if at all. She got out of bed and opened the door.

Grady was on the couch with a bottle of water in his hand. He glanced over at her when she came out and grimaced. Not exactly the reception she'd hoped for from the man she'd had a crush on for the last two years.

"I thought you'd be asleep," he said without looking at her.

"I can't fall asleep," Caitlin mumbled. "I can't stop thinking about what happened." She eased into the chair across from him, pulled her knees up, and wrapped her arms around them. What she really wanted to do was sit beside Grady so he could put his arms around her and comfort her. She stared at him for almost a full minute, willing him to call her over, but he ignored her. Apparently, it was up to her to break the silence.

She sucked in a deep breath and exhaled slowly before she spoke. "So, now what?"

"What do you mean, now what?" he grumbled.

Caitlin rolled her eyes. "I mean, do we just hang out here and wait?"

He nodded. "Yep, that is exactly what we are going to do. At least until I hear from your father."

She looked around the small cabin, then back at Grady. "So, this is it? A great room, a bedroom, and a bathroom?"

"Yes."

Why did Grady have to be a man of few words? Getting information out of him was like pulling teeth out of a rabid lion. She took a deep breath and reminded herself not to roll her eyes. "It's kind of close quarters, don't you think?"

Grady shrugged, but he didn't answer her.

Caitlin sighed. "The two of us stuck in one room for God knows how long? You don't think that's a recipe for disaster?"

"No," he replied.

Of course he didn't. It probably didn't faze him at all, while she felt like she was going to crawl out of her skin. She crossed her arms over her chest and glared at him.

"Jesus Christ, you're frustrating," she mumbled.

Grady opened his eyes and smirked at her. "Now you know how I feel when I'm with you."

"What the hell is that supposed to mean?" she retorted.

"You're not the easiest person to get along with, Caitlin," he explained. "You take frustrating to a whole new level."

"Whatever," she muttered. She looked around the room, a thought dawning on her as she took in their accommodations. "Hey, where are you going to sleep?"

He pointed at the couch as he got to his feet. "Right here, on the couch."

"That doesn't sound very comfortable," Caitlin said.

"I'm not concerned about comfort," he snapped. "I'm worried about protecting you."

She resisted the urge to stick out her tongue. Did he have to sound like keeping her safe was such a chore? It wasn't her fault her ex-boyfriend had been murdered in her apartment.

She clenched her fists in her lap and did her best not to scream. This conversation was not going as she'd hoped. "Don't you … don't you think we'll drive each other crazy?" she asked.

Grady shook his head. "No, I think we can stay out of each other's way for a few days."

Fat chance of that happening, especially in such close quarters.

"Does the TV work?" she asked as he walked past her.

Grady stopped, glanced at the television, then back at her. "I think so. It's satellite. The remote is in the drawer of the coffee table."

"Okay," she said, though she didn't move. She couldn't take her eyes off him. The raw anger running through his body made him even sexier than usual. It was like a fire burned in his eyes, and she couldn't look away.

He ran a hand through his gray hair and stared at the ceiling for a full thirty seconds before he asked, "Are you hungry?"

"Yes," she murmured.

"I'll make us some food," he said.

After Grady went into the kitchen, Caitlin got up and opened the drawer on the coffee table. The remote was there, next to a handgun. She took out the remote, sat down, and scrolled through the channels, looking for something mindless to watch. She settled on reruns of *Friends*.

It wasn't long before the smell of eggs and toast wafted her way, making her salivate. She got to her feet and went to the kitchen. There was a plate on the table, along with a full glass of orange juice. Grady sat on the other side of the table, shoveling food into his mouth. He didn't even glance at her.

Caitlin eased into the chair across from him and picked up her fork. She was hungry, but she didn't realize how much until the first bite of food hit her tongue. Hunger took over. She polished off everything on the plate, plus two more pieces of toast and two glasses of orange juice. She stifled a burp with the back of her hand.

When she was done, Caitlin got up, gathered their dirty dishes, and took them to the sink. She filled it with hot, soapy water and washed everything. After she finished, she turned around and leaned against the counter. Grady was still at the table, watching her.

"What?"

"I didn't know you could do dishes," he said with a smirk.

Caitlin rolled her eyes. "I know how to clean. I'm not helpless."

"I didn't say you were," he replied. "But I've never seen you clean, well, anything."

She flipped him off, pivoted, and went into the living room. As she walked, she yanked her hair out of the bun and put the ponytail holder on her wrist. Caitlin considered sitting on the chair and watching TV, but instead she went into the bedroom and slammed the door behind her. She climbed into bed and immediately fell asleep.

Caitlin awoke to a dark room. She sat up, groggy, confused, and unsure what time it was. For a second, the thought flitted through her head that maybe everything that happened had been a dream. A horrible, impossible dream. But then she heard Grady talking in the other room and realized it was all real.

She got out of bed and opened the door. He wasn't in the living room, though she could still hear his voice. Caitlin glanced into the kitchen and saw him leaning against the counter with his cell phone pressed to his ear. She slipped into the bathroom and quietly shut the door.

She washed her face and hands, then she brushed her teeth. Her hair stood up all over her head like she'd slept standing on it, so Caitlin pulled it up into the bun like she'd had it earlier. She didn't know what time it was or how long she'd been asleep; everything was upside down. A knock on the door made her jump and squeal.

"Caitlin? Are you okay?"

It was Grady, of course. It wouldn't be anyone else.

"Yeah, I'm fine." Her heart was in her throat, but she was fine.

"I need to talk to you," he said.

"Okay, give me a minute," she yelled. She looked in the mirror one more time, but there was nothing she could do to combat the puffy eyes or her pale, washed-out face. Not that it mattered. She could look like a runway-ready supermodel, and Grady wouldn't blink twice in her direction. She was his boss's daughter. Shit, she was the *mob* boss's daughter. The mobster's daughter. Off-limits.

With a sigh, Caitlin yanked open the door and saw Grady was on the couch. She crossed the room and dropped into the chair. "What time is it?"

"Almost seven. You slept most of the day away. Do you want something to eat?"

She shook her head. "No. You wanted to talk to me? What's up?"

"I spoke to your father," he said.

"Great," she muttered. "And what did dear old Dad have to say?"

He snarled. "Knock it off, Caitlin."

She crossed her arms and stared at the floor. He was right, of course. She had a tendency to treat her father unfairly. "I'm sorry," she mumbled. "What did he say?"

Grady sighed. "He wants us to stay here until further notice. He's setting up a meeting with Moretti."

Her head came up. "What? Why is my father going to talk to the man who thinks I killed his son? What if something happens to him?"

"Your father has people to protect him," he said. "He's trying to protect *you* by meeting with Moretti."

Caitlin exhaled. "Okay. So, how long do we have to stay here?" she asked.

"Why?" Grady grumbled. "Are you eager to get back to your blood-splattered apartment?"

He might as well have punched her in the chest. "That's not fair," she whispered.

He sat forward, his elbows on his knees, his hands clasped together tightly. "I know it isn't fair. But I don't think you understand the severity of this situation. Your life is in danger."

Caitlin rolled her eyes. "I know."

He growled in frustration and jumped to his feet. "God damn it. Quit rolling your fucking eyes. I swear to God, you are so damn immature sometimes. This shit is for real; this isn't a game. Someone wants you dead. *Dead.* Do you understand what I'm saying?"

"Of course I understand," she retorted. "I'm not stupid. I am scared. Shit, I'm not just scared; I'm terrified, Grady. I know you think I'm not taking this seriously, but how the hell could I not? I'm in a cabin in the middle of the woods with a man who can barely tolerate being in the same room as me. I'm scared, lonely, and I want to go home. Not home as in my apartment, but *home*. With Mom and Dad and Olivia. I want all of this to be over so I can move on with my goddamn life. And the last thing I need is a fucking lecture from you. Please stop treating me like I'm some insolent brat and treat me with a little respect."

"Then stop acting like an insolent brat," Grady countered. He grabbed his gun from the table, tucked it into his waistband, then he stormed past Caitlin and out the back door.

"Fuck," she muttered. She pushed a hand through her hair, swung around, and went back into the bedroom.

Chapter 8
Caitlin

Caitlin stood in the middle of the room, unsure why she was back in the bedroom. She yanked off the shirt and sweatpants she'd slept in and picked up a bag from the floor. She grabbed the first thing she found, which turned out to be the skirt and one of the T-shirts they bought from the store. The shirt was tighter than she liked, and the skirt hit mid-thigh, but it would have to do. She put the clean clothes on and brushed her hair until it didn't look like a rat's nest, then she braided it. When she was done, she nosed around, looking in drawers, the closet, and even under the bed. That was where she discovered a stash of books, old romances with the same long-haired guy on all the covers; Olivia called them bodice-busters. She chose one and tried to read it, but she couldn't concentrate.

All she could think about was Grady—her feelings for him, his disdain for her. They couldn't go on like this.

Maybe I need to tell him how I feel.

She could lay it all out and be honest about how she felt. There was no way she could stay cooped up in this place with him for an undetermined amount of time, not with constant tension in the air. She would tell him. Once she calmed down, and he came back.

Decision made, she climbed onto the bed, arranged the pillows behind her head, and read until she heard the back door slam.

She waited a few minutes, wondering if Grady would approach her first. When he didn't, she got up, opened the door, and peered out. He stood on the other side of the room in front of the inlaid bookcases, head tipped at an angle, looking at the variety of books on the shelves. He turned when she stepped into the living room.

"Where did you go?" she asked.

"Nowhere," he replied with a shrug. "I walked around the perimeter. Checked things out while I got some much-needed air."

Caitlin eased into the chair and folded her hands in her lap. "I want to apologize. I know I can be ... difficult."

Grady snorted.

She winced. "I'm trying to say I'm sorry."

He ambled across the room, stopped a foot or so away from her, and crossed his arms. The gesture made his biceps bulge. "Go on."

She got to her feet and stood face to face with him. She was tall enough that they were almost eye to eye. "I know you think I'm a brat. There's a reason I act like that when I'm with you. I—I do it on purpose. It makes it easier to push *you* away."

"What do you mean, push me away?" he asked. "What are you talking about?"

Caitlin inched closer. "The way I feel about you—"

Grady took a step back, his hands up. "Caitlin, don't. Stop before you say something you'll regret."

She shook her head. "The only thing I regret is not telling you this sooner." She sucked in a deep breath and slowly exhaled. "I fucking hate you, you asshole, but every part of me wants you. I can't stop thinking about you. I can't stop thinking about how much I *want* you. Need you."

Grady clenched and unclenched his fists and shook his head. "You don't know what you're saying."

"Yes, I do. For the last two years, you have been the only man I can think about. Why do you think I was always getting in trouble? Because I knew you would come to my rescue."

"What about Bobby?" he asked. "Or any of the other boyfriends you've had?

Caitlin laughed, though there was no joy in it. "Bobby was a filler, a way to forget about you. They all were. But it didn't work. I can only think about you."

He sighed. "You don't know what you're saying."

"I know exactly what I'm saying," she whispered. "I know what and *who* I want."

Grady pushed a hand through his gray hair and stared at her. "I can't be what you want."

Her heart thumped so hard she was sure he could hear it. When had she fallen in love with him? When had this man, a man her father would never let her be with, become the only man she wanted?

"Grady," she whispered. "Please." She moved a step closer.

Suddenly, he lunged, took her by the shoulders, and dragged her close. His mouth closed over hers in a kiss that stole her breath from her lungs. Her arms slipped around him, and a sigh escaped her.

Just as quickly as the kiss started, it ended. Grady pushed her away, spun around, and darted into the kitchen. He perched on the edge of the kitchen table, head down, chest heaving, and eyes closed. His hands gripped the table so hard she heard it creak.

Caitlin couldn't play this game anymore, this back-and-forth shit. She followed him and stopped less than a foot away from him. "How long are we going to fight this?"

He shook his head. "It's wrong."

She took another step forward and planted herself between Grady's legs. She put her hands on his thighs and stared into his eyes. "It's not wrong. Not if we're both desperate for it. I know you want me. More importantly, *you* know it, but something is holding you back."

Grady grunted. "Yeah, you're Sean O'Reilly's daughter."

"I don't give a shit what my father thinks," Caitlin said. "You shouldn't either. This has nothing to do with him and everything to do with us. The feelings we have for each other. The crazy *need* we have for each other. I know you feel it as much as I do." She leaned over and brushed a kiss across his lips. "Admit it," she whispered.

He fidgeted, pulling his head back so they weren't touching. "It doesn't matter what I feel or what I want. You're my boss's daughter."

Caitlin slid her hands further up his thighs. "Why can't we just forget about that for one night?"

"Because in the morning, it will still be our reality," Grady murmured.

She sighed and stared into his gray eyes. "Tell me you don't want me, and I'll walk away right now. I'll go in that tiny, little bedroom over there, close and lock the door, and we can pretend it never happened. Look me in the eye and swear to me you don't want this as much as I do."

He stared at her, sweat on his brow, his fists clenched at his sides. She waited, wondering if he would say it, tell her he didn't want her. If he said those words, she would walk away.

Ten seconds passed. Twenty. Thirty. Forty-five seconds. A full minute. Silence.

Caitlin licked her lips. "I need your mouth on me, on my body." She ran her hands up his thighs until she reached the growing bulge under his jeans. She rubbed him through the thick denim, his cock hard under her hand. "I want to feel your cock inside me, filling me up."

Grady groaned. "Jesus, Caitlin, your mouth."

"Let me show you what I can do with my mouth," she whispered.

He grabbed her, put his arms around her, and pulled her tight against him, his erection pressed against her stomach. His hands eased under the edge of the short skirt she wore and kneaded the soft skin of her ass. He caught her lips in his.

Caitlin sighed as his tongue slipped into her mouth. He tasted like heaven.

Grady broke off the kiss far too soon. He held her at arm's length. "There's no going back," he said. "If we do this, we do it my way. Do you understand, princess?"

She nodded.

"You do what I say, when I say. This will not be like fucking your pansy-assed former boyfriends, baby. I take what I want, how and when I want it. But I promise you, it will be just as good, if not better, for you. It will be the best goddamn sex you have ever had in your life. Now, are you sure this is what you want?"

That was the hottest damn thing anyone ever said to her. She was wet and throbbing.

"Answer me."

"Yes," she whispered. "Jesus Christ, yes."

Grady yanked her back between his legs, hooked his thumbs in the flimsy panties she wore, and dragged them down, hurriedly pushing them down her thighs until she could kick them off. His hand dipped between her legs, and his long, thick fingers pushed into her.

"Fuck," she gasped. She wrapped her arms around his neck, squirming and pushing herself down on his hand, urging him on.

Grady nipped at her neck and caressed her breast through the thin T-shirt. "Christ, Caitlin, you are so fucking sexy." He slid his hand up her chest and wrapped it around her throat. He forced her to look at him. "I want to hear what you sound like when you cum, princess."

As he gently squeezed her throat, his fingers plunged deep into her. He used them to fuck her until her legs gave out and her body was his to control. All she could do was dig her fingers into his shoulders and hold on. Caitlin threw her head back, loud, obscene gasps and moans falling from her lips. He released his grip on her, put his arm around her waist, and held her close, using everything he had to give her as much pleasure as possible. Her body tensed, and a shuddering moan left her as the orgasm built inside her. She finally let go with a loud, "Yes!"

Caitlin barely had time to catch her breath before he pushed her to her knees. "Show me what you can do with that mouth," he said.

She unbuttoned and unzipped his jeans, yanking them down until his cock was free. She took the base in her hand and held it tight as she wrapped her lips around him. Her tongue swirled across the tip, then she slid her mouth down his shaft. A moan escaped her as she moved, taking more of Grady's length with every bob of her head, until her nose was pressed against him, and his cock was down her throat.

Caitlin glanced up at him through her lashes. She watched him as she moved her mouth up and down his shaft. He wrapped a hand around the back of her head and twisted his fingers in her braid.

"That's it, baby," Grady growled. "Take it all."

He shifted forward, his hips thrusting, shoving his dick into the warm heat of her mouth. Fuck, she liked it. She wanted him to fuck her senseless, wanted his cum down her throat, inside her, all over her. She wanted him to own her, every damn inch of her. Desire pooled in her stomach as she sucked him into her mouth. She pushed a hand between her legs, desperate for something to relieve the ache between her legs.

Grady must have known what she needed. He grabbed her arm and pulled her to her feet. "Take off the skirt and the T-shirt."

She didn't hesitate to do as he asked. He leaned her over the table, her ass in the air, dropped to one knee, put his warm hands on the inside of her thighs, and kissed a trail up her leg, his tongue briefly diving into her wet pussy before he got to his feet. He wrapped an arm around her and put his hand between her legs. His fingers danced over her, teasing her until she thought she might pass out from need.

He gripped her hips as he leaned over her. His hard cock pressed against her ass. She couldn't resist wiggling it against him. He grabbed her braid and pulled her head back.

"Tell me what you want me to do to you, princess," he ordered.

Caitlin squirmed and rolled her eyes. He knew what she wanted; she didn't have to say it.

A stinging slap landed on her ass, taking her by surprise. "Answer me," Grady demanded.

She'd never been so turned on. God, it was even better than she imagined. Every second that passed made her more desperate to have him inside her, filling her up. "I … I want you to fuck me," she whispered.

"Beg for it," he said. He smacked her ass again.

"Please fuck me," she begged. "Fuck me now!"

The tip of Grady's cock rubbed against her entrance, and then he slid into her, stretching her wide. He moved slowly at first, giving her time to adjust. He put a hand on her shoulder and held her in place as he thrust into her. Once she took him completely, he flexed his hips, slamming into her hard, every movement hitting her sweet spot. He pulled her upright, slid his hand down her stomach, and circled her clit with two fingers.

Caitlin gasped as he used his fingers on her, and his thrusts hit the perfect spot. She gripped his arm and moved with him, an intimate, scintillating dance like nothing she had ever experienced before. Her climax started deep inside her, spreading like a wildfire through her until she exploded, coming with a loud scream. Moisture ran down her thighs as Grady pushed her back over the table and pounded relentlessly into her. The orgasm rolled through her, draining every ounce of her energy.

A few seconds later, he slammed into her one last time, burying himself deep inside her, his cock twitching, his breath heavy on her neck, his arms tight around her as he let go.

Caitlin collapsed face down on the kitchen table and tried to catch her breath. Grady's lips grazed her shoulders and neck, kissing and nibbling the bare skin. He helped her upright and cradled her against his chest.

She fisted his T-shirt in her hands and breathed deeply, Grady's scent filling her head.

He took hold of her chin and forced her to look at him.

"You know we're fucked, right?" he murmured.

"I don't care," Caitlin replied. "I don't regret it. I won't ever regret it." She swallowed. "Do you?"

Grady shook his head, but he wouldn't look in her eyes. He let go of her, bent down, picked up her clothes, and put them in her hands.

"You should get dressed. I'm going to start a fire. Warm it up in here."

Chapter 9
Grady

What the hell did I do?

Grady laid on the couch, staring into the dark. Caitlin had gone to bed shortly after midnight. It had been obvious she wanted him to go with her, but he had only nodded at her. She sighed loudly, went into the bedroom, and shut the door harder than necessary.

It had been an awkward evening, spent in silence. Neither of them knew what to say to the other. He was relieved when she announced she was going to bed, and he had no intention of following because he needed time to process what happened without Caitlin staring at him from the other side of the room.

There was no way he would ever fall asleep, so he got up. He remembered something Sean had said about stocking this place with alcohol, but he didn't know if it had happened. Under one bookcase was a small cabinet, where he found bottles of scotch, whiskey, and bourbon. He grabbed a bottle of Jameson, poured two fingers of the amber liquid into a glass, and downed it. Grady coughed at the sudden burn in his throat, but that didn't stop him from pouring more into the glass. He returned to the couch, bottle and glass in hand.

It wasn't like him to drink heavily, especially when he was on duty, but these were unusual circumstances.

I fucked Caitlin.

He scrubbed a hand over his face. Over the past two years, he'd grown more attracted to the younger woman, but he had pushed it down and refused to acknowledge it. That didn't stop him from dropping whatever he was doing to help her. Knowing Caitlin had intentionally been getting herself in trouble so he would come to her was rescue was—weirdly—a turn-on. But getting involved with the boss's daughter was a death sentence. Sean would kill him if he found out.

"Knock it off," he mumbled. "Stop thinking about it."

But he couldn't. He could almost feel her warm, soft body in his hands. The taste of her was still in his mouth, and the scent of her was on his skin. Her moans and screams of pleasure echoed in his head. Every time he closed his eyes, he saw Caitlin on her knees in front of him, his cock in her mouth, tears streaming down her cheeks as she sucked his dick. Just thinking about it made him hard.

He pushed the thought away, refusing to acknowledge his growing feelings for Caitlin. He didn't believe in love. Emotions no longer ruled his life; not since Oona betrayed him.

That was another thing he didn't want to think about, so Grady poured another drink. Anything to help him ignore the wave of emotions fighting to overtake him. Before he knew it, the bottle was empty, and he was drunk. He dropped the glass on the table, stretched out on the couch, and fell asleep.

Oona stared up at him, tears streaming down her face.

"Please, Grady, you don't have to do this." She swallowed, her throat moving. "We can go away, me and you. Someplace where nobody knows us. We can start over. We don't have to stay here."

"You tried to kill me," he whispered.

She shook her head. "I never wanted to hurt you. I was supposed to kill Sean O'Reilly. You got in the way."

Grady pressed the gun to Oona's head.

He bolted upright, the gunshot a memory echoing in his ears. He rubbed his temples, grimacing at the pounding in his head, likely because of the alcohol. His neck was stiff, and his mouth was dry. After going to the bathroom and brushing his teeth, he stood in front of the bedroom door, one hand on the knob, ready to open it and go inside.

He was determined to talk to Caitlin, to discuss what happened. They couldn't be together, feelings be damned. He had to explain to her how it was wrong, a terrible idea, and could have consequences neither of them wanted in their lives. The dream about Oona reminded him why he didn't get involved with anyone.

He had a list of the reasons they couldn't be together, ready to go. Arguing wasn't an option; Caitlin would listen to what he said, and then she would *do* as he said. Period.

Grady dropped his hand and took a step back. She was a force to be reckoned with when she didn't get her way or if she wanted something, evidenced by what happened between them last night. But he didn't have a choice; he had to be the one to stop this madness before it went too far.

It already went too far.

Grady reached for the door just as it opened. Caitlin let out a startled squeak and stumbled back. Her knees hit the bed, and she fell on it.

"Jesus Christ, what the fuck are you doing?" she snapped. "You're sneaking around at the crack of dawn? Were you trying to give me a heart attack?"

He sighed. Why the hell did she have to be so damn annoying and intriguing at the same time? Her blonde hair was still braided down her back, though a few strands were loose, falling around her face. The shirt she wore left absolutely nothing to the imagination, hugging her curves, her nipples poking against the fabric. It was obvious she was cold and not just because she rubbed her arms as she stared at him.

"We need to talk," he said.

Caitlin jumped to her feet. "I don't want to talk. Not if you're going to say what I think you are."

The dim light streaming through the window put an ethereal glow around her, making her look like something not of this world. She was a beautiful woman. Grady dropped his eyes and stared at the floor as he spoke. He couldn't look at her or his control would snap.

"What we did was wrong," he mumbled.

"You don't sound like you believe that," she retorted.

"You're younger than me," he said. "And you're my boss's daughter." He didn't even believe himself when he said it.

Caitlin stepped into his personal space and put her hand on his chest. "Grady, look at me. Please?"

He sucked in a deep breath and looked into Caitlin's bright blue eyes.

"Stop thinking about this like you're my father's *leascheannasaí*. For once in your life, let yourself *feel* something. You don't have to be the tough guy with no emotions all the time." She inched a little closer. "Not with me."

Grady shook his head, but he couldn't shake away the need for her. He wanted her, wanted to possess her, own her, make her his in every way possible. He'd been barreling full force down this path for the last two years, and now she was there for him to take and make his own. He couldn't resist the need, and he could not resist *Caitlin*.

"Screw it," he muttered, then he grabbed her by the waist, slipped his hands under her T-shirt, and dragged it over her head. He dropped it to the floor, caught her lips in his, and kissed her hard.

If she wanted him, she was going to get the full Grady treatment. He didn't hold back with sex, and he sure the hell wouldn't start now. He would give her tonight, show her what he liked, what he wanted, and if she wasn't on board, then they would both know it wouldn't work.

Caitlin moaned into his mouth.

He broke off the kiss. "Fuck, it's sexy when you moan for me," he murmured. He cupped her breast and thumbed the nipple. "I want to fuck you."

She smirked. "I guess you don't think it's wrong anymore, do you?"

Grady grabbed her chin and held it tight. "I said it was wrong. I didn't say I don't want to fuck your brains out. I don't know what the hell it is about you, Caitlin O'Reilly, but I need you like I need the goddamn air I breathe."

Her eyes widened, and she trembled in his arms.

He dragged her closer until her mouth was only inches from his. "You need to understand something, *princess*. If we do this, if we commit to this insane path, you are mine and mine alone. I like things a certain way, and if you can't deal with that, then we won't go any further. Do you understand?"

"Yes," she whispered.

Grady grinned. "Good. Now, tell me you want me to fuck you. Beg me to fuck you."

Caitlin swallowed, and her chest heaved. "Please fuck me."

"Hm, I'm not sure that's good enough," he muttered.

Her voice dropped to a low whisper, and she stared up at him as if he could give her everything she wanted. "I want you to fuck me, Grady. I want your cock inside me. Make me scream. I'm begging you."

"That's better." He slipped his hand between her legs and teased her with the tips of his fingers. "Mm, you're fucking soaked. Does all of this make you wet, baby? Does being told what to do turn you on?" He dragged his lips from her jaw to her ear and sucked the lobe between his teeth. "Answer me."

Caitlin moaned. "Yes." She whimpered, her head fell back, and her hips flexed, chasing his fingers. "Please, don't tease."

He laughed. "That's the fun part, princess. You know what? I think I need to make you scream. What do you think about that?"

He didn't give her a chance to answer; instead, he wrapped his arm around her waist and held her flush against his body. Grady thrust two fingers into her pussy and pumped them, enjoying the gasp of surprise that came from Caitlin. He kept at it for several seconds, taking her right up to the edge before he abruptly stopped and pulled away.

"What the hell?" she muttered, stumbling toward him.

"Take off your underwear and get on the bed," he ordered.

Caitlin shot him a dirty look, but she did as he said. He stripped off his clothes, leaving them in a pile on the floor. He grabbed Caitlin's ankle and dragged her to the end of the bed.

Grady dropped to the floor and kneeled in front of her. He ran his hands up her calves and over her trembling thighs, taking in every inch of her. He dragged his tongue up her inner thigh, stopping to blow a heated breath across her wet core, drawing a moan from her. His tongue snaked out of his mouth.

"I could stay here all night," he whispered. "Teasing." He brushed light kisses across her hip, his thumb grazing her sensitive nub. "Tasting." He licked her warmth, groaning as her taste covered his tongue. "Sucking." The tip of his tongue tapped lightly at her clit, circling it before he pulled it into his mouth, sucking it between his lips. Her hips shot off the bed, grinding against his face.

He swirled his tongue around the sensitive nub of nerves, making her squirm, then he thrust it into her warm, wet entrance, his fingers sliding into her, caressing her walls. She was close, he knew; he could *feel* it. He pulled away.

Caitlin groaned and shot him an irritated look.

Grady ignored it. "Get on your knees," he ordered.

She obeyed immediately. What a surprise; she *could* listen.

He got on the bed, laid on his back, and gestured for her to straddle him. Once she was seated on his chest, he guided her up his body until his head was between her legs. He rubbed her ass and squeezed it gently, then he pulled her down until she hovered over his face.

"Ride me, baby," he said as he yanked her down onto him, his tongue stroking her several times before he slid it inside her.

Caitlin put her hands on the wall behind the bed and eased forward. Grady buried his tongue inside her, his mouth completely covering her, sucking, licking, tasting. She moved, slowly at first, then faster, writhing and moaning obscenely.

His cock jutted out from his body, aching and throbbing. He couldn't hold out much longer.

Caitlin closed her eyes, arched her back, and fucked his face. Her cries of pleasure got louder and louder, and he knew she was about to orgasm.

Grady pulled away, his fingers replacing his tongue, and held her right on the edge.

"Jesus, baby, you taste good." He squeezed her ass with one hand. "I love it when you ride me." He swept his fingers across her sweet spot and grinned when she gasped.

"Oh my god, please," she begged. "Let me cum."

He chuckled. "Oh, not until I say so. I'm not done with you yet." Grady moved and flipped her to her back, his fingers still inside her, moving and teasing.

Caitlin gasped and moaned as he kissed her body, touching every inch of bare skin. He took her aching breast into his mouth and sucked on her hard, pebbled nipple, teasing it. Her back arched, and she whimpered.

"Beg, princess," Grady purred. "Tell me how bad you want to cum. Tell me how bad you want me to fuck you so you can cum."

"Please don't tease me anymore," she cried. "I need your cock inside me. I need you to fuck me. I want it so much, and you know it. You can feel how wet I am, how turned on I am, and that's all because of you. Please make me cum. I want to cum on your cock. I'm begging you to let me finish."

Grady moaned. He kissed her, his cock jerking against her hip, then he got to his knees, pulled her legs around his waist, and lined himself up with her entrance. He sank into her, an inch at a time, making her wait, watching her lose her mind as he teased her.

"When you cum, you better scream my name." He yanked her against him, filling her completely. Grady held himself there, inside her, his cock twitching.

"Please," she begged.

He slammed into her, their hips colliding, his grip on her so tight, it would probably leave marks. It didn't matter because he was fucking her, pounding into her, as unfathomable, incoherent noises fell from her lips.

"Jesus, Cait, I love the way you sound when I'm inside you." He panted as he thrust into her, the muscles in his arms and neck taut with tension. "Touch yourself. I want to see you touch yourself while I fuck you."

Caitlin slid her hand between her legs, found the swollen nub of nerves, and rubbed it with two fingers. Grady's cock brushed against them with every flex of his hips, both of them now consumed with lust, the sensations overwhelming.

"Cum for me," he ordered. He rammed into her, trapping her hand between their bodies, her fingers pressed against her clit.

The orgasm he'd denied her for so long exploded through her. She came, screaming Grady's name. He pumped his hips, forcing her fingers to press into her as his cock pulsed, his own climax consuming him as her walls tightened around him. The pleasure was so intense, he thought he might pass out.

When it was over, Grady collapsed to the bed beside her, their legs tangled together, his arm thrown over her waist and his face pressed to the side of her neck. He kissed her throat and traced circles on her skin.

Caitlin rolled over, rested her hand on his cheek, and kissed him.

She was impossible to resist. He'd tasted the forbidden fruit, and it was better than anything he could have imagined. Unfortunately, nothing good would come from it.

Grady abruptly rolled to his back and got out of bed. "I need a drink," he said. He grabbed his clothes and walked out of the room.

Chapter 10
Grady

His heart thudded in his chest. Feelings complicated things. They didn't just complicate things; they *changed* everything. His best friend was almost murdered the last time he let his feelings control him. He had been shot and nearly lost his life. All because of a woman, a woman Grady thought he loved.

When Caitlin put her hand on his cheek, his frozen heart cracked and for a second, he considered what might happen if he allowed her in. He shut down that thought as soon as it entered his brain and bolted.

Grady darted out of the bedroom, went into the bathroom, splashed some water on his face, and dressed. Then he headed straight to the liquor cabinet, grabbed the bottle of Glenlivet scotch, and took a drink from it. He then poured a small amount in the glass on the coffee table and picked it up.

He exhaled and walked to the open bedroom door. "Caitlin?"

She squinted at him from the bed. "Yeah?"

"You want a drink?" Grady asked. "Water or something?"

She pointed at the glass in his hand. "What's that?"

"Scotch," he replied. "I drank all the whiskey." Did she even care he drank all the whiskey? Probably not.

She pulled the sheet around herself and got out of bed. "Isn't it a little early for alcohol?"

He shot her a dirty look. Was she joking?

"Okay, no jokes in the morning. Noted." She grinned, and the ice around his heart melted a bit more. "You know what, I'll have a glass of that," she said.

Grady raised his eyebrows, but he kept his mouth shut. No arguing with her; she was a grown woman and could do what she wanted.

Caitlin followed him to the living room and stood right beside him while he poured her a glass of scotch. She took it and held Grady's gaze as she downed it. To his surprise, she didn't even flinch.

"You good?" he asked.

"Mm-hm." She held the glass out and gestured for more. Grady obliged.

Once he refilled her drink, she sat down on the couch and cleared her throat. "Are you going to do this every time we have sex?"

Grady groaned, crossed his arms over his chest, and leaned against the wall next to the bookcase. "Do what?"

"Run off after we fuck and make some excuse to get away from me," she replied. "Making a fire, getting a drink. What's next? Running a marathon?"

He sighed. She would not let him off the hook easily. "In case you haven't noticed, I'm not great at expressing myself."

"Oh, I noticed."

Grady glared at her. Caitlin had the good sense to close her mouth. She nodded at him to continue.

"This thing between us is complicated," he continued.

"No shit," she interjected.

"Dammit, will you shut up and listen to me?" he snapped.

"Sorry, sorry." She made a motion like she had zipped her lips closed.

"Thank you." He pinched the bridge of his nose. "I'm supposed to be protecting you, not fucking …" He stopped and took a deep breath. "Sorry, I mean, I'm not supposed to be *having sex* with you. It complicates an already complicated situation."

"Maybe if we talk to my father—"

Grady shook his head. "Do you think we should talk to your father? Considering everything that is happening right now, something like this might push him over the edge."

Caitlin nodded and mumbled, "You're right. It will piss him off."

He sat on the edge of the chair and sipped his drink. "Tell me about Bobby."

"What do you want to know?" she asked.

"Did he have a relationship with his father? Why was he working for the Moretti family? Did he need money? Or maybe he pissed the Italians off and had to work off a debt or something?"

She shrugged. "I don't know. He rarely mentioned his father and when he did, he never said who his father was, just vague references to 'my father.' I didn't know Moretti *was* his father until you told me. I know he sold drugs, but he never talked about it."

"How did you know about the drugs?" Grady asked.

Caitlin gave him a weird look. "Seriously? I've spent years around people who … well, let's just say people who weren't on the up and up. I notice things, and I know when people are doing something they aren't supposed to do. Late-night phone calls, not letting me see what was in his backpack or check his phone, plus we never stayed at his place, and weird people were always coming around or calling him at all hours of the day and night. I knew."

"That might have pissed off his father," Grady muttered.

"Enough to kill his own son?" She shook her head. "I don't think so."

He sat back and closed his eyes. "None of this makes sense. None of it. I can't believe Aldo would risk jeopardizing a deal that has been years in the making."

Caitlin narrowed her eyes. "What deal?"

"Your father worked tirelessly to get the Italians to agree to a partnership between the two families. They were going to work with us in our East Coast dealings. I don't know how he did it."

Caitlin's eyes widened and her lips twisted in a grimace. Before he could ask her what was wrong, his cell phone rang.

He didn't just want to ignore it; he wanted to throw it out the window and run over it with the Bronco. Or maybe use it for target practice. He snatched it off the table and hit the button.

"Yeah?"

"Grady?"

He gritted his teeth. He wasn't interested in talking to his boss less than twenty minutes after he'd had sex with the man's daughter.

"Grady? Are you there?"

"Yes, sir?"

"You haven't checked in," Sean said. "Is everything okay?"

He forgot he'd promised to check in at six a.m. He glanced at his watch; it was almost ten.

Shit.

"Everything is fine," Grady replied. "How are things on your end?"

"Not good," Sean muttered. "Moretti is on the warpath. Understandably. His son is dead, and he was found in my daughter's apartment. He is convinced Caitlin is responsible for Roberto's murder. I tried to tell him what happened, but he hung up on me. I'm sending Finn and Declan to New York to talk to him in person. Listen to me. If Moretti finds her, he will kill her. You have to keep her safe."

"I'll protect her with my life," Grady said.

"I know." Sean sighed and his voice shook when he spoke. "No matter what happens, your only job is to protect my daughter."

"I will," Grady replied.

"I don't trust anyone but you. Do you understand?" Sean asked.

"Yes, sir," he whispered.

"If you do this for me, if you keep Caitlin safe and alive, then consider your debt to me paid."

"You don't have to do that," Grady said.

"Yes, I do." Sean cleared his throat. "I can't help but wonder if this is because I called off the wedding."

A chill raced down Grady's spine. "Wedding? What wedding?"

Caitlin abruptly got up and went into the bathroom. The shower turned on a few seconds later.

The room closed in on him, and he couldn't breathe. He squeezed the phone in his hand so hard he heard a crack. Sean was unusually quiet.

"What wedding are you talking about?" Grady asked again.

Sean cleared his throat before he spoke. His voice was low, practically indiscernible. "Caitlin's wedding. She was supposed to marry Moretti's oldest son, Massimo."

The room spun, and Grady's vision went black. His head throbbed, but it wasn't from alcohol.

"Why didn't you tell me?"

"Because it was none of your business," Sean said. "It was between me and Moretti."

"I'm your *leascheannasaí*. If you can't trust me—"

"It had nothing to do with trusting you," Sean snapped. "You know I trust you, with my life *and* with my family's life. There isn't anyone on Earth I trust more. But it was a delicate situation. It's Moretti; he doesn't trust anyone. He insisted we keep the negotiations between us. I did as he asked."

Grady sat on the couch. "Why? What were you trying to gain by marrying Caitlin off to the Morettis?"

"Aldo's trust," Sean replied. "And an ally. Instead, I made him an enemy. He was furious when I called off the wedding. He couldn't understand why I cared how my daughter felt about her impending nuptials. In his eyes, all that mattered was merging our families into one of the most powerful on the East Coast. When Olivia married Declan and he took over the Muldoon family, Aldo saw it as an act of war. He swore he would make us pay for ruining his plans."

Grady groaned. "Do you think Bobby's murder—"

"I don't know what to think," his boss said. "I can't imagine Moretti would kill his own son to get back at me. It had to be someone who knew how tenuous our working relationship was and used Caitlin and Roberto

Corelli to start shit. What I do know is Aldo will have no problem killing Caitlin because he thinks she killed Roberto. As a bonus, it will be the perfect way for him to get revenge for fucking up the marriage plan."

"You should have told me, boss."

Sean sighed loud enough for Grady to hear it through the phone. "I know, but like I said, it wasn't any of your business."

"It is my business, especially now," Grady interjected. It was his business because Caitlin belonged to *him*. She was his, and no one would ever touch her again, especially one of those damn Morettis. He pinched the bridge of his nose. He couldn't think like that; emotions made everything more difficult.

"I'm sorry," Sean murmured.

"Great, you're sorry. But that's not good enough. This situation is significantly more complicated than I thought. Things have escalated to a level I cannot control."

"You can and you will. Keep Caitlin safe, Grady." Sean was quiet for a long moment before he spoke again. "I will not call anymore. I'm worried someone might track the calls back to your location."

The phone went dead in Grady's hand. He tossed it on the table and rested his head against the couch. He desperately wanted another drink, but he needed to stay sharp. He'd already had more than enough alcohol.

Instead, he got up, went to the kitchen, opened the fridge, grabbed a bottle of water, and drank half of it. When he turned around, Caitlin stood between the living room and the kitchen, staring at him. She was dressed in jeans and a button-down shirt with little blue cartoon dogs all over it, and her long blonde hair was in a braid that hung over her right shoulder. Her face was clean and shiny. She gnawed on the nail of her left thumb, a habit she'd had since she was a little girl.

"What did he say?" she asked.

Grady gave her a brief rundown of his conversation with her father. Tears welled in her eyes when he told her how worried Sean was about her.

"Shit," she muttered. "It is my fault."

He shook his head. "No, it's not. None of this is your fault."

Caitlin sighed. "You can keep saying it, but I don't have to believe it. If I hadn't gotten involved with Bobby in the first place—"

"Knock it off, Cait. You cannot let yourself go down that road."

"You don't understand," she whispered. "It is my fault." She took a step closer to him and released a shuddering breath. "Do you know why I've been so difficult for the last few years? Why I've broken every rule, pushed every boundary?"

Grady shook his head. "You mean it wasn't just to get me to come to your rescue?"

Caitlin's cheeks turned bright pink. She must have forgotten she told him that. She took a deep breath and continued. "That was part of it. But I also thought if I was awful enough, if I was impossible to be around, or if my father thought he couldn't rein me in, he would leave me alone to live my life."

"Did you know," he asked, "about the marriage and the wedding being called off?"

Caitlin nodded. "Yes."

"You never said anything."

"You're right, I didn't. Daddy asked me not to tell you."

Anger rushed through him at her words. He slammed the bottle of water on the counter, sending droplets flying everywhere. "God dammit! I cannot believe he put you in this position."

Caitlin moved closer, stepping into the kitchen, leaving two to three feet of distance between them. "I've forgiven him. I swear. But I hated him for it for a long time. Then everything with Olivia came to light and, for the first time in my life, my father apologized to me. He swore he never intended for either me or Olivia to get hurt. Shit, he was distraught over what happened to Liv. Horrified. He called off my wedding to the Moretti kid and promised me nothing like that would ever happen again."

Grady snorted. "And you believe him?"

She nodded. "I want to believe him. My father and I are still rebuilding our relationship. It's not going to happen overnight." She giggled. "Not to mention, this whole situation throws a monkey wrench into things." Another giggle burst out of her and then Caitlin laughed, her entire body shaking as the laughter overcame her. She put her hand over her mouth, but she couldn't stop. She sank to the floor, wrapped her arms around her knees, and laughed until tears streamed down her face.

"Jesus. Christ," she muttered, gasping for air between each word. "My life is a … a soap opera … or a, a terrible movie. People are trying to kill me … and … it's all because my father is a mobster."

Grady crouched in front of her and wiped a tear from her cheek with his thumb. "Hey, look at me."

When she brought her face up, he realized the tears weren't from laughter. The pain and fear in her eyes completely melted his icy heart. He would do everything in

his power to keep her safe, and he would give her anything she wanted.

Caitlin stared up at him and whispered, "I'm scared.
I've never been this scared in my life. Those people mean
business. They want me dead."

Grady took her arm and helped her to her feet. He
kissed her forehead before he pulled her into his arms
and hugged her tight.

No one would ever hurt her. They wouldn't dare,
because he would destroy anyone who dared to harm her.

Chapter 11

Grady

Caitlin paced the room, gnawing on her thumbnail. She paused and looked at his gun on the coffee table between them, then at him. "You said you grabbed my gun, right?"

Grady snorted. "I didn't have much choice. I couldn't leave it for the police to find it."

"I haven't shot it in almost a year." She stopped in front of him. "I'm out of practice."

"What are you saying, princess?" he asked.

"If a bunch of fucking hitmen are gunning for me, maybe I need some practice. Don't you think?"

She wasn't wrong. It certainly couldn't hurt. But she couldn't shoot his .357 Magnum, not when she had never shot a gun before.

"Yeah," he said. "It is a good idea. Go grab your backpack and meet me outside. I've got ammo in the truck."

Grady went outside and opened the back of the Bronco. Under a pile of blankets, he had a duffle bag of weapons—all legal and registered. Caitlin put her backpack down beside him and took out her gun. She handed it to him, and he loaded the clip.

A search of the shed behind the house produced empty paint cans, soda bottles, and a few cardboard boxes. He dragged everything out, and, together, he and Caitlin set them up on a fence at the edge of the property.

"You ready?" he asked when they were done.

"Yep," she said.

"Come here."

She did as she was told, moving to stand right in front of him.

"We're going to start with a rundown of the basics. In case you forgot the five rules of gun safety."

Caitlin snorted. "Rules? That's kind of ironic, don't you think?"

Grady kept himself from shaking her by sheer will. "What exactly do you mean?"

"Aren't you kind of a 'shoot first, ask questions later' guy?" she asked.

"Have you ever seen me shoot my gun?"

She opened her mouth to answer, then snapped it shut. "Um, no, I guess not. But it's not like you or any of the men who work for my father follow any rules."

Grady rolled his eyes. "With guns, you always follow the rules, or you get dead. Period."

"Fine."

He sighed; nothing with Caitlin was ever easy. Even when she *wanted* to learn or practice something, she made it difficult.

"Number one: Treat every gun as if it were loaded. Number two: Always point it in a safe direction. Which goes along with numbers three and four: Never point it at anything you don't plan to shoot and be sure of your target and what's behind it. You don't want to shoot someone because you weren't paying attention to what was behind them. And the most important one is to keep your finger *off* the trigger until you are ready to shoot. Got it?"

Caitlin nodded. "Yes."

Grady held out the gun. "Do you remember how to load it?"

"I think so." She took it and the magazine, slid the magazine into place, then used the buttons on the side of the gun to pop it out. She turned around, pointed it at the target, and put a bullet in the chamber.

He moved behind her, wrapped his arms around her, and put his hands over hers. "Step back," he said. "Spread your feet," he ordered, kicking at her right heel. "Bend your knees a little. Don't lock them or you'll go down."

Caitlin did as he instructed. She spread her legs and stepped back, her body flush against his. Her hair tickled his nose.

That goddamn irresistible need for her reared its head. Grady closed his eyes, took a deep breath, and exhaled. All he had to do was concentrate and ignore it.

"Relax," he whispered. He wasn't sure if he was talking to her or to himself.

"I'm trying," she muttered. "It's been a long time since I did this."

He held her trembling hands and together, they brought the gun up. He pointed it at the cardboard box. "Put your finger on the trigger. Take a deep breath and as you exhale, squeeze it."

She did as he said, breathing in, her breast brushing his arm as she inhaled. As the breath escaped her, she squeezed, jumping as the gun went off. The bullet veered left, completely missing the target.

"I missed," she grumbled.

"You'll get better," he said. "It takes practice." He released her and backed up. He couldn't be that close to her and concentrate.

"It's louder than I remember," she said. "And it has more kick."

Grady chuckled. "If I remember correctly, the last time we went shooting, you used a .22. That's a pew-pew gun."

Caitlin put her hand over her mouth and giggled. "What the heck does that mean?"

"It means if you shoot somebody with a .22, especially somebody big, you're just going to piss them off," he explained. "Unless you shoot them in the eye or something. You might slow them down, but it won't be for long. Your Sig Sauer has more power."

For the next two hours, he worked with Caitlin, teaching her how to aim and shoot. Hopefully, that would at least give her a chance to get away.

After a while, she cleared the chamber, removed the magazine, and handed the gun to him. "I'm done. I can barely hold my arms up. And I'm starving. We haven't eaten since late last night. I'm going to make some food. Are you hungry?"

Grady nodded.

"Great," she said. "I'll get started. I'll see you inside."

He watched Caitlin until she entered the small cabin and the door closed behind her. He didn't follow; instead, he stayed outside to clean up. Now and then, he saw her moving around the kitchen through the window. By the time he cleaned up the targets and the spent shells, the sun was above the mountains. He put the guns in the back of the SUV, except for his .357 and Caitlin's Sig Sauer.

He holstered his gun, took the magazine out of hers, and went inside. Caitlin didn't look up when Grady walked past her into the small living room. He put her gun on the coffee table and the magazine beside it.

"The food is ready," she said from the kitchen. "It's nothing fancy, just grilled cheese and soup."

"Sounds good." He returned to the kitchen and washed his hands.

When he turned around, Caitlin was right behind him, only inches away. She stepped to the side to get out of his way, head down, hands shoved in the pockets of her jeans.

"Come here," he murmured.

She didn't hesitate; she stepped into the circle of his arms, rested her head on his shoulder, and sighed. Grady kissed her forehead, hugged her tight, and rubbed her back.

"I'm scared," she whispered.

Caitlin didn't admit weakness; hell, she didn't acknowledge weakness. It worried him.

"I promise I will keep you safe, no matter what," he murmured. "You believe me, right?"

"I believe you," she said with a sigh. She grabbed one of her braids and twisted it around her fingers. "Am I worth all this trouble?"

You're worth it. Especially to me.

Not that he said that statement out loud. He couldn't, not yet, not after one night together. Besides, it would probably come across as trite and unrealistic, given the situation. Caitlin would think he was only saying it to make her feel better.

"That's not true," he told her instead. He hoped she would understand what he meant.

She kissed his cheek. "I'm hungry. Let's eat."

They sat at the table, across from each other, and ate in silence, both lost in their own thoughts. When they were done, she took the plates to the sink. Then she turned around, smiled at him, and pointed at the living room.

"I cooked, so you get to do the dishes. I'm exhausted. I think I'll take a nap."

Grady laughed, got up, and went to the sink. The TV came on in the living room, though he wasn't sure what Caitlin decided to watch because the sound was drowned out by the water running in the sink. Even though it didn't take him long to wash the dishes, she was asleep when he walked into the living room, stretched out on the couch with the pillow clutched in her arms and the blanket pulled up to her chin.

He took his gun off and put it on the coffee table next to Caitlin's, then he sat in the recliner, stretched his legs out in front of him, leaned back, and fell asleep.

Grady shot upright, wide awake, unsure of what had woken him up. It took him a minute to get his bearings in the pitch-black room. Once his eyes adjusted to the lack of light, he got up, went to the window, pulled the curtain aside an inch, and peered out. He didn't see anything, but something was off. Something didn't feel right. He turned on the small lamp on the end table.

Caitlin squinted at him from the couch, and propped herself up on her elbows. "What's wrong?" she asked groggily.

"I don't know," he muttered. "Something's wrong."

She gave him a funny look, got off the couch, and stretched. "Well, I gotta pee. Let me know if you find something." She went into the bathroom and shut the door.

He checked the small bedroom, but he didn't see anything. Leaving the bedroom light on, he walked through the cabin to the kitchen and stopped in front of the window over the sink. That was when all the lights went out.

The bathroom door banged into the wall. "Grady? Where are you?"

The flare of flashlights blazed in the woods behind the cabin. "Fuck," he muttered under his breath. "I'm in the kitchen. Get over here. Now."

She ran across the room, stood behind him, and put her hand on his arm. "What is it?"

"Someone is outside," he whispered. He reached for his gun, but it wasn't in the waistband of his jeans. It was on the coffee table.

"Shit." He grabbed Caitlin's hand and pulled her into the living room. "Go get your backpack." He picked up their guns. When she came out of the bedroom with her bag slung over her shoulder, he put her gun in her hand.

"No, I can't shoot somebody," she protested. "I'm not ready for that."

"Take it," he ordered. "Do not argue with me. Keep your finger off the trigger unless you need to shoot."

He snatched his phone off the table and flipped it open. No service.

"What is going on?" Caitlin whispered.

"I think they found us," Grady replied. "The Morettis."

"How?"

"I don't know. The lady at the convenience store, maybe? Or somebody in the family has a big mouth." The possibility of someone in the family betraying him, *betraying the boss's daughter*, was almost unthinkable. If that was the case, once Sean found out, whoever it was wouldn't live to see another day.

"What are we going to do?" she asked.

"We're going to get out of here." He pulled her close. "You stay close to me and do as I say. Understand?"

Caitlin nodded. "Y-yes."

"Come on," he said. "We're going out the back door. The Bronco is unlocked. You move your ass as fast as you can, get in the backseat, close the door, and stay down."

Walking through the kitchen, Grady caught another glimpse of the lights outside, three of them about twenty feet apart, less than fifty yards from the cabin. For all he knew, there were more people waiting outside, people he couldn't see, lying in wait for him and Caitlin to make a move.

He pushed off the safety of his gun and opened the door. Grady waited on the top step, off to one side. He looked left, then right, counted to three, then whispered, "Go!"

Caitlin darted outside, down the steps, yanked open the back door of the Bronco, and dove inside. The slam of the door echoed through the small valley. The lights moving toward the cabin turned in unison toward the Bronco.

As Grady stepped off the porch, a gunshot shattered the silence of the night. He ducked and lunged for the driver's side door. He opened it and climbed in. He hit the button to start the Bronco. The headlights came on automatically. Shouting filled the night air, though he couldn't make out what they were saying. He put the SUV in reverse and backed away from the cabin. Caitlin screamed.

"Fuck," Grady muttered. He put his palm on the wheel and spun it, turning the car 180 degrees. He hit the accelerator, and the tires spun, leaving a cloud of dust behind them as the vehicle roared down the road. Caitlin cursed as she bounced around the backseat, hitting her head on the door and falling to the floor.

The Bronco nearly toppled over as he took the corner onto the paved road leading back to town. He glanced in the rearview mirror. A light blue sedan trailed behind them by a hundred yards. Unfortunately, he didn't know his way around well enough to lose them. Once they got to Sharon, he thought he might shake them.

Grady opened the glove box and tossed papers on the floor until he found what he wanted. An old, beat-up flip phone. He flipped it open, hit the number five button, and waited for somebody to answer. It didn't take long.

"Grady? Why are you calling me? What's wrong?"

"I need your help, Dante."

"What kind of help?" his friend of over thirty years asked.

"The kind I can't discuss over the phone," he replied. "Where are you? Because I'm coming to you."

Dante grunted. "Understood. Remember where we went after the game against Worcester? Senior year, with the Albany twins?"

"Yeah," Grady said.

"Good. I need some time. How far out are you?"

He checked the clock on the console. "I don't know. Not far. How long do you need?"

"Eighteen to twenty-four," Dante replied.

"Will do. I'll find someplace to hole up. When we leave, I'll call with an ETA."

"Sounds good," his friend replied. "Listen, when you get there, park along the street, under some trees. Stay in the shadows. If something happens before you arrive, call me. I'll call you if anything goes down."

The phone went dead in Grady's hand. He tossed it in the cup holder and checked the rearview mirror. The light blue sedan was still back there, though it was several cars back; that would work to his advantage.

"Who was that?" Caitlin asked from the back seat. "On the phone?"

"An old friend," Grady answered. "He's going to help us."

"Can I get up now?"

"Not yet," he said. "We're being followed, and I want to lose them first."

"Shit," she mumbled.

When they reached Sharon, he was careful to keep his speed down. The last thing he needed was some hick cop pulling him over and getting them killed. He changed lanes and noticed the sedan did as well, though there were still two cars between them. Grady eased off the accelerator and kept his eye on the stoplight a hundred yards in front of them. It was green. He increased his speed and glanced at the countdown on the walk signal. Ten seconds.

There were no cars in front of him. He tapped the brake, slowing as they approached the green light. The light changed from green to yellow. Grady hit the brake again, as if he planned to stop. He checked the two cars behind him that were also slowing and coming to a stop. He inched forward, counted to three, and just as the light changed from yellow to red, he hit the gas and flew through the intersection. He made a quick right, a left, then another right.

The blue sedan was nowhere to be seen. He glanced in the review mirror at Caitlin crouched in the backseat.

"You can get up now," he said.

She huffed loudly, then deftly climbed into the front seat beside him, put her gun in the glove box, and buckled her seatbelt. When she was done, she folded her shaking hands in her lap and stared out the window.

"So, where are we going?" she asked.

"I have a friend who can help us," Grady said. "He has no ties to either family. He's neutral."

"What makes you think he'll help us?"

"Because we're friends," he explained. "And he owes me."

"That doesn't mean he'll help us. Can't we go somewhere else?"

"It's not open for debate," he snapped. "Someone found us when they shouldn't have. Those men had night-vision goggles, guns, everything necessary to kill you. *Kill* you, Caitlin. And probably me. I need to find out how the hell they found us."

"Okay, okay," she muttered. She crossed her arms and stared out the window.

"That's it? That's all you have to say?"

"What do you want me to say?" she snapped. "Christ, I don't want to think about any of this, let alone talk about it. I want all of this to just go away."

Grady tightened his grip on the steering wheel. Just when he thought she was taking things seriously, she showed her true self. Typical Caitlin. Ignore the problem like it doesn't exist. Pretend everything was fine. It drove him crazy. He couldn't wait for this nightmare to end and things to go back to normal.

Chapter 12
Caitlin

Grady gripped the steering wheel and stared straight ahead, with a furrowed brow and tight lips. He didn't speak.

She'd angered him, which wasn't hard to do. A rough lesson she had learned over the years. She rubbed her forehead and watched the miles pass through the window.

"Where are we going?" she asked.

"Final destination?" Grady answered. "Worcester."

"That's only forty-five minutes from home. Why don't we just go to Weston?"

He grunted. She swore she heard his teeth grinding. She glanced at him out of the corner of her eye. He'd loosened his death grip on the steering wheel, but he still had a scowl on his face.

"I told you I think someone in the family gave up our location," he said. "We shouldn't go home. We don't want to take the problem to where your mom and dad are, right?"

Problem? Was that she was?

She cleared her throat. "What about the lady at the convenience store? Maybe it was her?"

Grady shook his head. "She didn't know where we were going. All she could do was tell someone what direction we headed. There are a lot of places to hide. It was somebody who *knew* we were in Sharon and knew about the cabin. Fortunately, that narrows it down. It will be easy for Sean to figure out who did it."

"My father will kill them," Caitlin said.

"Not if I get to them first," he mumbled.

"Your friend—Dante—is in Worcester?" she asked.

"No, we're meeting him there," he corrected her. "But not tonight."

"What? Why not?"

Grady's grip on the steering wheel tightened until his knuckles turned white. His normally handsome face was marred with a scowl that made him look like a killer from a horror movie.

"Dante needs time to get things ready. We'll meet him in Worcester tomorrow night." He shot a glare at her and offered no more information.

The motel was in Ashford, definitely off the beaten path, practically in the middle of nowhere. It was aptly named the Ashford Motel.

Grady left her in the Bronco while he went inside to secure a room. She put her gun on her lap, safety off, hand resting on the gun with her finger off the trigger. She worried about shooting a hole in the Bronco's floor, or maybe one in her leg, since every little noise made her fidgety. When the driver's side door opened, she snatched up the gun and pointed it right at Grady's head.

"Christ, put that thing down," he snapped. "Before you shoot me."

"Sorry," she mumbled. She lowered it back to her lap and flicked the safety on.

"Come on," Grady said. "Let's get inside where it's warm."

Caitlin nodded, shoved her gun in her backpack and climbed out of the SUV. She followed him down the sidewalk and into the room. She breathed a sigh of relief as they stepped into the cozy, heated interior. For the last hour, she'd been in the Bronco, shivering as the chilly night air washed over her. The SUV's heater couldn't offset the rush of cold air streaming through the busted windows.

She dropped her backpack on the floor and looked around. One full-sized bed, barely big enough for Grady, let alone both of them. There was a recliner in the corner that she might be able to sleep in, though it didn't look comfortable.

"I'm going to make a phone call, then I'll see if I can find some food," he said. He tossed the room key—an actual key on a ring with the number twelve on it—on the bed. "Lock the door behind me and do not let anyone in except me. I'm not taking that with me, just in case."

"Just in case what?" she asked.

Grady stared at her for a long moment. "In case I don't come back." He spun on his heel and marched out the door.

Caitlin threw the lock and flipped the door's security latch. She stood in the center of the room, taking everything in. It was tiny and cramped. The bed was in the middle with end tables on either side, covered with an ugly green-and-orange floral print bedspread and two flat pillows that looked like they were straight out of the 1970s. In between one of the end tables and the wall was a checkered chair and matching footstool. The white part of the checkered pattern had faded to a dull yellow color. On the wall opposite the bed stood a lamp, along with an armoire and a desk combination. A TV sat on one shelf, the remote on the one above it. A faint, flowery scent permeated everything.

She crossed the room to the bathroom. Thankfully, it was clean. On one side was a shower stall surrounded by cloudy glass and on the opposite side was the toilet and the sink. Two bottles of shampoo and conditioner, along with a bar of soap and a small tube of toothpaste, were balanced on the edge of the sink. Four stark white towels hung on the towel rack.

A shiver raced through her. A hot shower might help warm her up. She stripped off her clothes, shut the bathroom door, and turned on the water. It took several minutes for it to heat and once it did, she grabbed the soap and got in. Ten minutes later, she got out, dried off, and wrapped a towel around herself.

Back in the bedroom, Caitlin sighed and sat on the edge of the bed. Once again, she had no clothes. She dried her hair as best she could, ran her fingers through it to comb it out, and pulled on her T-shirt. After she folded her jeans and underwear, she put them in the drawer. She picked up the remote, pulled the covers back, climbed in, and turned on the TV.

Forty-five minutes later, a pounding on the door interrupted her rewatch of one of her favorite rom-coms. She shut off the television, got out of bed, and peered through the tiny peephole. It was Grady. She unlocked the door and yanked it open.

He strode in, and she locked everything again. He dropped a white, grease-covered bag on the desk portion of the armoire and pulled out the chair.

"I found a diner up the road. I bought some burgers, fries, and a couple of milkshakes," he said.

"Vanilla?" she asked.

He nodded. "Of course I got vanilla. Did you think I forgot?"

Caitlin smiled. She should have known he wouldn't forget she preferred vanilla shakes to chocolate. He knew everything about her, and he never forgot.

She pushed the footstool over to the end of the desk, sat down, and opened the bag of food. It smelled incredible. Within minutes, she'd devoured everything but a few fries. She stifled a belch with the back of her hand.

"Hungry?" Grady asked as he popped one of her leftover fries into his mouth.

"I was," she replied.

He got to his feet. "I'm gonna take a shower," he said.

While he showered, Caitlin cleaned up their dinner mess, returned the footstool to its place, then sat down on the bed. She contemplated turning on the TV again, but she wasn't in the mood to watch anything.

The bathroom door swung open, and Grady came out in his jeans and T-shirt. His hair was damp and his cheeks pink from the hot shower. He made himself comfortable in the chair and propped his feet on the footstool, leaned his head back, and closed his eyes.

Caitlin went into the bathroom after him, washed the smell of hamburgers off her hands, and used her finger with a bit of toothpaste on it to clean her teeth. When she came out, Grady was in the same position he'd been in when she went into the bathroom.

She dragged in a deep breath as she perched on the edge of the bed. "Now what?" she asked.

Without bothering to open his eyes, he mumbled, "I'm getting *really* tired of that question, princess."

"Well, I'm tired of not knowing what the hell is going on," she retorted. "It's my fucking life and I don't know what's happening."

"Maybe you should just trust me to handle things," he said. "My job is to protect you. Let me do my job."

Caitlin snorted and rolled her eyes. "Yeah, well, you're doing a shitty job of keeping me safe."

Grady kicked the footstool away and bolted from the chair, moving so quickly Caitlin's head spun. He moved like a hunter, a warrior, a fighter—strong, feral, frightening. Goosebumps broke out all over her skin, and a low heat spread through her belly as he pushed her down on the bed and straddled her.

"Your attitude is getting on my nerves," he snarled. "If you weren't Sean's daughter, I'd spank your tight, little ass until it was nice and pink."

Caitlin's heart skipped a beat as her breath caught in her throat. The thought of him spanking her, *marking* her, his handprint on her ass, sent waves of desire rippling through every nerve ending.

"What if I *want* you to hurt me?" she whispered.

Grady's eyes widened. "What did you say?"

Emboldened by an intense need to have him control her, to have him punish her, Caitlin swallowed her fear and murmured, "I said, what if I want you to hurt me?"

"I don't know if you're ready for that," he replied. "The things I like to do—"

"Try me," she challenged.

He loosened his belt, yanked it free of his pants, and grabbed her hands. He wrapped it around her wrists several times, then cinched it tight. It annoyed her, but not enough for her to complain. He pushed her arms above her head and said, "Do not move."

His hands slid beneath her shirt, pushing it up above her breasts. "You're not wearing anything under this, are you?" he asked.

Caitlin shook her head.

Grady's lips moved over her neck and down her chest, mouthing at first one nipple, then the other. He nibbled a line down her stomach until he was between her legs, then he pulled them over his shoulders and rubbed his bearded cheeks over her thighs. He covered her with his mouth, his tongue gliding through her soft folds and flicking at her clit. He groaned as her taste spread over his tastebuds.

Caitlin curled her fingers around the leather belt and pushed herself against Grady's face, the anticipation at what was about to come making her overly eager. Grady growled, released her, and got to his knees.

"Are you a little anxious, princess?" he asked. His jaw clenched tightly, but his hazel eyes flashed with a mix of lust, want, and glee. "You need to lie still and take it like a good girl. Do you understand me?"

Desire washed over her, her eyes falling shut and her thighs squeezing together as her pussy clenched with need. "Y-yes," she stammered.

He grinned, then he dropped his head, took her breast in his mouth, and suckled it, pulling a breathy moan from her. He caressed her inner thighs, moving closer and closer to her center until his finger slipped inside her.

"Oh my god," she gasped. "Please don't stop."

Grady looked up at her, and his eyes sparkled with barely contained laughter. He went back to kissing her, a deep, brain-numbing kiss that made her tingle with desire and her toes curl.

Caitlin groaned when he pulled away again. "Jesus Christ, stop teasing me!"

"Oh, sweetheart, this is only the beginning. You are going to beg to cum like you wouldn't believe before I finish with you." He grinned an impish grin. "If you're a good girl and do as you're told, the orgasm will be worth the wait."

Heat flooded every inch of her, flushing her skin a bright pink.

Grady started at her ears, nibbling at the lobes, gently kissing her neck right beneath them, moving along her jaw, peppering her neck and shoulders with kisses and bites. He took her nipple in his mouth and sucked greedily as he cupped her other breast, kneading it roughly. Then he moved down her stomach, his fingers tracing circles all over her, his lips following his hand, his beard scratching her sensitive skin.

When he reached the apex of her thighs, he paused long enough to make her moan, then his fingers slid through her slick folds. He blew a warm breath over her clit, sending a shiver racing through her.

Caitlin's hips came off the bed and she tried to grab him, forgetting her hands were tied. She dropped them and moaned in frustration, egged on by Grady tracing her swollen nub and his tongue lapping at her. He sighed as he buried his head between her thighs, his middle finger slipping inside her as he sucked her clit into his mouth, sending a jolt of intense desire shooting through her. Her legs opened, and she pushed her hips up, allowing Grady to slide his hand beneath her to hold her against his mouth.

The orgasm built and pleasure spread through her body. She knew she was about to cum—her toes curled, her fists clenched, her nails digging into the palms of her hands, her breath tearing in and out of her throat. She drew in a deep breath, ready to let loose with a litany of praise for the man giving her so much gratification.

But instead of bringing her to orgasm, Grady pulled away and bit the insides of her thighs, his finger still pumping in and out of her, keeping her right on the edge. She was on fire, coming undone, but not quite there.

"Fuck me," she mumbled. "Don't stop. I want to cum."

"Not yet, princess," he whispered before he dove back in, his tongue sliding into her soaking wet pussy alongside his finger, thrusting as he brushed his thumb across her sensitive nub.

Caitlin writhed beneath him, close to orgasm again, right at the peak, ready and willing to let herself go. But Grady slowed his movements until she teetered on the edge once more. She wanted to cum so badly, tears had formed in the corner of both of her eyes and every nerve ending burned with the need to let go.

"Please," she begged. "I ... fuck ... I need to cum." She squirmed and cursed.

Grady rose to his knees, his face damp with her slick, his chest heaving, the hard line of his erection visible through his jeans. "Oh, princess, you are not being a very good girl," he murmured.

He reached back, grabbed the neck of his T-shirt, and pulled it off. He put one hand by her head and leaned over her, his mouth mere inches from hers, their breath mingling.

"You need to remember who is in charge." He nipped at her throat. "I'm going to punish you, Cait. I want you to take your punishment like a good girl. Can you do that?"

Caitlin groaned. "Oh, fuck."

Grady took hold of her face with his large hand and pulled her to him. "Damn that mouth," he said. He kissed her, a hard, bruising kiss that left her moaning for more. "Answer my question. Can you take it like a good girl?"

This was a side of him she had never seen. It wasn't that she was scared of him; he would never hurt her. But this Grady was raw, feral, and more man than she ever imagined. He took what he wanted, no questions asked. To her surprise, she liked it. She sucked in a deep breath and released it slowly.

"Yes," she whispered.

Grady rolled Caitlin over so her bound wrists were stretched above her head, and her ass was in the air.

He rubbed her soft skin. "I think two or three will be enough," he mumbled, then he hit her right butt cheek. The sting was immediate, heat spreading across her ass and pooling in the pit of her stomach. Her nipples hardened, and a low moan of desire escaped her.

He caressed her, his rough, calloused hand caressing the red spot left by his hand. He shifted, then there was another slap, this time on her left butt cheek.

Caitlin gasped and fell forward, her breasts skimming the threadbare bedspread. Jesus Christ, she wanted to rub her entire body all over the bed, anything to relieve the tension building inside of her.

"One more," Grady whispered as he lifted her, his hand coming forward and connecting with her again, the sting both painful and unbelievably satisfying.

His hands were on her in a heartbeat, caressing her ass, stroking it gently. He crouched behind her, his lips drifted over her reddened skin, and two of his fingers pushed into her wet pussy, pushing her up to the edge and over it, the orgasm rolling through her in waves, taking her to unimaginable heights of pleasure.

Grady leaned over her back, his fingers still moving inside her as he loosened the belt, and it fell from her wrists. He held her close and whispered praises in her ear. Caitlin balanced on her elbows as he opened his jeans, pulled out his cock, and buried it so deep inside her that his pelvic bone pressed against her ass.

She pushed back against him, groaning as his cock brushed her sweet spot with every thrust into her. He wrapped an arm around her waist and his hand found her clit, rubbing the swollen nub of nerves with two fingers as he pounded into her from behind. She clutched the bedspread with both hands, a scream of pleasure building in her. It wasn't long before her walls clamped down on him, drawing his own orgasm from him as another rushed through her, his hips stuttering in their movements as his control slipped.

When Grady released her, Caitlin fell face down on the bed, completely satisfied and utterly exhausted. She pressed her face against the bedspread and hummed contentedly.

The bed shifted, but she didn't turn to see what he was doing. She heard water running in the bathroom sink, then he returned to her side, rolled her to her back, and used the warm washcloth to clean her wet thighs and between her legs, all while pressing soft kisses to her cheeks and forehead, murmuring sweet praises in her ear. Once she was cleaned up, he wrapped her in the bedspread and pressed her vanilla milkshake into her hands before he disappeared into the bathroom.

When he emerged a few minutes later, he wore a pair of ridiculous silk boxers with huge red lips all over them.

Caitlin giggled and rolled her eyes.

"Don't laugh," he mumbled. "I had to buy them at the convenience store down the road. It's all they had." He crawled into bed beside her, pulled her into his arms, and kissed her temple. "How are you doing?" he asked.

"I'm good," she whispered. "What about you?"

"I needed that," he said. "Thank you." He cleared his throat. "I told you I liked to be in control. I hope I didn't scare you."

She shook her head. "No. Surprised me a little, but you didn't scare me. I … I kind of liked it." Heat rushed to her cheeks. "I've never done anything like that before."

Grady sucked in a sharp breath, but he didn't utter a word. Instead, he hugged her closer, both arms wrapped around her, her head tucked under his chin.

Caitlin closed her eyes and let herself enjoy the brief respite from the insanity her—their—life had become. Maybe that had been just what she needed, too.

Chapter 13
Caitlin

The next day, they ate breakfast at the same diner where Grady picked up dinner. Caitlin had pancakes, surprised at how good they were. He had one egg, a slice of sourdough bread, and drank four or five cups of black coffee. She lost count.

She assumed they would head for Worcester after breakfast, but they returned to the motel. Grady turned on a football game and made himself comfortable.

"Would you *please* sit down?" he muttered after ten minutes of her pacing the room and shooting glares in his direction.

"Why aren't we leaving?" she asked.

"We're not meeting Dante until after dark," he replied. "We have to wait."

Caitlin sighed and dropped onto the bed. "What am I supposed to do until then?"

Grady glared at her. "You're a grown woman, Cait. You should be able to entertain yourself for a few hours."

She laid down. "I'm sick of being cooped up."

He rubbed his forehead. "Don't you think I feel the same way? Especially with an insolent brat."

"Funny, you don't think I'm an insolent brat when you're fucking me," she snapped.

"Don't try to get a rise out of me," he muttered. "I'm not in the mood to fight with you."

That was exactly what she was trying to do—get a rise out of him. Fighting with Grady turned her on. If she could drag him into an argument, maybe she could get him to have sex with her. She stretched out on the bed and put her arm over her eyes. Her mind drifted as she listened to the football game in the background.

"How do you think they found us in Sharon?" she asked. "It wasn't our phones; we got rid of them. Was it somebody who works for my father? I can't imagine anyone daring to defy him like that. It's a death sentence."

"You're damn right it's a death sentence," Grady muttered. "I'll fucking kill him myself."

Caitlin barely heard him. The wheels in her head were turning. "You know, I'm positive Moretti didn't have anything to do with Bobby's death. Bobby never told me who his father was, but he always hinted that they had a good relationship. Why would Moretti have his goons kill Bobby?"

The volume on the television went down. "What are you getting at?"

"What if Joey and Gino killed Bobby on their own? Without Aldo knowing? Is that a possibility?"

Grady snorted. "Not unless they have a death wish. That's Moretti's kid. Why would they intentionally put themselves in danger like that?" He sat up. "Hey, do you have Finn's number?"

"I think so," she replied. "I have an address book on my laptop in my backpack. Why?"

"He mentioned he knew a couple of guys in the Moretti family," he said. "We heard something was going down, but not what. Maybe this has something to do with that."

Caitlin climbed off the bed, opened her laptop, and sat back down. It was almost dead, but she had enough power to get Finn's phone number for Grady. He dialed, put the phone on speaker, and set it between them.

"Finn Duffy," her cousin answered.

She wanted to answer, but Grady gave her a look that silenced her. She crossed her arms and glared at him.

"Finn, it's Grady."

"Jesus, I am glad to hear from you. How's Caitlin?"

Grady nodded at her.

"I'm good," she said. "Tired of running, but no injuries."

"Thank God," Finn replied. "Your father is worried sick about you. I'll let him know we talked."

"Have you heard anything out of New York?" Grady interjected.

"Yeah, I have. Hold on." A door closed in the background, then Finn was back on the phone. "My buddy, Matt, works on the fringes of the Moretti family. He said there was a major shakeup a few weeks ago. Apparently, Joey LaGuardia and Aldo had some kind of falling out. Joey accused Aldo of shorting him the payment on some drug deal and Aldo went ballistic. Sounds like he told Joey if he didn't like the way Aldo was running things, he could leave. And Joey did. Took a couple of guys with him, most notably Gino and Fredo, two of Aldo's best enforcers. According to Matt, it's a fucking mess over there."

"Joey and Gino killed Bobby," Caitlin said.

"That's what Uncle Sean said," Finn added. "But he can't get through to Aldo, or anybody in the Moretti family, for that matter. They've gone dark on us. If we could get the word to Aldo that it was Joey and Gino, then Moretti might call off the dogs. Uncle Sean sent Declan to New York yesterday to see if he could meet Moretti. We haven't heard from Declan since the jet landed."

Grady sighed and ran his hand through his hair. "Shit."

"Shit is right," Finn muttered. "Olivia is freaking out."

"I thought you were going with him," Grady said.

"I was, but at the last minute, Uncle Sean asked me to stay here," Finn explained. "He didn't want both of us to go."

Caitlin grabbed Grady's arm. "We have to go back to New York. I'll go to Moretti, tell him I didn't do it, tell him it was Joey and Gino. Jesus, if anything happens to Declan, Olivia will be heartbroken. We can help."

Both Grady and Finn shouted, "No!"

"You can't do that, Caitlin," Finn yelled through the phone. "Moretti will kill you the minute he sees you."

Grady took her hand and squeezed it. His eyes were wide, and he shook his head. She slumped onto the bed and tried not to scream. Dammit, she could help, but the macho assholes wouldn't let her.

"Declan will take care of it, Cait," Finn said.

Grady snatched his phone off and stalked out the door, slamming it behind him. Caitlin wanted to punch something.

Ten minutes later, he returned.

"Well?" she asked.

"I'll check in with Finn later today," he said. "We're sticking with the plan. We'll go to Worcester tonight and hole up until Declan talks to Moretti."

She sighed; there was no use arguing with him. She wouldn't win. "Okay," she whispered.

He must have expected her to argue, because he gave her an odd look, then he returned to the chair, put his feet up, and turned up the volume on the television.

Grady shook her awake a little after eleven and told her it was time to leave the motel. She gathered her meager belongings and followed him to the Bronco. Earlier in the day, he had disappeared for almost three hours and when he came back, the window in the back had been replaced. She climbed into the SUV, turned on the radio, and flipped through the stations until she found one playing music that wasn't forty years old. Grady's jaw clenched and a muscle in his cheek twitched, but she pretended she didn't see it. She turned the radio up, crossed her arms, and stared out the window.

Less than an hour later, they turned onto Salisbury Street. To her right was an enormous park. Grady pulled off the road and stopped under some trees. He rested his forearms on the steering wheel as he looked out the front windshield.

"Where the hell is he?" he muttered under his breath. He killed the engine. The music cut off in the middle of a Beyonce song. Grady picked up the phone in the cup holder and hit a button. She was close enough she could hear the man on the other end of the line when he answered.

"We're here," he said.

Caitlin heard the other guy tell Grady to watch for a white Ford pickup to arrive in the next ten minutes. He promised to be ready and ended the call.

He reached under the seat and grabbed his gun. "Wait here," he ordered before he opened the door and slipped out.

She took her gun out of the glove compartment and rested it on her leg. Caitlin kept the safety on and was careful to keep her finger off the trigger. The back of the Bronco opened, and Grady rummaged around, then he slammed it closed. He tossed a duffle bag on the backseat before he got in the front.

Caitlin didn't bother to strike up a conversation. It was obvious he was on edge, making small talk an impossibility. He stared out the window while she watched him.

Ten minutes after he hung up, a white truck pulled up beside them and stopped. Grady rolled his window down.

"Ready?" someone said.

Caitlin tried to get a look at him, but he wore a baseball cap pulled down low over his eyes, a long-sleeve shirt, and gloves. His voice was deep and gruff.

"Where are we going?" she asked.

Grady glared at her, which immediately silenced her. She shut her mouth, crossed her arms, and glared at the back of his head. A chill washed over her. In the rush to leave the cabin, they'd left everything behind. The thin T-shirt she wore did nothing to keep her warm and the open window made the Bronco's heater worthless.

Grady stepped out of the Bronco to speak to the driver of the truck. After a few minutes, he got back in, started the SUV, and made a U-turn to follow the pickup as it drove toward the freeway.

They went north on Interstate 190. They weren't taking her home to Weston. She itched to ask where they were going, but she knew he would glare at her again, so she didn't bother.

Thirty minutes later, after a slow drive through the small town of Lancaster and a trip several miles down a secluded road, they followed the truck down a dirt road and parked in front of a two-story farmhouse.

Grady shut off the engine, jumped out, and went around the front of the Bronco. He took Caitlin's elbow, helped her out, then he led her inside. Over her shoulder, she noticed the truck moving toward a large barn about a hundred yards from the farmhouse.

She shook her head. As far as she was concerned, all this subterfuge was unnecessary. They'd left the people chasing them behind in Sharon, so they should be able to breathe easier.

As soon as they were inside, Caitlin yanked her arm free of Grady's tight grip and stepped away from him.

"Stop pushing me around like some kind of prisoner," she snapped.

Grady clenched his jaw and walked away from her.

She glanced around, then she followed him through an open archway that led to a living room and kitchen.

The kitchen exuded a warm, rustic charm she might have appreciated under different circumstances. In the center of the room was an expansive, weathered oak table with six chairs around it. An iron chandelier hung above it, casting a soft glow over everything. The creamy white walls appeared to be freshly painted and covered in old-fashioned botanical prints. Open shelves held mismatched crockery, copper pots and pans, and glass jars of what looked like dried herbs or spices. The only modern thing in the kitchen was a coffeepot next to the deep porcelain sink.

A fire burned in a massive stone fireplace that dominated one wall. Grouped around it were an overstuffed sofa and two faded floral armchairs. A large area rug covered the wooden floor. It didn't look like a place where a man like Dante would live. The room radiated warmth, while his demeanor was cold and aloof. She couldn't reconcile the two in her head.

Caitlin went to stand in front of the fireplace, sighing when the heat hit her back. She rubbed her arms and waited for Grady to give her some kind of explanation.

"What is this place?" she asked.

A voice spoke from behind her. "This place is off the beaten path and perfect for hiding people who don't want to be found."

"Caitlin, this is Dante," Grady said.

"O'Reilly's daughter, right?" Dante asked.

She nodded. There wasn't anything to say; everyone knew who she was, yet she was constantly kept in the dark. She'd hoped after what happened between them, things might change, and she wouldn't be treated like a schoolgirl who didn't know her ass from a hole in the ground. Apparently, she was wrong.

"Is there someplace I can clean up?" she asked.

"Follow me," Dante said. "Grady, why don't you make a pot of coffee while I show Miss O'Reilly the upstairs bathroom?"

Caitlin didn't look at Grady as she followed Dante back into the front living room. He led her up a set of carpeted stairs to the second floor.

"The bathroom is at the end of the hall." He pushed open a door directly behind him and pointed at an antique dresser against the wall. "There are some shirts and sweatshirts in that dresser that might fit you. Probably a pair of sweatpants, too."

"Thanks," she mumbled.

Dante left her and went downstairs. Caitlin used the bathroom, washed her hands and face with the bar of soap on the sink, then went to the bedroom and searched through the dresser until she found a button-down shirt and an oversized sweatshirt that looked like it might fit her. She put them on and started back downstairs. Halfway down, she heard Dante say her name and froze.

"Tell me about Caitlin."

"What do you want to know?" Grady asked.

"When did you start having sex with her?"

Grady choked on something and coughed. When he finally spoke, his voice was gruff and deep. "What the fuck are you talking about?"

Dante laughed. "So, you are sleeping with her?"

The silence hung heavy in the air. It was a full thirty seconds before Grady answered.

"Sleeping with her is a recent development. It just kind of happened."

She rubbed her forehead. *It just kind of happened.* Jesus, men didn't change even as they aged. Why couldn't he admit there were feelings involved?

Grady said something she couldn't hear, then Dante asked, "Do you love her?"

More silence, then Grady spoke. "I don't believe in love. Can we change the subject, please?"

Caitlin sat up straight, stung. What the fuck did that mean? *He doesn't believe in love?* Then what the hell was she doing? She'd been half in love with him for two years, hoping and praying he felt the same. She didn't want to hear anymore, so she tiptoed down the stairs. The front door was only a few steps away, and the men in the kitchen were talking. They probably wouldn't notice if she went outside and got some fresh air.

Years of practice sneaking out of her father's house and evading her ever-present bodyguards made it easy for her to open the door and slip out without making a sound.

The wind was sharp and biting. Stark, silver light from the moon cast odd shadows over the ground and the faint smell of wood smoke filled the night air. Caitlin loved fall, but wintry nights like this were not her favorite, especially when she only wore a sweatshirt and a pair of sweatpants.

The barn loomed in the distance, so she headed that way. The heavy doors were locked. She peered in the window and saw the Ford pickup truck and the Bronco parked side by side. A glance back at the house told her nobody was coming after her. She walked the length of the barn and around the back, where she found a blue sedan next to a garden overrun by weeds. Caitlin tugged on the door handle, and, to her surprise, it opened, so she slipped inside and pulled the door shut.

"Wouldn't it be nice if I could drive away and disappear?" she wondered out loud.

Maybe that wasn't such a bad idea. What if she just disappeared? Not with Grady's help or her father's, but on her own. She didn't have to tell anybody where she was going. Hell, she could drive in whatever direction she wanted and stop whenever she wanted. Nobody had to know.

Of course, money was an issue. She couldn't use her credit or debit cards because they could easily be traced. She would need cash and a lot of it. And there was only one person besides her father who could help her in that department: her cousin Finn.

A plan formulated in the back of her mind, one she might actually make work. All she had to do was figure out how to get away from Grady.

Chapter 14
Grady

It was half an hour before Grady noticed Caitlin hadn't come downstairs. He shoved himself away from the table and went to the bottom of the stairs.

"Caitlin!" he yelled.

No answer.

"Dammit," he muttered. He stomped up the stairs, making as much noise as possible, hoping if she fell asleep, it would wake her up. He checked the bathroom and the two bedrooms, but she was gone.

Grady swung around, barreled back downstairs, and yanked open the front door. Dante came racing after him.

"What's wrong?" he asked.

"Caitlin is gone," Grady replied.

"She couldn't have gotten very far," Dante said. "Not without a car." He pushed past Grady and down the porch steps. "Go check the barn. I'll walk toward the road. If she's trying to leave on foot, it's a long hike. Here." He dug the keys out of his pocket and tossed them to Grady. "If she's not there, pull the truck around and we'll look for her." Dante slowly jogged up the driveway.

Grady shoved his hands in his pockets and hurried toward the barn. This was so typical of Caitlin; she never thought about anyone but herself. If she got a bug up her ass and took off, then she would do it without a second thought, consequences be damned.

He stopped at the barn and peered in the window, but he didn't see anything, so he walked around the side of the building. Fortunately, the full moon was bright enough for him to see where he was going without a flashlight.

In the back, he found an old sedan parked in the middle of a weed-filled garden. Sitting inside the car was Caitlin. When she saw him, she climbed out and stared at him over the roof.

"What the hell do you think you're doing?" he asked. "You can't just disappear like that."

She rolled her eyes. "I didn't disappear. I went for a walk because I needed some air."

Something was wrong. Something she wasn't telling him. He wasn't sure what it was and, knowing Caitlin, she wouldn't offer any information.

"You need to come back inside. Now," he ordered.

Obviously irritated, she marched past him and headed for the house. He hurried after her, grabbed her arm, and stopped her.

"What is wrong with you?" he asked.

"Nothing," she muttered. An obvious lie. She took a step, then turned around with her hands on her hips. "How long are we going to be here?"

"I don't know," Grady answered. "As long as nobody finds us, we can hole up here for a while. If something happens, we'll have to move someplace else."

Caitlin sighed and pushed a hand through her hair. "What are we going to do, jump from safe house to safe house, hoping and praying we can stay awhile? That's so stupid."

"We don't have a choice."

She darted back to his side. "We could go away, me and you. Go someplace where no one knows us. Mexico, Canada, shit, Europe. Any place but here." Caitlin put her hands on his chest and stared into his eyes. "We could start over. As long as you're with me, everything would be okay. Right? And we would be together."

Grady's eyes closed. Those were the same words Oona said to him all the years ago. But unlike Oona, at that moment, all he wanted to do was throw Caitlin in his truck and run away with her. He would have done it, too, if he thought they could break away without a fight.

He cupped Caitlin's cheek and brushed his thumb across her lips. "You don't know how tempting that is, sweetheart. But it would never work."

Her face fell, and her eyes widened. "What do mean, 'It would never work'?" she whispered.

"Grady!" Dante yelled.

"Over here!" he responded.

Dante jogged around the corner of the barn. "You found her. Thank God. We should get inside."

Grady took Caitlin's hand and dragged her to the house. He knew he'd hurt her feelings, but they couldn't afford her drifting off into some fantasy about the two of them running away together. It wasn't plausible; it wouldn't save her; and her father would never allow it. It was time for her to come to terms with reality.

Once they reached the porch, Caitlin yanked her hand from his, stalked through the house, and sat down on the overstuffed couch in front of the fireplace, her back to him. He ignored the obvious tantrum and parked himself at the table. He pulled his phone from his pocket, dialed Sean's number, and waited for the inevitable ass-chewing.

"Jesus Christ, where the fuck have you been?" Sean yelled. "Where is my daughter?"

"She is safe," Grady replied.

"Where are you?" Sean asked.

God, the urge to tell his boss where they were overwhelmed him. He usually told Sean everything; it didn't matter that the man was Caitlin's father. Grady's need to protect Caitlin outweighed the biological factor. He exhaled slowly before he answered.

"It's probably best if I don't tell you, sir," Grady said.

"Goddamn it," his boss snapped. "That is my daughter."

"I think someone told the Morettis where we were. I'm not sure who I can trust."

"Somebody who works for me?"

"Yes, sir. I believe so."

Sean swore loudly, then he exhaled with a huff. "Understood. But I want my daughter brought home. As soon as possible."

"Yes, sir," Grady replied.

The phone went dead in his hand. Sean O'Reilly was a man of few words.

He shoved the phone into his pocket and looked at Caitlin. She had taken off her sweatshirt, stretched out on the couch, and thrown a blanket over her legs. Her eyes were closed, and her breathing was slow. She appeared to be asleep. He gestured to Dante, who got to his feet and followed him into the other room.

"I need a new phone," Grady said. "I still don't know how they found us in Sharon. It could be the phones, if it's someone we know. I need to dump this one and get new burners."

"I'll go," Dante said. "You stay here with her."

Grady took out his wallet and gave his friend a handful of cash. "Can you buy her some clothes: a coat, jeans, maybe a couple of T-shirts? She has nothing."

Dante nodded. "Yeah, I got this." He glanced at the couch where Caitlin slept before lowering his voice. "I'll be gone two, maybe three hours. See if you can't fix whatever the hell is wrong between you two. This is going to be a lot harder if we have to fight her every step of the way."

Dante was right; if they were at odds and fighting, Grady wouldn't be able to keep her safe. Her natural tendency to push back against authority could cause problems. They needed to talk.

Grady waited for Dante to leave before he approached Caitlin. He stood at the end of the couch and watched her sleep. Except she wasn't asleep.

He grabbed her foot and shook it. "I know you're awake."

Her eyes opened, and she rolled onto her back. "I don't want to talk to you."

"Tough shit," he replied. "You're angry with me, aren't you?"

Caitlin grunted something incoherent and pushed herself upright. She wrapped her arms around her legs and rested her chin on her knees.

"You didn't answer my question? Outside? Tell me why us being together would never work."

"Caitlin—"

She shook her head. "Answer the question, Grady."

"You know all the reasons this can't work, Cait. Our age difference and your father are the biggest and most pressing." He ran his fingers through his hair. "I don't do relationships, baby."

Now she was on her feet in front of him, that damn defiant, petulant look on her face. She put her hands on her hips and jutted out her chin. His cock twitched as he considered spanking her ass to rein in her attitude.

"Why won't you admit you don't believe in love?" she demanded.

He didn't think. He moved, his hand going around her throat, forcing her back a step. "Were you eavesdropping?"

She stiffened, but she didn't pull away. "Yes," she whispered. Tears welled in her eyes. "Just tell me you don't love me. Shit, tell me you don't *care* about me, and I'll let it go."

God, he wanted to kiss her, own her, possess her. But he couldn't lose control, not when Caitlin's life was on the line. Grady pushed her away and walked across the room.

"Dammit!" she screamed. A pillow from the couch flew past his head, followed by another hitting him in the back.

He turned, and she was right there, inches from him, her blonde hair flying around her face and her blue eyes on fire.

"Don't walk away from me," she shouted.

"You're being ridiculous," he snapped. "You need to calm down."

Caitlin raised her hand and before he could stop her, she slapped Grady, the sound resonating through the farmhouse. His head rocked to the side and his cheek stung where she had scratched him with one of her fake fingernails.

He froze for a split second before he turned to look at her. He reached for her, wrapping his arms around Caitlin's waist and pulling her close. But she wasn't having it. She struggled to get away and when that didn't work, she balled her hands into fists and pounded on his chest, screaming in angry, incoherent bursts of nonsense.

"Knock it off."

"You used me!" she screamed. "I let myself be vulnerable, and you fucking used me."

Grady grabbed her by the upper arms, swung around, and held her against the wall. "I didn't use you, baby. I fucked you because you *wanted* it."

Caitlin stared up at him and her lip trembled. "Yes," she whispered. "I need you, and it fucking kills me."

"Don't you think it's killing me, too?" he asked. "I can't keep my hands off you. I know I shouldn't want you, but I can't fucking resist you."

She grunted, but before she could say anything, he kissed her.

"Let me go," she mumbled when they broke apart.

"You need to listen to me, princess. I am not playing games with you. I'm not one of your stupid twenty-something boyfriends who thinks with his dick. I am trying to keep you safe. If anything happens to you, it would kill me. Which means I have to be smart. I will not allow my emotions to cloud my judgment. I can't keep you safe if I think with my heart instead of my head."

Grady released her. Instead of bolting like he thought she would, she pressed herself against him, wrapped her hands around the back of his neck, and pulled him into another kiss. When they broke apart, Caitlin was panting, and her chest heaved with every breath.

"I want you to fuck me," she whispered.

He groaned. "You're such a little brat." He put his hand around her throat and squeezed.

She gasped and threw her head back against the wall. "You're a bastard, Grady McCarthy."

He pressed his body against hers, his cock aching to take her. "I know." He squeezed harder. "Say it again."

"Fuck me."

Grady grabbed the front of her shirt and popped open the buttons, exposing her breasts. He smirked, ducked his head, and caught the skin beneath the edge of her jaw in his teeth and bit her, hard. He cupped her breasts and kneaded them roughly, then he pushed her shirt off her shoulders and shoved his knee between her thighs, his entire body now flush against Caitlin's, his cock hard against her belly.

"You're going to scream my name, baby girl," he murmured. He slid his hand down the front of the sweatpants, into her underwear, and brushed his fingers against her pussy.

"Hmm, fuck," she cried, her hips jutting forward, chasing his fingers. "Please."

"Yeah, that's my girl." He chuckled. "You are so fucking wet. Your body is begging to be fucked."

An odd, guttural sound escaped her, signaling he wasn't wrong. He shoved the sweatpants down her legs until she could kick them away, then he caressed her pussy, his eyes on hers, watching as the lust and desire took over her body. He pushed two fingers into her and pumped them agonizingly slow, smiling when she groaned.

With his free hand, Grady cupped her breast and plucked at the nipple until it was a small, hard pebble. He wrapped his lips around it and sucked greedily. Caitlin squirmed in his arms.

He twisted his fingers in Caitlin's cheap black panties and, with one yank, tore them off. He pushed her knees further apart, his hand cupping her, two fingers buried deep inside her, thrusting hard.

Grady smirked. "Are you going to cum for me, Cait? Are you going to cum like a good girl?" He pressed his thumb against her clit, circling it until her entire body shook, and she clutched his broad shoulders. Her thighs trembled and then she came, crying out his name.

He ripped open the front of his jeans and pulled his cock free. He stroked himself several times before he wrapped his arms around her waist, lifted her, and lowered her onto his shaft, entering her with one quick flex of his hips, a groan rumbling from his chest.

Caitlin moaned as he filled her. She pushed herself down on him, her arms around his neck, holding tight. Grady spread his feet, held her with one arm and with the other, he braced on the wall above her head. He slammed into her, burying himself in her wet heat, grunting as her walls tightened around him. He pressed his face against her neck and inhaled, her scent making him heady with insane desire.

Grady tangled his fingers in Caitlin's long, blonde hair, yanked her head back, and sucked at her neck. She came with a shuddering cry of his name. He thrust harder and faster, his grip on her so tight he knew he was leaving marks. His body tensed as he came.

He held her in his arms for a moment, his forehead pressed to hers, their breath mingling. Could it be like this all the time? Him and Caitlin, just the two of them somewhere in the world, away from prying eyes? He shook off the thought. It was a pipe dream; it would never happen. He couldn't protect her alone.

He set her on her feet and tucked himself back into his pants, regret worming its way into every fiber of his being. Caitlin distracted him because she occupied his every thought, making it hard to do his job properly. It had to end.

"We shouldn't have done that," he said.

"You keep saying that." Caitlin snatched her clothes off the floor and quickly put them back on. "You fuck me, then you immediately regret it."

"I can't help myself," he muttered, shaking his head. "You're like a drug, princess."

"It's called self-control," she muttered.

"I know!" he roared. "Jesus Christ, don't you think I am aware of that? I have no self-control with you. I can't keep my hands off you. It's fucking insanity, and I need to get my fucking act together."

"You know what? I'll make it easy on you," she snapped. "Do *not* touch me again." She spun around and darted up the stairs.

"Fuck," he muttered. He clenched his fists by his side as he stormed out the back door of the farmhouse. He stood on the porch sucking in deep breaths.

How the fuck did this happen?

Chapter 15
Caitlin

Caitlin sat on the bed for more than an hour, waiting for Grady to come upstairs to talk to her. Any second he would make his way up the stairs, grunt a half-assed apology, and she would forgive him. They were both under a lot of stress. It didn't help that she intentionally pushed his buttons to get a rise out of him, knowing damn well it would end in sex. She couldn't stay angry with him when she was the reason he lost control.

As the minutes ticked by and he didn't appear, the realization came over her that Grady didn't plan to seek her out and apologize. Maybe this time she'd succeeded in completely pissing him off.

But wasn't that what she wanted? To push him away? It would make it easier to leave him when this ended.

Except, what if it never ended? It wasn't unreasonable to see her life stretching out before her, one crazy problem after another, the inevitable drama always a part of her life because she was a mobster's daughter. And there was Grady, in the background, pushing her away while trying to keep her close, her emotions nothing more than a yo-yo on a short string.

Caitlin didn't think she could live like that, on the edge, unsure of her future. The idea of escaping all of this and escaping from her shitty life took hold until she couldn't stop thinking about it. Would anybody really miss her? Leaving meant her father had one less thing to worry about, and Grady was free to find someone else or keep being alone. She could disappear, and once this blew over, she could stay gone. It would be best for everyone involved.

Finn was the answer. She just had to talk to him, make him understand it was the right thing to do. If she could get him to see reason, she could get the money and find some place far away.

She left the bedroom and went to the top of the stairs. It was quiet, no voices or other sounds coming from the first floor, so she tiptoed downstairs, pausing every few seconds to listen. When she got to the bottom, she peered around the corner.

Grady sat on the chair with his feet stretched out in front of him and his hands folded on his stomach. His eyes were closed, and he snored quietly. Caitlin watched him for a few minutes, but he didn't move an inch. Now was her chance. She stepped into the kitchen.

Grady's jacket was on the table. She checked again to make sure he was asleep, then she darted across the room on her tiptoes and dug through the pockets until she found the keys to the Bronco. She grabbed her sweatshirt off the back of the couch and slipped it on over her shirt, then she picked up her shoes.

Outside on the front porch, she dropped the shoes on the dying grass and stepped into them. She glanced over her shoulder to make sure Grady hadn't snuck up behind her, then she jumped over the creaking steps and headed for the barn.

The doors were wide open; Dante must have opened them when he left and forgot to shut them. Or he figured there was no harm in leaving them open. Caitlin ran the rest of the way to the barn, wrenched open the Bronco's driver's side door, and climbed in. It took her a minute to figure out how everything worked and to adjust the seat, then she started the Bronco. She didn't wait to see if Grady would come running; instead, she put the SUV in gear, hit the gas, and flew out of the barn. She kept her foot off the brake as she careened around the corner onto the main road and sped up.

Caitlin pushed her hair off her face and watched for a sign. While she knew her way around the Boston area fairly well, she wasn't familiar with Lancaster. She pulled up the GPS on the center console and programmed in the address to Finn's club, the Emerald Diamond.

Boston was an hour away. She kept checking the rear-view mirror, expecting Grady and Dante to come roaring up in Dante's big-ass truck. It wouldn't be long before they figured out where she went.

Less than twenty minutes from the club, she saw her reflection in the window. *Shit.* Her hair was a mess, and she didn't have any makeup on. And there was no way she could go in the Emerald Diamond wearing sweatpants and an oversized sweatshirt. She had no money, so it wasn't as if she could stop somewhere and buy clothes. But maybe there was something she could do about it.

Back when she was in high school, she had gone to a party at a frat house and while she was there, this guy threw up on her. Afraid to go home covered in puke—and grossed out by it—Caitlin had strolled into a laundromat and swiped the clothes from one of the unsuspecting patrons, then dumped her stuff in the trash. There was no reason she couldn't do that again. She just needed to find a laundromat and, hopefully, somebody her size.

It took her thirty minutes of driving around before she found a twenty-four-hour laundromat. For once, luck was on her side. A woman who looked to be in her mid-to-late twenties was inside, doing her laundry. Now she had to wait.

The woman was Caitlin's size, shorter by maybe two or three inches, but close enough that in the end it wouldn't matter. When she got up and walked to the back of the laundromat, Caitlin jumped out of the Bronco, jogged to the front door, and slipped inside, just as the woman went through a door marked *Restroom.*

Her laundry was folded in neat piles on a table between the washers and dryers. Caitlin sifted through them, grabbed a pair of dark jeans, a black-and-silver T-shirt, a worn denim jacket, and a pair of stark white socks. Inside a large tote bag sitting beside the baskets, she found a small, zippered pouch of makeup. She picked that up as well, then she darted back out the door and ran to the Bronco. She threw everything on the passenger seat, then drove several miles until she saw a convenience store. When she emerged from the restroom ten minutes later, she looked presentable enough to get by the bouncers at the Emerald Diamond.

When Caitlin pulled into the Emerald Diamond's parking lot, it was full. While she desperately wanted to use the valet service at the club, it would be difficult to explain the bullet holes in the Bronco. Instead, she drove to the back and parked next to her cousin's Mercedes, then she walked to the front of the building. The bouncer manning the door was a guy she recognized, so she eased past the line of people waiting to get in and strolled up to him.

"Hi, Adam," she said.

A smile spread across his face. "Caitlin, hi! What are you doing here? I thought you were in New York going to school."

"Yeah, I'm, uh, taking a few days off," she replied. "Hey, is Finn here tonight?"

Adam nodded. "Yep, he's at his regular table. Do you need me to walk you in?"

She shook her head. "No, I'm good."

The bouncer unhooked the velvet rope and gestured for her to enter. She ignored the dirty looks and cries of protest from the patrons she bypassed, patted Adam's arm, and pushed open the club door.

The music slammed into her like a freight train. Her ears pulsed and the neon lights bouncing around the room made her head momentarily swim. Caitlin forgot it was Friday night. The place was packed, which explained the full parking lot. She took a deep breath and plunged into the crowd.

Finn's table was at the back of the club, in the VIP section, as far from the entrance as one could get. She elbowed her way past dancing couples, groups of college girls wiggling to the music, and the men watching them. By the time she got to his table, she had declined four offers to dance and at least six offers to buy her a drink.

Her cousin stood with his arms crossed, talking to a pretty brunette in an Emerald Diamond polo. Caitlin recognized her as one of his employees—Lainey, something. Another woman sat behind Finn, glaring at the back of his head. Caitlin couldn't help but laugh. Little did she know

Finn was taken—the man was in love with his work and maintaining his position in the O'Reilly family hierarchy.

The woman's glare shifted to Caitlin as she approached. The table was on a raised platform, separated from the tables of those unable to afford the VIP experience. She walked up the steps with confidence she didn't feel. When she was close enough, she reached out and touched her cousin's arm. He turned, his eyes widening in surprise when he realized it was her.

"Caitlin?" Her cousin pulled her into a hug. "What are you doing here?" He held her at arm's length. "Does your father know you're here?"

She shook her head. "No, and you can't tell him."

Finn pursed his lips and turned to the girl next to him. "Hey, Lainey? Can you grab us a couple of drinks? A beer for me and a white wine for my cousin."

The girl in the Emerald Diamond polo nodded and headed for the bar. Finn looked at the woman seated behind him. "Will you give us a minute, please?"

She shoved herself to her feet with a heavy sigh. "Whatever," she muttered, then disappeared into the crowd.

"Sorry about that," he said, nodding toward the woman he'd asked to leave. He took Caitlin's arm and led her to the couches clustered around a table in the corner.

The deep thrum of the bass vibrated through her body as she sat down and folded her hands in her lap. The noise and the people blurred into the background as Caitlin contemplated how to ask her cousin to help her.

Before she could speak, Lainey reappeared and put their drinks on the table. She smiled at them before she hurried away. Once she was gone, Finn patted Caitlin's arm, drawing her attention back to him.

"Where's Grady? Why aren't you with him?" he asked.

"I … I can't be with him anymore. I'm safer on my own. Look, it's a long story. Just trust me, okay? I need to disappear."

"What the hell do you mean, disappear?"

"I want to go where no one will find me," Caitlin said. "But I need money."

"You can't barge in here and ask me for money," Finn replied.

"I'm serious." She leaned closer so he could hear her over the music. "You're the only person I can ask."

He sat back, his blue eyes scanning the crowd. His usual smirk was gone, replaced with worry. "It's a death sentence, Cait. If you disappear, Moretti will send everyone after you. He won't stop until you're dead. What do you think that will do to Uncle Sean? Or Aunt Maeve?" His gaze flicked to her, hard and unyielding.

"I can't think about my parents right now." She clenched her fists and her nails bit into her palms, stinging. It kept her tears at bay. "If I disappear for a while, maybe this will all blow over."

Finn shook his head, running a hand through his dark blond hair as the flashing lights threw blue and purple shadows across his face. "Running won't fix it. Moretti's reach is longer than you know. Shit, it's longer than any of us know. He'll find you and when he does, he will destroy you. And then he'll come after your family to finish it."

"Are you going to help me or not?"

Her cousin's jaw tightened. "You know I can't. We need to call your father."

The club roared on around them. Caitlin envied them, these people whose lives were their own. She wasn't given the same luxury, not when she was a mobster's daughter.

"Please, Finn?" Her voice cracked on his name, her emotions overwhelming her, exposing her, laying her soul bare.

"Be reasonable. Let's go up to my office and call your father."

She shook her head. "If you won't help me, I'm leaving." She got to her feet with her wine glass in her hand. She downed the wine in two swallows. As she turned to leave, she saw Grady. How the hell had he found her so fast?

"Caitlin!" He yelled so loud she heard him over the music. He attempted to push through the crowd to her.

There was no way she would leave with him. He'd probably drag her back to her father or dump her at the mansion. As far as she was concerned, that wasn't happening. She glanced around, desperate to find an out. Twenty feet away was a door. Her out. She bolted.

A gunshot rang out. Caitlin ducked, then looked over her shoulder. She didn't see Grady, not that she could through the crowds of people rushing for the front door.

Finn grabbed her arm and dragged her toward a different door, his gun in his left hand, his body in front of hers. "Come on! We need to get you out of here!"

A loud crash drew her attention; it was Grady grappling with one of the Italians from New York—Joey LaGuardia. Jesus, what was he doing here? Joey rolled away from him, grabbed his gun, and fired, missing Grady but hitting the mirror behind him, which shattered.

Caitlin ducked as glass exploded around her, a scream in her throat. She had to get out of the club before Joey got to her.

Grady raced toward her and Finn, holding his left arm. When he reached them, he pointed at the door. "Go! Through the kitchen and out the back entrance."

She did as he said, running full speed. She hit the metal bar with both hands and the door flew open. Hopefully, there wasn't anyone behind it. The kitchen was empty. On the other side of the room, she saw the door leading outside. She glanced over her shoulder, wondering if she should wait for Grady. Another shot rang out, deciding for her. Forget the money, forget Grady, forget this goddamn family. She had to get away, or she was dead.

Chapter 16

Grady

"Grady?" Somebody kicked his leg. "Grady!"

"What?" he mumbled.

"Caitlin's gone."

It took a minute for the words to register. Caitlin. Gone. He lurched to his feet. Dante stood in front of him with his arms crossed.

"Caitlin's gone?" Grady repeated.

Dante nodded. "She took the Bronco. I don't know when she left, though. How long have you been asleep?"

Grady checked his watch. "A couple of hours, maybe?" He went to the kitchen sink, splashed cold water on his face, then he wiped it off with a paper towel.

"Any idea where she'd go?" Dante asked. "Her father?"

Grady shook his head. "No, she'd never go to the mansion. She said something to me about disappearing, taking off, just the two of us. I told her no, and it pissed her off." He didn't mention they'd had sex. "She took off because she thinks she can hide. But she needs money to disappear."

"Where will she get it?" he asked. "Is there somebody she could ask for money?"

"Yeah, her cousin Finn," Grady replied.

Finn Duffy was the son of Sean O'Reilly's older sister. He had dropped out of college after his mother's death and joined the family business. Talented and ambitious, he rocketed through the ranks, making not only himself, but his uncle as well, a millionaire several times over. If Caitlin needed cash, she would hightail it to Finn's club in Boston, the Emerald Diamond.

"He owns a club in Boston," Grady continued. "That's where she'll be."

"Do you want me to go with you?" Dante asked.

Grady shook his head. "No. You know if Sean or any of his men see you, you're dead. I'll go alone."

His friend didn't argue. He was aware of his limitations with the O'Reilly family, and he wasn't about to cross any lines. "What are you going to do when you find her?"

"I'm taking her to her father," Grady replied. "I'm done playing games with her. She's Sean's daughter and his problem."

"Take the Ford." Dante tossed his keys to Grady, who caught them with one hand.

It took just over an hour for Grady to make the drive into Boston and to the Emerald Diamond. The place was packed, no surprise on a Friday night. He utilized valet parking and told the kid who parked the truck to keep it close.

At the door, Grady gave his name to the bouncer, who immediately let him past the velvet ropes. He walked through the crowd and headed for the bar. After he sat down, he asked a pretty brunette for a beer.

He knew Caitlin was here; she had to be. As soon as he found her, he was taking her home to her father. Sean could deal with this bullshit; Grady was over it. In fact, once she was safely home at the O'Reilly mansion, Grady thought he might need a very long vacation.

He waved over the pretty brunette tending bar. Her name tag said Veronica.

"Can I help you?" she asked.

"Is Finn Duffy here tonight?" he asked.

Veronica nodded and pointed to a section of tables over his left shoulder. Grady looked over and saw Sean's nephew and a tall blonde getting to their feet. Caitlin. It looked like she was ready to leave. Grady set his beer down and stood up.

Caitlin brought a drink to her mouth and downed it in a couple of swallows, then she turned his way. When she saw him, her eyes widened.

Out of the corner of his eye, Grady noticed a commotion at the front door. His hand went to the gun under his jacket when Joey LaGuardia pushed past the bouncers at the door and headed straight for Finn and Caitlin.

"Caitlin!" Grady yelled.

She ignored him and bolted for the door behind her. She had no idea what awaited her.

"Goddamn brat," he swore under his breath. When he turned back, he searched the crowd for Joey.

La Guardia worked his way through the crowd, avoiding flailing elbows and kicking the ankles of the people on the dance floor. If Grady didn't move, he would get to Caitlin first. Joey was closer to her than Grady, less than twenty feet away.

Desperate to stop him, Grady yanked his gun from the holster under his jacket, shoved several dancing kids to the side, and fired a shot into the floor. Screams erupted and people fled for the exits.

"Caitlin!" he yelled. She ignored him and kept moving toward the door.

Grady swore under his breath as he ran across the room. He vaulted over a small table and kicked a chair out of his way. Just as Joey reached the edge of the platform, Grady launched himself at the other man. He hit Joey on the knees and forced him to the ground. Joey's gun flew from his hand and slid under a table.

Grady jumped to his feet and stomped on the Italian's ribs. The man grunted, rolled away, and scrambled to grab his gun. He snatched it from beneath the table, shifted to his back, and fired.

The bullet grazed Grady's arm and hit the mirror on the wall behind him, shattering it. Grady cursed, swung around, and darted across the raised platform to where Finn stood at Caitlin's side with his gun drawn.

"Go, Caitlin!" he shouted. "Through the kitchen and out the back entrance."

"Get her out of here!" Finn yelled. "I'll take care of that guy."

Grady nodded and raced after her. He found her in the middle of the kitchen, fists clenched at her sides, tears on her cheeks, her eyes darting from him to the door at the back of the building.

She sucked in a deep breath. "You're bleeding," she said.

"I know," he replied. "I got shot." He holstered his gun.

Concerned flashed across her face. "What?"

Grady shook his head. "I'm fine. Don't worry about it."

"How did they find me?" she asked.

"I don't know."

"How did *you* find me?"

"I know you, Cait. I know how you think. I also knew Finn might help you." Gunfire exploded behind them. "We need to go. I need to get you out of here. Now."

He took Caitlin's hand and led her out of the back of the club. He didn't know what was happening behind him, but he couldn't worry about that. Caitlin needed to be moved somewhere safe.

Outside the door, they found themselves in a small parking lot. As they stepped outside, he was hit from behind and Caitlin screamed.

Grady stumbled forward. As he straightened and turned, another blow landed on his chin. He grunted and fell on his ass.

"Put the girl in the car," someone said.

"Grady!"

"Shut her up!"

A boot connected with Grady's ribs and he dropped, his head connecting with the asphalt. Right before he blacked out, he saw two men shoving Caitlin into the backseat of a dark-colored SUV.

"Grady? Grady, are you okay?"

He pushed Finn's hands away and struggled to sit up. "I'm fine."

"Where the hell is Caitlin?" Finn asked.

"They grabbed her," Grady muttered. "Help me."

Finn grabbed his hand and pulled him to his feet. Everything spun, and he stumbled back a few steps. Finn latched onto his arm to keep him upright.

"You're not fine," the younger man snapped. "You're going to fall down."

"I just need a minute." Grady bent over and put his hands on his knees. He sucked in a deep breath. "Fuck." He stood upright and tried to ignore the buzzing in his ears and the way the alleyway spun around him.

"Where's LaGuardia?" he asked.

"He rabbited. Slipped out with the freaked-out kids." Finn took his phone out of his pocket. "I'm gonna call Uncle Sean."

Grady nodded. "Tell him we need men. As many as he can spare."

"Got it," Finn said. "Go back inside. My guys are clearing out the club. The cops are coming, of course, but I can handle them. You can wait upstairs in my office."

"Let me know what your uncle says. And tell him I will get her back. I swear." Grady walked toward the club, took his phone out of his pocket, and called Dante.

"Did you find her?" Dante asked.

"They got her," he replied. "Joey LaGuardia grabbed her."

"So, he's taking her to the Morettis?"

"Joey LaGuardia doesn't work for the Morettis anymore," Grady explained.

"What the hell are you talking about?" Dante said.

Grady told him what Finn had said about Joey, Gino, and Fredo.

"If Joey doesn't work for Moretti, then who the fuck sent him after Caitlin?" Dante interjected. "LaGuardia doesn't have two brain cells to rub together. There is no way he would ever think of this himself. He's working for somebody."

"You got transportation?" Grady asked.

"Yeah," Dante replied.

"Good. Come to the Emerald Diamond. We need to figure out what we're going to do."

Grady wove through the customers still in the club. Finn's men moved through the building, instructing people to leave as quickly as possible. He got to the stairs, but halfway up, a wave of nausea overtook him, and he lowered himself to the steps. When the police followed Finn through the back door, he continued up the stairs.

In Finn's office, he found a small refrigerator filled with bottles of water and protein drinks. He took a bottle of water and sat on a couch under a bank of windows overlooking the bar. With a grunt, he removed his jacket and checked the gunshot wound on his arm. He'd told Caitlin he was only grazed, but it was deeper than a scratch. It looked like it needed stitches.

The door opened and Finn stepped in. "Hey. The cops are gone." He shut the door and crossed the room to stand in front of Grady. "How's the arm?"

"You got a first-aid kit?" he asked.

Finn went to his desk, opened the bottom drawer, and took out a blue first-aid kit. He tossed it to Grady.

"How'd it go with the cops?" Grady asked.

"They think it was a customer who shot up the place," Finn explained. "I gave them a vague description that might have resembled Joey LaGuardia. Fortunately, no customers were hurt, so they came in, talked to me, and left. It doesn't hurt that I'm Sean O'Reilly's nephew."

"What did your uncle say?" He opened the first-aid kit, took out an alcohol swab and a large gauze pad.

"You mean after he stopped yelling?" Finn scrubbed a hand over his face. "He wants his daughter back, unharmed, and he wants to know how you're going to get her home. How *are* you planning to do that?"

"We have to find her first," Grady muttered. "Why was she here?"

"She wanted money," Finn explained. "To disappear."

"That's what I thought." Grady hissed as the alcohol hit his wound.

"I got the plate number." Finn tapped at the keyboard on his desk and watched the computer screen. "Twenty minutes, and I'll have an address."

"It's a start." Grady cleared his throat. "I have a friend, he's … uh, coming here to meet me. He's going to help me find Caitlin. It's Dante Bianchi."

Finn's eyes widened. "*The* Dante Bianchi? The guy who tried to kill my uncle ten years ago?"

Grady sighed. "It wasn't him." He pinched the bridge of his nose to stop the memories from flooding his head.

"If it wasn't him, who was it?" Finn asked, genuinely curious.

Grady had kept this secret for ten years. He'd told himself it was to protect *her*, the woman he had loved, but maybe it was to protect himself. If Sean found out the truth, it would be the end of their friendship forever.

I think when I fucked his daughter, I effectively ended that friendship.

He didn't look at Finn as he spoke; instead, he concentrated on cleaning and bandaging his wound.

"Did you know I was engaged once? A long time ago?" Grady asked. "Her name was Oona Coleman."

Finn shook his head. "I had no idea. I thought you were a loner."

Grady shrugged. "I am. Now."

"Okay, so you were engaged. What does that have to do with Dante trying to kill Uncle Sean?"

"It was Oona, my fiancée. Oona tried to kill your uncle."

Grady stared at the steam from his coffee cup rising in lazy curls. The busy hum of the diner was familiar and comforting, though it didn't ease the tension gnawing at the edges of his mind. Oona sat beside him, her hand on his arm, but even the touch of the woman he loved couldn't help the unease racing through him. Something was off; he felt it in his bones.

"Have you talked to my loser brother-in-law?" Sean asked.

Grady turned his attention back to his boss. "No, he won't return my calls. I'm going over there later today."

The diner's door swung open, the bell hanging over it jingling loudly, bringing a gust of icy air with it. Dante, who stood at the counter flirting with the new waitress, looked over his shoulder at the man who had come in. Grady also glanced that way as well, but nothing seemed out of place.

Oona patted his arm. "We should leave."

"Leave? Why?" he asked.

"I ... I'm not feeling well." She shifted in her chair. "Let's go."

"You just got here," Sean said. "Why do you want to leave already?"

Oona shot a glare his way, picked up her mug, and took a drink of her coffee. She tapped her fingers on the table and looked around, then she jumped to her feet. "I'll be right back." She hurried toward the restrooms on the other side of the diner.

Less than a minute later, a blast ripped through the building, shattering the quiet morning like a pane of glass hit with a crowbar. The force threw Grady from his seat and his body slammed onto the floor as the world exploded around him. The roar was deafening, drowning out everything else.

Grady couldn't move or think. His ears rang, his vision blurred, and he tasted dust and blood in the back of his throat. He blinked, and things slowly came into focus. Sean was a few feet away, not moving. Grady forced himself up, staggering to his feet as he attempted to ignore the pain shooting through his body. He limped to his friend's side.

"Sean!" His voice was rough, gravelly, panicked. "Sean, can you hear me?"

His boss's eyes flickered open, dazed but aware. He groaned when Grady grabbed his shoulders and tried to pull him up. He didn't know why, but something deep inside of him told him to move, to get Sean out of the diner now.

Out of the corner of his eye, he saw movement. Oona stood in front of him, pale, eyes wide. In her hand was a gun, pointed at Sean.

Disbelief mingled with confusion. Why was his fiancée pointing a gun at his boss?

"Oona?"

Her hands shook, but she didn't lower the weapon. "I'm sorry, Grady," she whispered. "I'm so, so sorry."

Grady's heart pounded in his chest, and his mind raced. Not Oona. It couldn't be her. But her finger moved to the trigger, and the world around him slowed as she pulled it.

Before he could process the betrayal cutting through him, he shifted left, throwing himself between the woman he loved and his best friend. A searing, white hot bolt of pain drove through his side, taking his breath away. He stumbled but somehow stayed on his feet. He clamped a hand over the wound and warm, sticky blood oozed through his fingers.

Grady turned to Oona and saw the horror in her eyes as she realized what she had done.

"No!" she screamed. Tears streamed down her face. "Grady, I—."

"Run," he gasped. "Go, Oona. Run."

She hesitated, her eyes darting between Grady and an unconscious Sean. "I can't. You don't understand. I have to finish it."

"Go!" Grady yelled. A fresh torrent of blood pulsed from his wound. "Before they come. They will kill you, Oona. I swear to God, they will kill you, and there is nothing I can do to stop them."

Love and guilt warred within her, reflected in her eyes. She knew as well as he did there was no turning back. If she didn't leave, she was a dead woman.

Dante, his face unreadable, emerged from the shadows. "You heard him, Oona. Go," he ordered, his tone leaving no room for argument. "Do it. Now."

Oona looked at the gun still in her hand, then at Grady. Her lips trembled. Finally, she turned and ran through the diner's shattered door.

Grady's legs gave out, and he collapsed on the floor. Dante was at his side in a second, his hands pressing on Grady's wound.

"You're an idiot," Dante muttered, his voice thick with emotion.

"Yeah, well—" He coughed, unable to catch his breath. He tasted blood on his tongue. "Sean is my friend. I had no choice. Nobody else was gonna do it."

Dante's face tightened, but he kept his mouth shut. He glanced at Sean, still unconscious on the floor. "Did you know she could do something like this?"

Grady groaned and shook his head. "I had no idea." He clutched Dante's arm. "Do not let her get caught. Promise me you'll help her get away."

Dante grimaced, then he nodded. "I'll take the blame," he said in a low voice. "I can handle it. I'll disappear, make myself scarce. That should get the heat off Oona."

The wail of sirens filled the air, piercing in the explosion's aftermath. Grady clung to consciousness, though he knew it wouldn't last much longer. He closed his eyes and pictured Oona running from the mess she created. His heart split in two, and a steel barrier formed around the remaining piece, suffocating any love he had left for the woman who tried to kill his friend.

As the darkness closed in on him, Grady's last thought was of her and her betrayal.

Never again. I can't let myself get close to anyone ever again.

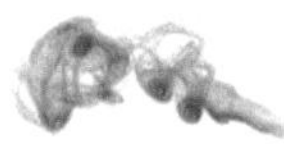

"Dante kept his word," Grady said. "He took the credit, claiming he had been hired to kill Sean, but he'd been injured in the blast and failed. He disappeared, but after that, he became the O'Reilly family's number one enemy. Two years later, Oona showed up at my place. She came to me, distraught, out of money, and nowhere to go. She explained the Muldoons paid her to murder Sean and, if possible, me. After she failed, she went to them, and they turned her away. Oona begged for my forgiveness and vowed to make it up to me."

"What did you do?" Finn murmured.

Grady raised an eyebrow and stared at him for a long moment before he said, "I took care of her."

Finn's eyes widened. "You … you killed her? I thought you loved her."

Grady nodded. Killing Oona had been the hardest thing he had ever done; it had made the steel fortress he'd put around his heart virtually impenetrable.

Until Caitlin.

He cleared his throat. "I had two years to think about what happened. My love for Oona died the day she shot me. It took me some time to figure that out. The day she arrived at my house and begged me to run away with her was the day I realized I didn't love her anymore. I felt nothing for her. Nothing at all."

A chime came from Finn's computer. He turned to it and typed something on the keyboard.

"I got the address," he said. "It's in Lincoln."

Grady stood up. "Good. When Dante gets here, he and I will go. Anybody your uncle sends as backup can follow." He picked up his jacket, but one arm was soaked in blood and rapidly stiffening. "I need a shirt and a jacket if you have one."

Finn hit a button on the phone on his desk. A young woman answered. "Ronnie, bring me an extra-large polo and one of the black leather jackets in the back closet." He disconnected the call and turned to Grady. "Anything else?"

"Guns. I need guns."

Chapter 17
Caitlin

"**S**hut her up!"

A big, sweaty guy who smelled like garlic put his clammy hand over her mouth, cutting off her scream, and another small, lanky man grabbed her legs. They dragged her across the alley and shoved her into an SUV. She landed with her upper body on the seat and legs on the floor, grabbed the seatbelt, and struggled to pull herself upright, ripping two of her fingernails almost off. Somebody snatched the back of her jacket and roughly lifted her onto the seat. Her head hit the door on the other side, and she yelped in pain.

Caitlin scrambled to grab the handle, but the man behind her pulled her backward until she was on his lap and his arm was around her waist. She screamed and kicked her feet.

"Let me go!"

Fat fingers twisted in her hair and yanked her back. She squealed and flailed her arms in a poor attempt to get him to release her.

"Shut the fuck up," he ordered.

"Fuck you," she muttered.

"Don't tempt me, you little bitch," he snapped. He shoved her away, sending her flying across the SUV.

She hit the window, causing her ears to ring and her eyes to blur. She groaned and grabbed her head. When she looked at the man next to her, he had a gun pointed at her.

"Give me a reason," he muttered.

"You're… you're Gino Russo," she whispered.

"Fuck," he mumbled under his breath. "Just shut up, okay?"

Caitlin slumped in the seat and crossed her arms over her chest. The front doors opened and, through her blurred vision, she saw two men climb in. Then the SUV started and they pulled away from the club.

"Can I kill her now?" Gino snarled.

"No," one man in the driver's seat replied. "Not yet."

She recognized the voice—Joey LaGuardia. She swallowed the scream rising in her throat.

"Why not?" her new friend asked.

"Because the boss wants to see her. We're taking her to the house in Lincoln."

She was in a car with two murderers, the men who came into her apartment and murdered Bobby. Caitlin wrapped her arms around herself and squeezed herself into the corner, as far from Gino as she could get. She stared out the window, watching familiar landmarks flashing past. They were close to Weston, less than twenty minutes from home.

The thought flitted through her head that she could throw herself out of the vehicle at a stoplight and bolt down the street. It would take time to stop and by then, she'd be gone. She was fast, definitely faster than a couple of old mobsters. The guy in the passenger seat—the short, skinny one—might catch her, but honestly, he looked weak. A blow to his throat or sternum would likely put him down.

Caitlin slid her hand along the side of her leg, inching it toward the door handle, eyes glued to the front window, looking for the telltale red circle.

"If you touch that, I will shoot you in the knee," Gino said. "It won't kill you, but it will hurt. And I'll fucking love it. Trust me."

She clenched her fist and tucked it under her other arm. She closed her eyes and prayed Grady would find her.

Joey LaGuardia drove like a man possessed, recklessly weaving through traffic at breakneck speed. They arrived in Lincoln less than ten minutes after they pulled away from the club. To Caitlin's surprise, they continued through town, finally turning on a tree-lined street a mile out of Lincoln. A few minutes later, the SUV turned onto a dirt road, speeding over the ungraded road, hitting every bump along the way. She hit her head on the top of the vehicle at least twice, and her stomach rolled. She pressed her fist to her mouth and prayed she wouldn't vomit all over the car.

Just when she didn't think she could hold it in any longer, the vehicle slid to a stop outside of a two-story ranch house. As Gino dragged Caitlin out of the backseat, she took in her surroundings, memorizing everything she saw. The house was gray or maybe light blue—it was hard to tell in the dark—with neatly trimmed grass and hedges surrounding it, and a porch stretching the length of the house. A large tree grew along the north side, its branches brushing against the roof. Lights glowed in the downstairs windows.

Gino gripped her arm tight, forced her up four short steps, and through the unlocked front door. He gave her a hard shove as soon as they stepped over the threshold. Her feet tangled together, and she fell to her hands and knees. She gritted her teeth and reminded herself fighting back wasn't a good idea. It was her against three assholes, and at least one of them had a gun. She was determined to get out of this alive, which meant she had to bide her time.

A hand twisted in her hair and dragged her to her feet. She winced and bit her lip to keep from crying out. Caitlin wouldn't give them the satisfaction. The hand slid to the back of her neck and squeezed.

"Walk slowly," Joey said. "And don't try anything."

Caitlin nodded. "Okay," she whispered.

They walked through a dark living room, down a long hallway, and into a tastefully decorated dining room. A man she didn't know sat at the head of the table, papers spread out in front of him, a small laptop open next to his right hand, and a cup of coffee by his left hand. He was in his shirtsleeves with his tie loosened, his suit jacket hung on the back of his chair, and his black hair was tousled, as if he'd been running his fingers through it. He wore an expensive watch on his left wrist and an emerald ring on his middle finger. When she stepped into the room, he looked up and raised his eyebrows.

"Ms. O'Reilly?" he said.

Caitlin nodded. She detected an accent, though she couldn't place it with only two words.

"Have a seat."

Joey yanked out a chair and gestured for her to sit, then he stepped back and leaned against the wall. She eased into the padded seat and folded her hands on top of the table. Her head throbbed where she'd hit it on the window.

"Nice place you've got here," she mumbled.

The man smirked. "It isn't mine. We are … borrowing it. Along with the cars outside. I didn't have time to acquire my own accommodations, so it was easier to borrow someone else's."

Caitlin imagined that this man's version of borrowing and hers were very different.

"Ms. O'Reilly, my name is Lev Chertok," he said.

Russian. His accent was Russian. "What do you want from me, Mr. Chertok?" she asked politely.

"I want nothing from *you*," Lev said. "In fact, I believe your usefulness has run its course."

Caitlin swallowed past the lump rising in her throat. She squeezed her folded hands together and wiggled one of the loose nails on her right hand. She prayed her captor didn't notice.

"What do you mean?" At least her voice was steady. She focused on him, especially his eyes. Men always spoke the truth with their eyes.

Lev dropped his pen on the table and stared at her for a moment before he spoke. "I assume by now you have ascertained that I am Russian, correct?"

She nodded.

"Have you heard of the Bratva, Ms. O'Reilly?" he asked.

"The Russian mafia," she whispered.

"Yes, the Russian mafia. For many years, my family has tried to gain a foothold in both New York city and Boston. But your family and the Muldoons controlled Boston and Moretti controlled New York. We fought for crumbs, never able to take control of any faction of either of the cities." He picked up the coffee cup, took a sip, and gently set it back on the table. "When the Muldoon and O'Reilly families merged, things became more difficult. Long-standing feuds ended, and new alliances were forged. Our worst nightmare. We turned our attentions to New York until rumors of another alliance emerged. It appeared the negotiations between the Morettis and O'Reillys were going well, until Sean O'Reilly changed course and the rumored marriage between Moretti's son and you, Ms. O'Reilly, was called off. Is that rumor true?"

She was tempted to lie, but there was no point. He knew everything. "Yes, it's true," she said. "My father arranged for me to marry Massimo Moretti. But he changed his mind."

Chertok nodded. "I thought so. Do you know why?"

"Yes," Caitlin replied. "My sister was… abused by the man she was supposed to wed. She escaped and disappeared for three years. After she came home and he learned of the abuse she suffered, he called off the marriage to Moretti. He didn't want the same thing to happen to me."

"How very noble of him," Lev scoffed.

Caitlin shifted uneasily in her seat. The Russian obviously didn't think her father was noble. It sounded as if he hated Sean O'Reilly.

"Your father's nobility and need to protect you may have helped me. The shaky alliance between your families only needed a … a—what is the American word—nudge to completely dismantle it." He pointed a finger at her. "You and Roberto Corelli were pieces in a much bigger game, Ms. O'Reilly. Your father and the rest of his Irish friends have been too comfortable for too long. And the

Italians think they are untouchable. You were the key to setting everything in motion. The first domino to fall."

"Bobby's death."

"Yes," Lev replied, his voice thick with satisfaction. "Poor Roberto. The perfect scapegoat. I had a flawless plan—the mobster's daughter takes out the Italian prince. Mass chaos ensues."

"But why?" Caitlin's voice cracked. "Why would you want to destroy everything?"

"Because while the Morettis and the O'Reillys tear each other apart, my plan is to come behind them and pick up the pieces. Their businesses, their power, all of it will be mine. I have been lingering in the shadows too long, and now it is my time to step into the light."

"You're insane," Caitlin whispered.

Lev snorted. "Maybe. It remains to be seen."

A smile spread across her face; she couldn't stop it. The woman in her who denied authority at every turn, who got enjoyment out of pushing people's buttons, rose to the occasion. "I messed everything up, didn't I? Because I know the truth. I saw Joey and Gino kill Bobby, and I ruined everything. I can tell Moretti the truth and stop the war from happening."

"Which is why you have to die." He said it like he was ordering a sandwich in a diner. Calmly, without a hint of emotion. "It won't happen exactly as I initially planned. But you will die, Ms. O'Reilly." He slowly stood up. "You see, you could not bear the weight of the murder you committed, so you ran. The guilt and the lies you told about Joey and Gino overwhelmed you, so you killed yourself."

She moved to get up, but Joey grabbed her shoulder and pushed her back into her seat.

"You won't get away with this," Caitlin murmured. "My father, or Grady, one of them will figure it out. They are going to come for you."

Lev's face was cold and unyielding. "Let them come. By the time they do, it will be too late."

He walked around the table, stopped beside her, and set a piece of paper in front of her. He held out a pen, tapped the paper, and said, "Take it."

She shook her head. "No."

Lev snapped his fingers. Joey grabbed the back of her neck and squeezed so hard a gasp of pain left her. He grabbed her wrist and forced her to open her hand. The Russian leaned over her, the sickening scent of his cheap cologne overwhelming her, and put the pen in her hand, forcing her fingers to close around it.

"You're going to write a note to your father," he ordered. Another piece of paper appeared in front of her. He set it on the table. "Copy it word for word."

Caitlin pinched the pen between her fingers and stared at the words she was expected to copy. Joey's fingers tightened on her neck. Black dots filled her vision and pain shot across her shoulders. He pushed her until her face was inches from the paper. Tears leaked from her eyes.

"Okay, okay," she cried. She did as instructed, her tears falling on the paper, and quickly copied the other note. She dropped the pen when she was done.

Daddy, I'm so sorry, but I can't go on like this. I'm the one who killed Bobby. I lied when I said it was those guys in New York, because I was scared. I didn't know what to do, but I know I don't want to go to jail. Please forgive me, Daddy. I'm sorry.

Joey released her. She sat up and rubbed the back of her neck.

"Thank you. The tears made it very authentic. We will send this to your father after … well, after." He rapped twice on the table, summoning Gino and the other man who had taken her from the Emerald Diamond.

"Fredo," Lev said. "Please take care of Ms. O'Reilly."

The other man—Fredo, apparently—took her arm and dragged her to her feet. One of the fake fingernails she'd ripped off fell to the floor and bounced under her chair.

"Wait! What are you going to do to me?" she asked.

Her blood ran cold as Lev grinned at her, turned around, and walked out of the room without a glance back.

Fredo pushed her through the house and out the back door. He pushed her down the stairs and across the lawn to a Toyota Corolla. He opened the passenger side door and gestured for her to get in the car. Another fingernail fell to the ground.

She did as he wanted, and he slammed the door. As he walked around the front of the car, she yanked on the handle, but it was locked. Fredo climbed in beside her.

"Don't bother," he muttered. "It won't open." He started the Toyota, put it in gear, and drove away from the ranch house.

Chapter 18
Caitlin

Fredo parked the Toyota, shut it off, and then climbed out. He walked around the car, opened her door, and pointed his gun at her.

"Get out," he said.

She hauled herself out of the compact car and checked her surroundings. The only light came from the car's headlights, which barely permeated the inky black darkness. They were parked at the end of a dirt road, in front of a picnic area with three tables and two trash cans. Beyond that, she couldn't see anything but trees. The chill in the air bit into her skin and the white puffs from her breath floated away with it. It howled loudly, whipping through the branches and through her thin leather jacket, sending shivers down her spine.

Fredo shoved the gun into her back. "Walk," he ordered.

Caitlin did as he asked, leaves crunching under her feet as they walked away from the picnic area, walking deeper into the forest. Her heart pounded as she stumbled through the underbrush. Fredo was right behind her, wheezing, his hot breath on her neck. If he killed her and left her body out here, no one would ever find her. She swallowed the panic rising in her chest.

He grabbed her shoulder, yanking her to a stop. They were in a small clearing—a ten by ten space with no trees or bushes, like someone mowed down all the foliage. As she turned to face him, she saw two tiny pinpricks of light. The car.

"This isn't personal," Fredo said. "Just business."

Caitlin snorted. "I'm not involved in my father's business, so for me, this is personal."

He chuckled. "If you didn't want to be involved, you shouldn't have let Bobby Corelli stick his dick in you. I guess you're getting what's coming to you."

Adrenaline mixed with pure rage surged through her. This bastard had no right to treat her like she was some kind of whore. She took a step back, intent on charging him, but in a moment of clarity, she stopped, took a deep breath, and let her knees buckle, feigning weakness and fear. She fell to the ground with a loud cry.

Surprised, Fredo lowered the gun and stepped closer, reaching for her. This was her chance. She dug her hands into the dirt, grabbed a handful, and threw it in Fredo's face, blinding him. He cursed and stumbled back, wiping at his eyes. She scrambled to her feet.

There was no time to waste if she wanted to live. She rushed at Fredo, who was still rubbing his eyes, and rammed her shoulder into his side, catching him off balance. They both crashed to the ground, Caitlin on top. She clawed at his face as he tried to push her away.

Cursing and thrashing, Fredo rolled them over, pinning her beneath him. He raised the gun, but she grabbed his wrist with both hands and twisted it with all her strength, shoving the gun up and away. It went off, the shot deafening in the deathly quiet night, but the bullet missed her, instead hitting a nearby tree.

Caitlin bucked her hips, causing him to topple over. She got on her hands and knees and attempted to crawl away. Suddenly, she felt something beneath her, something cold, thick, and hard. A rock. Fueled by desperation, her fingers closed around the stone.

As she turned back to throw it at him, Fredo grabbed her leg and dragged her toward him. She kicked her foot, but his grip was too tight. He crawled over her, trying to regain control. She screamed and swung the rock as hard as she could, smashing it into the side of his head.

The blow stunned him, but Caitlin didn't hesitate. Instead, she hit him again, harder this time. He collapsed, and the gun slipped out of his hand.

Breathing hard, she kicked herself away from him and picked up the gun. Blood covered her right hand, and the copper scent of it filled the air.

"You bitch," Fredo groaned. He clutched his head as he struggled to sit up.

Caitlin knew she couldn't leave him alive. He'd come after her and so would his boss. She raised the gun, holding it with both hands, and aimed it at Fredo's chest. She took a deep breath and, like Grady taught her, exhaled as she pulled the trigger, her hands steady as the shot echoed off the trees.

Fredo collapsed, and the scent of blood intensified. A wave of nausea washed over her. Caitlin dropped the gun, stumbled a few feet away, and vomited next to a tree. She wiped her mouth with the back of her hand and stood up. With no time to lose, she returned to Fredo's body to search him, finding the car keys, a cell phone, and a wad of cash. She shoved them in her pockets and picked up the gun.

She had to go. Now. It wouldn't be long before Lev wondered why Fredo hadn't returned, and Joey or Gino came looking for them. Caitlin glanced one last time at Fredo's body, then she turned and ran through the forest, the gun clutched tightly in her hand.

By the time she reached the car, Caitlin's stomach churned like an earthquake rumbling beneath the ground, leaving her off balance and uneasy. While she wanted to lie down and never get up, she knew she couldn't, though she sat in the dirt next to the car. She dropped the gun, rested her head against the driver's side door, and sucked in a giant lungful of air. Caitlin exhaled, then repeated the process until she no longer felt nauseous.

Caitlin had a choice: She could go home to her father, let him take care of everything, hide in the O'Reilly family mansion, and wait for him to fix her problems. It was what he would have wanted her to do.

Or she could go to New York.

If she went to New York, she could talk to Aldo Moretti and tell him what Lev Chertok had done, as well as the lengths the Russian had gone to in order to force a war between Moretti's family and her father's. He would believe her. He *had* to.

It was her life on the line. Hers. She couldn't trust anyone to save her anymore, not after everything that had happened. Not her father, not Finn or Declan. She was on her own. Which was fine, because dammit, she was an O'Reilly. It was time for her to act like one.

Decision made, Caitlin stood up, opened the door, and got in. She adjusted the seat, turned on the radio to drown out the thoughts in her head, and checked the gas gauge. Once she turned the car around, she drove back the way they'd come. With any luck, she'd be in New York in less than four hours. Hopefully, this would be over soon, and everything would be normal.

She snorted; her life would never be normal again. No one could go back after something like this, not even a mobster's daughter. She didn't want to think about that right now, though. Caitlin needed to get through the next twenty-four hours and fix this shit with Moretti before she worried about fixing her life.

Caitlin stopped for gas outside Hartford, Connecticut, using the cash she'd taken from Fredo to pay. While the tank filled, she tried to open Fredo's phone. Unfortunately, it needed a password or face ID. She should have opened it before she took off, but she hadn't been thinking clearly after she shot Fredo.

"After I killed him," she mumbled under her breath.

"I'm sorry, dear, what did you say?" a grandmotherly woman filling her truck at the pump opposite hers asked.

Caitlin smiled. "N-nothing," she said.

The woman gave her an odd look, quickly finished getting her gas, and left. As she turned to watch her go, Caitlin glimpsed her reflection in the car window. No wonder the woman left in a hurry. Caitlin's face and clothes were streaked with dirt. Her hair was a tangled mess, and she looked half-crazed.

She considered going inside to clean up, but she didn't want to raise suspicions if anyone saw her. She'd get a motel room in New York so she could clean up before she saw Moretti.

Back on the road, Caitlin's mind drifted to Grady. The only man she trusted. It had been colossally stupid of her to walk away from him. He protected her, put his life on the line for her, and she'd given him the middle finger by taking off. If there were anyone she wished were with her right now, it was Grady, and not because he could protect her. Her infatuation with him had turned to love.

Grady doesn't believe in love.

The thought sent a pang of regret rolling through her. As much as she longed for a relationship with Grady, it wouldn't happen, for a multitude of reasons, none of which she wanted to think about.

When this was over, she planned to go far away from Boston—maybe California or the mountains of Montana. It was probably the only way she would get over Grady. Distance. Because there was no way in hell her father would allow her and Grady to have a relationship.

Caitlin found a place to stay in New Jersey, the West View Motel in North Bergen. It was cheap and relatively clean, certainly better than sleeping in the car, which she'd considered. After she checked in, she went to a nearby thrift store and bought clothes. Back at the motel, she showered, standing under the hot water until it ran cold. When she was done, she dressed in ugly pink-and-green sweatpants and a large gray sweatshirt.

She had to figure out how to get in touch with Moretti. It wasn't like the mobster was listed in the phone book under "mafia families" or something. She picked up the phone and dialed her sister's number from memory.

"H-hello?"

"Liv, is that you?" Caitlin asked.

"Jesus Christ, Caitlin? Where the hell are you? Finn said somebody grabbed you—"

"Liv, will you listen to me? I can't explain where I am or how I got here. I need to talk to Declan." When her sister yelled, Caitlin held the phone away from her ear and waited for it to pass. When Olivia finished—or maybe she was just taking a deep breath—she interrupted.

"Liv, please. Tell me how to get in touch with your husband. I know he's in New York," she said.

"Are you in New York?" Olivia asked. "I'll call Finn, or … or Dad. He'll send someone to pick you up."

"Then I get locked in the mansion for my safety. A prisoner in my home. I want my life back, Liv. I have to do something."

"No, you don't. Let Dad handle it, or Grady, or for Christ's sake, Declan. Come home where you'll be safe."

"I can't do that."

"You mean you won't," Olivia snapped. "You're so god-damn stubborn."

"Olivia."

"Okay. Okay, fine."

Her sister recited Declan's number in a monotone voice. Caitlin jotted it on a pad of motel stationery she found in the drawer.

"Thank you."

"You're welcome. Tell Declan to call his wife. If I don't hear from you or my husband in twenty-four hours, I'm telling Dad."

"If I don't have this taken care of in twenty-four hours, I'm going to need Dad. I have to go. I love you, Liv."

Olivia sighed. "I love you, too. Be careful, please."

Caitlin hung up. She wanted to promise she would be careful, but she couldn't do that, and she didn't want to upset her sister any more than she already had. She picked up the phone again and dialed the number Olivia gave her. It went to voicemail.

"Declan, it's Caitlin. I'm in New York, and I need your help." She left the motel's number along with her room number, then dropped the phone back in the cradle. She stretched out on the bed and closed her eyes.

Four hours later, she woke to the sound of a phone ringing. She dragged herself upright and snatched it off the table.

"Hello? Hello?"

"Caitlin? It's Declan. Where are you?"

"I'm at the West View Motel in North Bergen, New Jersey. I need your help. I want to talk to Moretti."

Declan didn't hesitate. "Absolutely not."

It was the answer she'd expected. "Please? If I talk to Aldo, I can explain everything."

"What makes you think he'll listen to you?" her brother-in-law asked. "He wants you dead. I'm trying to convince him not to kill you."

"He'll listen because I know who is responsible for Bobby's death," Caitlin explained. "I know who sent Joey and Gino to kill him, who set me up, and why. I need to talk to Aldo. Can you help me or not?"

Declan sighed. "Yeah, I can help you. Let me arrange a meeting. I'll call when I know more. Meanwhile, stay put. Do you understand?"

"How long am I supposed to wait?" she replied.

"Until I set something up. I mean it, Caitlin. Stay there until you hear from me." The call disconnected.

She hung up the phone and prayed it wouldn't take long for Declan to arrange the meeting because she didn't have the patience to wait.

Chapter 19
Grady

Dante refused to enter the Emerald Diamond, despite Grady's assurances that Finn knew the truth and he was safe at the club.

"I'll wait in the truck," he'd muttered.

Grady tucked his phone in his pocket and picked up the duffle bag of weapons Finn had given him. His arm ached, as did his head, but he didn't have time to whine about his injuries. Caitlin needed him.

Finn followed him outside. "I'll send Uncle Sean's men as soon as they get here," he said. "They won't be far behind." He handed Grady a phone. "New burner. Numbers are programmed in. Send an update when you know anything about Caitlin."

Grady nodded. "Tell him I'll find her."

"For your sake, I hope you do," Finn replied.

Dante tapped the horn, so Grady shook Finn's hand, threw the duffle bag in the back, and climbed in the truck.

"Where are we going?" Dante asked.

"Finn got an address off a plate number," Grady said. "We're checking it out. House is in Lincoln."

"Plug it in the GPS."

Twenty minutes later, they pulled into the driveway in front of a two-story ranch house. "Park in those trees over there behind the garage," Grady ordered. "I don't want anyone to see the truck."

Dante did as instructed, parking as far back in the trees as possible. He shut the engine down before he climbed out.

Grady sucked in a deep breath and rubbed a spot in the center of his forehead. The unpaved road they'd traveled down hadn't done his headache any favors. He probably had a concussion, but he didn't have time to worry about his injuries while Caitlin was missing. After a few minutes, he pushed open the door and joined Dante.

"It's awful quiet. Looks deserted," Dante said. "You sure this is the right place?"

Grady nodded. "The SUV was registered to somebody at this address. They probably stole it. But it's a lead. We have to follow it."

Dante shrugged. "Alright, let's check it out. Weapons?"

"Guns are in the duffle bag in the back."

Dante hauled the bag out of the bed of the truck and set it on the tailgate. He pulled a .357 Magnum from the bag, loaded it with a full clip, and tucked a knife into his belt. He walked around the side of the house, his gun raised. Grady joined him after he loaded his own weapon.

He mounted the porch steps first and tapped on the front door. When no one answered, he tried the knob. "It's unlocked." He pushed open the door and stepped inside; it was empty.

"Caitlin?" he yelled.

He was met with silence.

"Stay sharp," Dante muttered, entering behind him with his gun drawn.

The house was eerily quiet, the only sound their footfalls on the shiny wooden floors as they crossed the room. Grady shined the flashlight around the room, stopping at a dark red splotch marring the white paint near a door leading down a long hallway.

"Is that—?"

"Blood," Dante finished.

"Fuck," Grady snarled. "Do you think it's Caitlin's?"

Dante shrugged. "We need to keep looking." He pointed down the hallway. "You check down there. I'll go upstairs to check the bedrooms."

Grady headed for the kitchen, the floorboards creaking beneath his feet. The house was clean and well-maintained, despite its obvious age. Photos hung on the wall—a family portrait, wedding photos, pictures of young children.

He paused outside the kitchen. It was empty, the sink full of dirty dishes, the first sign of life he'd seen since they stepped inside. He continued down the hall until he came to a large, tastefully decorated dining room. The chairs were pulled away from the table, and several wads of paper littered the floor.

"Grady!"

"Back here," he answered. "End of the hall."

Dante appeared a few seconds later. "I think I found the owners," he said. "Dead upstairs in a back bedroom. Each of them had a gunshot wound to the head. It doesn't look like anybody has been up there in a while, not since they stashed their bodies up there. You find anything in here?"

Grady shook his head. "Not yet."

Dante scanned the room with his flashlight. He was meticulous, examining the walls, floor, table, and each chair.

"She was here," he said after a few minutes.

"You don't know that," Grady mumbled.

"The lady upstairs had short, gray hair," Dante explained. He pointed to one of the dining room chairs. "There are blonde hairs all over this chair."

Grady shook his head. "It could belong to one of the owner's kids. Or somebody else. Long blonde hairs don't mean it was Caitlin."

Dante crouched beside the chair and snatched something off the floor. He dropped it on the table and shone his light on it. "What about that?"

It was one of Caitlin's fingernails. A manicured nail with a funky design on it. It sat on the table in front of him. There was a drop of blood on it.

"Yeah, that's hers. She was here," Grady whispered, his voice thick with emotion. "But where did they take her?"

"We'll find her," Dante said firmly. "Did you check those papers on the floor? Maybe something on those will give us a lead."

Grady rolled his eyes. "Yeah, maybe they drew us a map with a big red X and a note that says 'Caitlin is here.' Let's be realistic."

Dante shot him a dirty look. "Your sarcasm is unnecessary."

Grady picked up the discarded papers and dropped them on the table. The first two had illegible scribblings on them. Then he opened the third and spread it out so they could both see it.

"Son of a bitch," he muttered. "Look at this."

Dante stood next to him and shone his light on the paper. "What is this? A suicide note?"

"That's what it looks like," Grady said. "I think it's supposed to be from Caitlin, but that's not her handwriting." He rubbed the back of his neck. "What the fuck is this?"

"Come on, let's go check outside," Dante said.

They made their way down the hall and out the back door. There were tracks in the dirt, but no vehicles. Grady found another one of Caitlin's nails on the ground near the tire tracks.

"She was here," he said. "They took her somewhere."

"Yeah, but where?" Dante asked.

The crunch of gravel under the tires of an approaching vehicle made them freeze.

"Fuck," Grady muttered. He looked around. "Get in the garage."

They sprinted across the lawn and through the side door to the garage. Out the window on the other side of the building, he saw an SUV pulling to a stop in front of the house. The passenger door opened, and Gino Russo stumbled out of the car. He bent over, put his hands on his knees, and screamed at the top of his lungs.

"Fucking bitch!"

Dante looked up at him and mouthed, "What the fuck?"

Grady shrugged.

"Jesus Christ, Gino, calm the fuck down."

That was Joey, coming around the front of the SUV.

"That little bitch killed my brother!" Gino yelled. "Where the fuck is that Russian motherfucker? This is his fault. I'm going to fucking kill him, too. We should have killed that Irish bitch when we grabbed her instead of bringing her here. Fredo would still be alive."

"We'll find her." Joey slapped a hand on Gino's shoulder, holding him in place. "And this time, we'll kill her. I don't care what he says. She dies. Period." He hitched his pants up higher on his waist. "Lev is gone, probably on his way to the other house. We need to meet him there, like he said. You can deal with this shit when we see him, okay? Now get in the fucking car."

As he watched, the Italians returned to the SUV and left, the vehicle flying down the road like it was on fire.

"What now?" Dante asked.

"I don't know," Grady mumbled. "If Caitlin got away—"

"Let's assume she did," Dante interjected. "Where would she go? Home?"

"No, she won't go home. She's afraid her father will lock her up like a prisoner after all of this. She went to Finn to get the money to disappear. If she escaped, she may bolt. And if I know her—and I do—we won't be able to find her."

His cell phone vibrated in his front pocket. He yanked it free, expecting it to be Sean. Instead, it was Declan.

"Declan? Is everything all right?"

"I know where Caitlin is."

"What? Where?"

"New York," Declan replied.

Grady pinched the bridge of his nose as he spoke. "What the hell is she doing there?"

"She wants to meet with Moretti," he explained.

"No fucking way."

"I already arranged the meeting," Declan said. "Tomorrow night. Will you come? I won't go in alone, and Sean insists you be there."

"I can't believe her father agreed to this." He struggled to keep his anger under control. "Tell me where Caitlin is."

Declan sighed. "She doesn't want me to tell you. In fact, I didn't tell her I was calling you. I don't know what the hell is going on with you two and honestly, I don't care. My job is to protect Caitlin when she meets Moretti and to do that, I need your help. Will you come?"

"When? Where?" he asked.

Declan gave him the details, and Grady promised to be there. He disconnected the call, then tucked it in his front pocket.

"What's up?" Dante asked.

"I'm going to New York," Grady replied.

Grady arrived at the airport half an hour before the jet was scheduled to leave. Dante took him to his apartment in Boston, and they'd parted ways. He had a feeling it would be a long time before he saw his friend again. Dante was evasive about where he planned to go and what he planned to do. It was time for him to disappear again.

Once Grady cleaned up and changed, he packed a bag and headed downstairs. His Audi was in the garage, parked next to the empty spot where he kept the Bronco. He pulled out of the garage and drove to the airport.

What he didn't expect was for Sean to be waiting on the plane for him when he boarded, with a drink in his hand and a grim look on his face. Seated behind him were Angus, Conor, and a new kid named Calvin. All three of them looked anywhere but at Grady.

He paused at the door. "Sean."

"Have a seat," his boss replied.

He tossed his duffle bag on an empty seat and sat down across from the head of the O'Reilly family. He crossed his legs at the ankle and his arms over his chest.

"Tell me what happened," Sean said.

"Caitlin took off when I fell asleep," Grady explained. "She went to Finn to ask him for money and somehow Joey found her. I snuck her out the back door, where they hit me from behind and grabbed her. We found where they took her, but by the time we got there, she was gone. I *think* she killed one of them—Fredo Russo."

"Did you have any idea she planned to go to New York?"

Grady shook his head. No use telling him things that didn't matter or weren't important. He wouldn't want to hear superfluous ramblings, anyway.

Sean tapped his fingers on his leg and sipped his drink. "Is there anything else you want to tell me?"

His heart thumped in his chest. What did his boss know?

"What do you mean?" he asked.

"Finn said she was acting strange."

Grady took a deep breath. "She's in a world of shit, Sean. People are after her, trying to kill her. Of course, she was acting strange."

Sean raised an eyebrow. "Is that all?"

Thankfully, the pilot chose that moment to tell them he was about to take off. They buckled their seatbelts, and Sean handed Grady a glass of scotch. He downed it in a couple of swallows.

"When this shit is over, I'll tell you everything. I promise," Grady said.

"Everything?" Sean asked.

He nodded. "Even if you hate me."

Sean froze with his drink halfway to his mouth and narrowed his eyes. "Why would I hate you? What did you do?"

"We'll discuss it once Caitlin is home," he said. "Okay?"

"Okay," Sean replied. "But I'm holding you to it."

"Are you going to the meeting with Moretti?" Grady asked.

Sean shook his head. "One stipulation is that I am not there; that's why you're going with Declan and Cait. I trust you to protect them both and maintain the peace between the families."

Grady chuckled. "No pressure, though, right?"

Sean smiled. "No pressure. Just keep my family safe."

"Yes, sir," he murmured.

Chapter 20
Caitlin

The knock at the door startled her. She hadn't heard from Declan, so she'd put out the *Do Not Disturb* sign. No one should be outside.

"Shit," she muttered. There was nowhere for her to go. The window in the bathroom was maybe two feet by two feet, so she couldn't go out that way. Her eyes darted around, looking for a place to hide.

"Caitlin, open the door."

She got off the bed, tiptoed across the room, and peeked through the peephole. Grady stood on the other side.

"Open the door," he repeated.

She threw the lock and opened it slowly. Grady stared at her with his arms crossed over his chest, biceps bulging, and a half-smirk on his face.

"Hi," she mumbled. "Let me guess. Declan told you where I was?"

"Yeah," he said. "Can I come in?"

She nodded, waved him inside, and pushed the door closed behind him. He looked her up and down, taking in her various cuts and bruises.

"Jesus, he really did a number on you, didn't he?"

His voice was gruff, thick with emotion. They stood less than three feet apart, but it was like the Grand Canyon separated them. She opened her mouth to speak, but a sob escaped her, and tears streamed down her face. She gasped, put her hands over her face, took a step back, her knees hitting the bed. As she sank onto it, she stared up at Grady.

"I … I killed him."

Sobs wracked her body. Caitlin fell to her side, curled into the fetal position, and let the tears come. She'd held them back since she shot that guy in the woods. Since she *killed* Fredo.

He sat on the edge of the bed beside her, brushed her hair away from her face, caressed her cheek, and murmured soft praises to her. She cried until her throat hurt and her head pounded.

"I'm sorry I took off," she whispered. "It was stupid."

"Yeah, it was," he said. "But you're safe, which is what matters." He cleared his throat. "I hear you're meeting with Moretti."

Caitlin nodded. "I need to talk to him, make him understand I had nothing to do with Bobby's death."

"How do you plan on doing that?" Grady asked.

"Don't worry, I know what I'm doing."

"I didn't say you didn't. I want to know how you think you're going to convince Aldo Moretti you didn't kill his son when the evidence is stacked against you."

She had no intention of explaining to him—or anybody else for that matter—her plan to tell Moretti about Chertok's attempt to start a war between their families. She needed to be the one to tell him. Bobby's father had to hear it from her, or he wouldn't believe it.

"I need you to trust me." Caitlin took his hands. "Please. I know what I'm doing."

He sighed. "Alright, I'll trust you. But for the record, I don't like it. And I will be right there to make sure nothing happens to you."

"You're going to the meeting?" she asked.

"Yes," he replied. "It was one of the stipulations your father requested. Declan and I will be with you the whole time."

"When is it?"

Grady checked his watch. "In two hours."

Caitlin closed her eyes and nodded. Two hours until her fate was decided. If she couldn't convince Moretti she didn't kill his son, he would have her killed. She swallowed and got to her feet.

"I'll get ready."

Caitlin's heart thumped in her chest as the car pulled to a stop in front of Fred's Sin Bin. Declan parked under a flashing neon sign shaped like a woman. Every thirty seconds, it changed, so the woman went from standing up straight to bent over with her head between her legs.

"Is this a strip joint?" she asked.

"Yeah," Declan answered. "Moretti works out of the back office. His cousin owns the place."

He and Grady got out of the car. Declan opened the door and took Caitlin's hand to help her out.

"You ready for this?" he asked.

Caitlin gnawed on her lower lip. "I ... I think so."

"You do exactly as you're told, do you understand?" her brother-in-law said. "If something is off, me or Grady will take the lead. Don't do anything stupid and do not agree to do anything stupid. Okay?"

She nodded.

The door to the strip club opened, loud eighties music following a group of men stumbling out to the parking lot. They were almost as loud as the music. She watched as they followed the only sober guy to a lifted truck and got in.

"Let's go," Grady said. He put his hand on her back and walked beside her.

Inside, she was assaulted by air thick with the stench of stale cigarette smoke and cheap perfume. The low thud of bass-heavy music made Caitlin's eardrums vibrate. Dim, flickering lights cast an unpleasant glow over the worn plush chairs and sticky laminated tables. The bar was lined with half-empty glasses reflecting the gaudy colors of the rotating disco ball over the stage. Bleary-eyed patrons sat on mismatched bar stools, staring at the elevated stage in the center of the room. At each end of the stage, there was a pole where a woman in varying degrees of undress swayed to the music. Her cheeks heated as the woman on the far end winked at her.

A door at the back of the club opened and two men stepped out, their faces unreadable. Their eyes followed her as she walked past them, flanked by Declan and Grady.

A heavyset man sat at a table in the center of the room, his posture rigid and his face a mask of barely contained fury. His dark eyes bored into Caitlin. If she could have hidden from him, she would have. As they approached, he got to his feet, the chair scraping loudly against the con-crete floor. He was shorter than her, overweight, and bald. He glared at her as he crossed his arms over his chest.

They stopped in front of the table, and Declan stepped forward. "Mr. Moretti, you know Grady McCarthy. This is Caitlin O'Reilly."

Moretti tipped his chin at Grady, then he returned his focus to Caitlin. She wanted to fidget, but she stood perfectly still. She hadn't been scrutinized so closely since the last time she'd defied her father.

She inched closer. "Mr. Moretti, I'm sorry about your son."

The Italian narrowed his eyes. "You murdered my son."

She swallowed around the lump rising in her throat. "N-no, I didn't," she replied. "I know there is no reason for you to believe me. But I came here to tell you the truth."

Moretti sat back down and pointed to the chair across from him. "Have a seat. I'll give you five minutes."

She glanced at Grady. When he nodded, she pulled out the chair and perched on the edge with trembling knees. Behind her, Grady and Declan inched closer.

"Go on," Moretti said.

Caitlin tried to take a deep breath, but it caught in her throat, strangling her, making her head spin. She gripped her thighs, squeezing them until she got herself under control. "A man named Lev Chertok ordered the death of your son. He's... he's with the Bratva, the uh, Russian mafia."

"I know what the Bratva is," Moretti snapped.

"Yeah, um, sorry," she continued. "It was supposed to look like a murder-suicide. But I-I wasn't there, so Bobby was killed, and they made it look like it was me."

"Why?"

"Because Chertok wanted to start a war between our families," she explained. "He said while we tore ourselves apart, the Bratva would step in and take over everything."

"You're saying this Chertok person killed my son?" Moretti asked.

Caitlin shook her head. "No, it was Joey LaGuardia and Gino Russo. They work for Chertok. He told them to kill Bobby and set me up to take the fall."

Moretti's expression shifted, the fury in his eyes giving way to something much darker: cold, hard rage.

He fisted his hands, his knuckles turning white from the strain. He stared at her for a long moment before he looked at Grady and Declan. "Do you believe her?" he asked them.

Grady stepped closer and put his hand on Caitlin's shoulder. "She's telling the truth, Aldo. Caitlin wouldn't kill anybody. Joey and Gino did it and tried to frame her. Chertok wants us to tear each other apart. If we go after each other, if you continue down this path, he wins."

Declan nodded in agreement. "The Bratva have attempted to expand their territory for months. Chertok could try to make it happen. This could be another move in whatever game he is playing."

Moretti turned back to Caitlin. "If you are lying to me, young lady, there will be nowhere for you to hide."

"I am not lying," she said firmly. "I am here not only to save *my* life, but because I want this to end before someone else dies."

"Where is this Chertok at now?" he asked.

"Gone," Grady answered. "So are Joey and Gino."

"How convenient," Moretti scoffed.

"What?" Caitlin interjected.

The mobster slammed his fist on the table, the loud thump startling her. "The men you claim are responsible for my son's death have conveniently disappeared. Do you think I'm stupid, little girl?"

"Aldo—"

"Shut up, McCarthy," the mob boss snarled. "Do not speak again."

Grady's hand on her shoulder tightened, his fingers digging into the muscle. She needed to be cautious. The rage came off Moretti in waves, threatening to bowl her over.

"No, sir, I don't think that," Caitlin whispered.

"You come here with this crazy story but no proof, expecting me to believe you." Moretti slammed both hands on the table and stood up. "Find Chertok. Bring him to me. I want to talk to him so I can ask him in person if he ordered the death of my son. He needs to stand beside you and tell me he was the one responsible for Roberto's murder."

Caitlin shook her head. "That's crazy! I don't know where he is and even if I can find him, he'll never agree to come here."

Moretti flattened his palms on the table and leaned over it, inches from Caitlin's face. "I guess you better ask your father's *amici* for help. I will give you forty-eight hours." He straightened up and crossed his arms over his chest. "Escort Ms. O'Reilly and her friends out of my club."

The two men who greeted them earlier appeared at her side and waited as she got to her feet. Caitlin followed them back through the club, with Grady and Declan on her heels. No one spoke until they were in the car.

"Where do we go from here?" Caitlin asked.

"We find Chertok and deliver him to Moretti," Grady said.

Declan shook his head. "What if we don't?"

"We're dead," Grady replied. "And the O'Reilly family is fucked."

Her father secured an entire floor of the Ritz Carlton for everyone. Armed guards stood at the elevator and at the doors leading to the stairs at either end of the hall. As soon as Caitlin stepped through the doors, Sean swooped in and pulled her into a tight hug.

"Dad, I can't breathe," she whispered after two full minutes of being nearly suffocated by him.

"Sorry," Sean said. He released her and took a step back. "I've been so worried about you."

To her surprise, tears sprung into her eyes. "I know. I'm sorry you worried."

"Well, you're safe now." Sean straightened to his full height. "Get some rest. We're going home tomorrow."

Before she could say anything, her father turned on his heels and walked away, yelling over his shoulder for Declan and Grady to follow him.

Grady glanced at her as he followed his boss into a room near the elevators. The door closed, leaving Caitlin standing by herself.

"Ms. O'Reilly, your room is this way," one of her father's men said.

She followed him to the end of the hall, where he opened a door, then stepped aside. She smiled at him, mumbled, "Thank you," and took the key card he had in his hand.

Several bags from Macy's sat on the bed. Inside, she found clothes in her size—pants, shirts, socks, shoes, even bras and underwear. Her father must have hired a personal shopper for her. She would have to thank him later.

She stripped off the secondhand clothes and headed for the bathroom. The lingering scent of smoke and cheap cologne clung to every inch of her body. While showering, she scrubbed until her skin was raw. Once she was out of the shower, she rummaged through the bags of clothes until she found something to wear. After Caitlin dressed, she sat on the edge of the bed, staring at the silent TV.

Caitlin waited forty-five minutes before she got up and went into the hall. As soon as she stepped out the door, the man who had escorted her to her room appeared.

"Can I help you, Ms. O'Reilly?" he asked.

"Do you know where Grady is?"

He pointed to the elevator. "Mr. McCarthy is in the last room on the left."

"Thanks." She marched down the hall and pounded on Grady's door.

He flung it open a few seconds later, scowling. "What are you doing?"

"What did my father say?" Caitlin demanded.

He looked up and down the hall, then he grabbed her arm and pulled her into his room. Shutting the door, he released her and backed up, putting several feet between them.

"You're going home," he said. "First thing tomorrow morning with your father and Declan."

She narrowed her eyes. "What are you doing?" She took a step toward him.

Grady sipped from the bottle of beer in his hand. "I'm going to find Chertok."

"Alone?"

He nodded. "Yes. It's a delicate situation. The Bratva is easily offended. If they figure out we are searching for one of their people, bad things could happen. Therefore, it was decided I would go after him on my own."

Caitlin shook her head. "I'm going with you."

"Absolutely not." His tone left no room for argument. Not that she cared.

"I have to go with you," she argued. "You heard him. I am supposed to be there when he questions Chertok. He won't like it if I'm not."

"Let me worry about that," Grady replied. "I can handle Moretti. You need to go home, where you'll be safe."

She exhaled, blowing her hair off her forehead. "I'm not going home. I'm going with you." He opened his mouth to protest again, but she held up her hand, stopping him. "If you don't take me with you, I'll figure out a way to get out from under my father's thumb and find Chertok myself. This is my life. Not yours, not my father's, *mine*."

Grady sighed and sat on the edge of the bed. "Your father will kill me if I defy him."

"He's used to me defying him," she replied. "Blame it on me. I don't care. But you cannot leave me behind. I need to be there when Chertok meets Moretti. Who knows what will happen if I'm not? I don't want to find out. Do you?"

"Caitlin, you're asking me to go against your father's wishes, jeopardizing not only my standing in this family, but my life. Because I promise you, when he finds out, I will be lucky if I get to walk away with my head attached."

"I know," she whispered. "Believe me, I'm sorry. But I cannot sit back and wait. I need to do something—that something is helping you find Chertok."

Grady scrubbed a hand over his face. "All right, fine. You can go with me." He got to his feet, walked across the room, and leaned over her. "Do not make me regret it."

Chapter 21
Caitlin

Shortly after two a.m., Caitlin heard a light tap at her door. She slung the hotel gift shop tote she'd purchased earlier over her shoulder and opened the door a crack.

Grady held a finger to his lips and gestured for her to follow him. She had to step over the guard sprawled in the hallway, slumped against the wall unconscious. She looked questioningly at Grady's back, then hurried to catch up with him. Caitlin slipped into the elevator beside him and waited for the doors to close.

"What did you do to that guy?" she asked.

"Hit him over the head," he said with a shrug. "He should be out for a while. Or long enough for us to get out of the hotel. I need you to listen carefully. I got a car; it was delivered an hour ago. It's a dark blue Mercedes S580 with the valet. Once we're in the lobby, I want you to wait until I give you the all-clear. I think your father has men posted down there. If they see you, they *will* drag your ass back upstairs. We have to be careful. Okay?"

"Okay," she mumbled.

"If someone stops you, tell them you couldn't sleep, so you're going for a walk or something," he continued.

"That's why I told you to wear pajamas. I don't want it to *look* like you're trying to sneak out."

Her stomach twisted and turned. She was sick of the subterfuge, the dishonesty, all of it. The last thing she wanted to do was intentionally disobey her father or get Grady in trouble, but she had been pushed beyond reasonable expectations.

"Caitlin?"

"Hm?"

He inched closer. "What's wrong?"

She signed and sagged against the wall. "I'm tired. I want this to be over so I can go back to my life. Is that too much to ask?"

Grady brushed her hair away from her face. "You want to go back to life in New York? Law school, parties, dumb boyfriends?"

Caitlin stared up at him. "No, I don't want to run anymore."

"Then you should go home with your father. You'll be safe. Protected. Let me handle this."

She shook her head. "I need to do this. I'm sick of other people controlling my life, telling me what to do, what to say, how to act. This is the only way out. This is the only way it will end."

He kissed her: one hand on her waist, the other sliding around the back of her neck to pull her close. When the kiss was over, he rested his forehead against hers with a sigh.

"Caitlin—"

Her voice shook as she spoke. "This will never work, will it? You and me, I mean."

He didn't answer her because the elevator opened. Grady released her and stepped out, looking both directions before he gestured for her to follow him.

He hurried down the hall while she hung back and stopped at the front desk, talking to the woman behind the counter. She burst out laughing, which made Grady smile. A knot of jealousy coiled in Caitlin's gut. While she seethed at the sight of him flirting with another woman, he turned to look at her and pointed over his shoulder. Caitlin nodded and headed for the door. She saw the Mercedes through the large glass windows.

Across the lobby, a small, wiry guy stood in the corner, watching everything. Caitlin recognized him; he was one of Declan's men. She didn't know his first name, but his last name was Murphy. She stepped behind a wide pillar, afraid he would see her. She then glanced at the counter, but Grady was no longer there, and neither was the woman.

He appeared at her side instantly, grabbed her arm, and peered around the pillar. Caitlin didn't know what he was waiting for, but it must have happened because they suddenly moved, hurrying through the lobby. She saw the woman from the counter talking to Murphy. Distracting him.

They darted out the door, hurrying to the valet. He handed over the keys, and they got in the car. It wasn't until they pulled into traffic that Caitlin relaxed.

"Did you know that woman?" she asked after a few minutes.

"What woman?"

"The one at the counter who distracted Murphy," she explained.

Grady snorted. "No. I told her he was your ex-husband, and you wanted to get out of the hotel without him seeing you. She was more than happy to help."

"It looked like you were flirting with her," she mumbled.

"Were you jealous?"

She clenched her fists in her lap. "Maybe," she responded. "I don't know. I know I didn't appreciate it."

He glanced at her before turning his eyes back to the road. "It was what it was. I got what I needed from her."

Caitlin rested her head against the back of the seat and closed her eyes. She didn't want to think about him flirting with someone to get what he needed or him doing anything with anybody because she hated it. Not that she had any right to dislike anything he did with any woman. He didn't belong to her.

"Where are we going?" she asked after a few minutes.

"I know somebody," he replied.

Caitlin laughed. "Of course you do."

Grady chuckled. "Yeah, of course I do. We're meeting them in Jersey."

It didn't take long to arrive there in the middle of the night. They parked next to a Waffle House in God-only-knew what part of Jersey at five minutes after three. Before they went in, he took a cell phone from his pocket and handed it to her.

"Here. In case we get separated."

"Thanks," she murmured.

Inside the restaurant, most of the tables were empty, except for one in the front surrounded by a bunch of construction workers. Grady nodded at the waitress leaning on the counter, then he headed for the back. He stopped in front of a booth occupied by an older woman with short gray hair reading a magazine. When she saw him, she dropped her glasses on the table and jumped to her feet.

"Grady!" She bounced on her toes as she threw her arms around him and kissed his cheek with a loud smack, her exuberance rolling off her in waves. She released him, stepped back, and checked him out from head to toe. "You haven't changed one bit. Still a handsome fucker." She laughed as she sat down. "Sit, sit."

Caitlin slid into the booth, Grady right behind her.

The woman propped her elbows on the table, her chin resting on her hands, and stared at Caitlin with narrowed eyes. "She looks like Maeve," she pronounced. "Is this Olivia or Caitlin?"

"Francine, this is Caitlin," Grady said. "Caitlin, Francine Goldberg, friend, confidant, also the baddest bitch I know."

Francine giggled and slapped him on the arm. "You're too sweet. Stop it."

The waitress appeared at the table with three plates of waffles. She set them down, along with napkin-wrapped silverware. She picked up a bottle of syrup from one of the other tables, dropped it with a clunk, and left.

"I thought you might be hungry," Francine said. She pointed to a carafe next to Grady's elbow. "I ordered coffee, too."

Caitlin hadn't realized just how hungry she was until the stack of waffles sat in front of her. She slathered butter over the stack and drowned them in syrup.

"Alright, Grady, what was the dire emergency that required me to drag my ass out of bed in the middle of the night?" Francine said. "You know I don't want to get up once I'm asleep." She winked at him.

Caitlin bit her lip, holding back the biting comment she wanted to make. Who the hell was this woman to Grady?

He poured himself a cup of coffee and took a sip before he spoke, taking his time, as if he was trying to figure out how to ask his question. "The Bratva. What do you know about them?"

Francine stopped with a forkful of waffle halfway to her mouth. "What did you say?"

"You heard me," he said.

"Please tell me you are not involved with the Russians. They are fucking crazy. It's best if you stay as far away from them as possible."

"It's too late," Caitlin interjected.

Francine set her fork carefully on the table. She pushed a hand through her short gray hair, sighed, and then wiped her mouth with the napkin.

"What do you mean, it's too late?" she asked quietly.

Caitlin glanced at Grady, only to find him looking at her. She gave him a curt nod. He explained their situation to Francine.

"Jesus Christ," Francine muttered when he was finished. "I told you, they're crazy." She exhaled. "Okay, fine. Here's what I can tell you. Chertok is a minor player, a distant cousin to Dmitry Sokolov, the head of the Bratva on the East Coast. Lev's been trying to make a name for himself in New York, but he hasn't had much luck. Dmitry keeps him on a short leash."

"So, is he doing this to impress Dmitry?" Grady asked.

"That's my guess," Francine said. "Lev has always felt like he deserves more, but no one else does. He's kind of the bratty younger brother who never gets his way but will do anything for attention."

"How do you know so much about them?" Caitlin inquired. "The Russians I mean."

Francine raised an eyebrow and looked at Grady. "You didn't tell her?"

He shook his head. "Not my story."

"I was in the FBI," Francine explained to her. "For twenty-five years. For a long time, I was undercover as the girlfriend of a … well, a prominent member of the Bratva. I know everything about them. *Everything*. I got out less than a year ago."

"Can you get us a meeting with Dmitry?" Grady interjected.

Francine rubbed her eyes. "Probably. But I need time."

"We can't wait," Caitlin said.

"Okay. Let me see what I can do." Francine slid out of the booth. "I'll be right back." As she walked away, she pulled a cell phone from her pocket.

Caitlin waited until she rounded the corner before she turned to Grady. "How the hell do you know an FBI agent?"

"I know a lot of people, Cait," he replied. "I've known Francine since we were kids. She grew up down the street from me. I maintained that connection after she joined the FBI. In my line of work, it pays to be friendly with people in law enforcement."

"What makes you think she'll help us? Why wouldn't she just turn us in? Maybe that's what she's doing right now, calling the police to tell them she has the woman who killed Bobby Corelli in custody."

"She wouldn't do that."

"Why not?" she asked.

"Because she owes me a favor," Grady said. "And she's my friend." He took a drink of his coffee. "Eat your waffles."

Caitlin huffed, but she pulled her plate close and worked on the pile of waffles. They were almost gone before Francine returned to the table.

"Sokolov will meet with you," she said. "Tonight, seven p.m."

He shifted in his seat. "You can't get him to see us any sooner?"

Francine shook her head. "No. You're lucky he agreed to meet. Trust me, it's going to cost me." She sat down, opened her purse, took out a pen and a receipt. She scribbled something on the back of it and slid it across the table to Grady.

"Do not be late," she said. "He won't wait. He has no patience." She got to her feet and slung her purse over her shoulder. "I gotta go. Do me a favor? Call me when it's over. Otherwise, I'll worry you didn't make it out in one piece."

He smiled up at her. "I will." He grabbed her hand. "And Francine? Thank you. I know how hard it was for you to do this."

She bent over to kiss his cheek. "Consider my debt paid," she whispered. She stood upright and grinned at Caitlin. "It was nice to meet you, young lady. Try to stay out of trouble, okay?" With that, she left.

She pushed her plate away. "So, now we wait? Again."

The front door of the restaurant opened, and two police officers entered. Grady waited until they were seated before he got up and threw money on the table.

"We wait, but not here," he muttered. "Let's go."

She took his extended hand and let him lead her outside to the car. She didn't know where they were going, so she stared out the window, watching the lights. Ten minutes after they left, Grady turned into a large complex filled with office buildings, drove around the back, and parked under a tree, hiding them in the shadows.

"Where are we?" she asked.

"Close to where we're meeting with Sokolov," he replied. "The O'Reilly family owns this building, along with a dozen more on the East Coast. When we need a legitimate address for something, we use one of them." He pointed at a door directly in front of them. "That office right there is one we use frequently. I've got the alarm code. Come on." He got out of the car, went to the office door, and input the number into the keypad above the handle. When the light flashed green, he pushed it open. Inside, he entered another number into the keypad by the door, the alarm changing to "Disarmed."

"Come on in," he said, opening it wide. "We can hide here until morning. I don't want to chance checking into a hotel. I'm exhausted. I've been awake for over twenty-four hours. I need to sleep."

Overhead, an emergency light illuminated a reception area. A built-in desk stretched from one end of the office to the other. Leather chairs sat beneath blind-covered windows. She followed Grady past the reception desk, through a door, and down a short hallway. On her left were several offices, and on the right was a conference room with a table, chairs, and an enormous leather couch. He entered the conference room and went straight to the couch.

Grady stretched out, crossed his arms over his chest, and closed his eyes.

Caitlin was antsy, anticipation and adrenaline combining to make her jittery. She didn't know how he could be so calm when so much was at stake. She threw her tote bag on the table and tapped her hands against her legs as she paced back and forth in front of the couch.

"Can I ask you a question?" she said after a few minutes.

Grady sighed heavily. "I suppose."

"What are you going to do when my father finds out about us?"

"Run," he mumbled.

"Haha, funny. I'm serious."

"I don't know. I've been a little busy trying to keep you alive, which you haven't made easy by the way. I haven't had time to think about it."

"Are you going to tell him?" she asked.

Grady sat up. "I thought *you* said this thing between us would never work?"

Caitlin perched on the edge of a chair, folded her hands in her lap, and squeezed them tight. She closed her eyes as she spoke. "It won't. I want somebody to love me. I need somebody who loves me. If you don't believe in love, how can we ever be together?"

"It's not that I don't believe in love, princess." Grady rubbed the back of his neck. "Maybe I needed to find someone I could love? I've been so jaded for so long, unable to trust anybody, pushing away every woman who crossed my path. Until you."

"What are you saying?"

"You push all my god damn buttons. You purposely piss me off. Jesus Christ, you are the most stubborn woman I've ever met. But there's something about you I can't resist. I've tried. Everything about this … this thing between us is crazy and fucked up. I don't know what to do about it. I know I don't enjoy thinking about life without you."

Caitlin burst out of the chair, throwing herself at Grady, climbing into his lap and kissing him.

He grabbed her wrists, stopping her. "What are you doing?"

"That was the sweetest thing you've ever said to me," she whispered. "I got caught up in the moment."

He released her hands, his hands sliding down her back to her ass. "Kiss me again."

Caitlin giggled, cupped his cheeks, and kissed him. She licked his lips and pushed her tongue into his mouth as he pulled her hips down against his, the erection trapped behind the zipper of his jeans pressing against her warm core. She squirmed, grinding against him.

Grady smacked her ass hard enough to sting, though not too much. "Sit still," he muttered.

"No." She wiggled, her knees pressing against the couch on either side of him.

He spanked her again, sending a jolt of heat rushing through her. Caitlin grabbed the bottom of her shirt, yanked it over her head, and threw it aside.

"I want you to fuck me," she whispered.

"Jesus, princess." He attacked her, sucking dark marks all over her neck and chest. He unhooked her bra, slid it down her arms, and tossed it on the floor. He took her breast in his mouth, swirling his tongue around the pink tip before he sucked it between his lips and bit it gently. He pinched the nipple of her other breast between his thumb and forefinger until Caitlin moaned obscenely.

Grady's cock rubbed against her, noticeable even through the thin pajama pants she wore. God, she wanted him. Desperately.

"Grady," she gasped.

He stretched her out on the couch beneath him, pushing her legs open with his knee and settling between them. She moaned as desire flowed through her and fire pooled in the pit of her stomach. Caitlin fumbled with the button of his jeans, desperate to release him, to touch him. Once she got his pants undone, she slipped her hand past the waistband and took hold of him.

Grady groaned, his hips moving as she stroked his heavy cock. He leaned on his forearm, tangled his fingers in her hair, and yanked off her pajamas and underwear with his free hand.

Grady's hand was between her legs as soon as she kicked them off, cupping her sex and sliding a finger inside her.

"Fuck, you're so wet, princess," he murmured. He pressed his thumb against her clit as his finger moved, gently massaging her sweet spot.

Caitlin moaned and writhed beneath him. "I want you inside me," she begged. "Now." She clutched his hand, pushing her hips against it, desperate for more.

Grady chuckled. "Oh yeah, is that what you want?" Another finger eased into her, pumping wildly.

Her grip tightened on his hard shaft and her finger traced the thick vein on the underside of his cock as she rubbed her thumb across the tip.

He abruptly sat up, tore his shirt off, followed by his jeans and boxers. Then he was back between her open legs, entering her with one powerful thrust.

Caitlin gasped and her back arched as she opened herself to him. They moaned together as he entered her, his cock filling her completely.

His thrusts were erratic, fast, and vigorous. She kept pace with him, her nails digging into his ass as he plunged into her repeatedly. They both panted with exertion, sweaty and desperate, bodies moving in sync, rushing toward that elusive peak of satisfaction. But it was good. So, so good.

Insanely aroused, it took almost no time for Grady to bring her to orgasm. It burst through her like an explosion of light and completely overwhelmed her. He wasn't far behind, his hand tightening its grip on her hair as he came.

He collapsed on top of her with a heavy sigh. After a few minutes, he lifted his head and kissed her. When he was done, he sat up, pulling her with him.

"When this is over, I promise you, I will figure something out," he said. "I don't know what yet, but I'll think of something."

Caitlin kissed the corner of his mouth. "Thank you," she whispered.

Chapter 22
Grady

Grady woke up with Caitlin sprawled across him, her head tucked under his chin. He rubbed her back as he stared off into space.

His promise to her resurfaced, sitting on his chest like a dead weight. It was stupid and reckless. He never should have done it; her father would never allow it. Promising her they would somehow make their relationship work was practically a death wish. It was only a matter of time before he broke her heart. He hugged her tight, not wanting to think about it.

Caitlin stirred in his arms, so he checked his watch. They needed to get moving.

"Caitlin?" He brushed her hair away from her face. "Wake up."

She sighed and kissed his cheek. "What's going on?"

"It's almost time to go," he whispered.

She got to her feet and stretched. "Is there a bathroom around here?"

"Out the door, make a right, last door on the left," he replied. "Hurry. We don't have much time."

She gave him a dirty look, grabbed her tote bag, and marched away. He watched her until she went through the bathroom door.

Grady walked behind her, went into the men's room, and kicked the door closed.

Ten minutes later, he emerged after giving himself what his father had called a "spit bath." Caitlin was on the couch, her face scrubbed clean and her hair freshly combed. She looked like a teenager in her dark jeans and a red sweater with the tote bag thrown over her shoulder. It was a harsh reminder of how much younger than him she was. He was stiff and his joints ached after a night spent sleeping on the couch—and having sex on it—while she bounded around as if it was nothing.

"You ready?" he asked.

She nodded. "Yeah."

Once they were in the car, Caitlin buckled her seatbelt and stared straight ahead, utterly silent.

"I'm not sure I'm ready to do this," she mumbled.

"You wanted to come," Grady replied. "In fact, you insisted."

She snorted. "Yeah, well, I think I changed my mind."

"Too late, princess. There's no turning back now."

"Where are we going?" she asked.

"Close to the Hudson, there are deserted warehouses. They were bought a few years ago by a Russian conglomerate. It was assumed at the time it was for the Bratva. I guess we were correct. That's where we're meeting Sokolov."

Caitlin rolled her eyes. "How cliché. A mafia meeting in a deserted warehouse."

He chuckled. "Where do you think the movies, TV shows, and books get their clichés? From actual mafia members. I know a couple of guys who moved to Hollywood. They're working as consultants on a bunch of films." He shrugged. "It's a way of life, Cait. One we've lived for a long time. It's hard to change, hard to accept the modernization of the world we shaped for so long. It might be cliché, but it's our life."

She clasped her hands in her lap and stared straight ahead. He wished he was one of those men who could commiserate with people, soothe them with a kind word or gesture, but that wasn't him. Caitlin was deeply upset, but he could not comfort her. All he could do was protect her from harm.

In the distance, the warehouse loomed so immense, it blocked out the other buildings. A chain-link fence surrounded it, the gate hanging wide open, a broken lock dangling from the metal pole. Grady drove through it and parked in the empty lot.

As soon as they stepped out of the car, a tattooed bald man wearing a black Metallica shirt approached them with his gun drawn. Grady raised his hands over his head and smiled.

"I'm Grady McCarthy, and this is Caitlin O'Reilly," he said.

"I know who you are." The man had a thick Russian accent. "Dmitry is waiting for you." He turned abruptly, without another word.

"Grady," she whispered.

"Just follow him, Cait. Don't ask questions and do as he says."

She nodded and followed him, Grady right behind her. They entered the warehouse through a side entrance, the faint scent of mildew and oil tinging the air, mixing with the dust kicked up with every step they took. Light from the streetlights outside filtered through the broken windows high above, casting jagged shadows on the rusty corrugated metal walls. Stacks of wooden crates and corroded machinery covered the dirty floor. Their footsteps echoed as they crossed the vast space.

Standing in the middle of the warehouse, surrounded by several tattooed, menacing-looking men, was a short, dark-haired older man in a black trench coat. He stared at them as they walked toward him. Caitlin thought he looked vaguely like Lev Chertok; they were definitely related.

The bald guy in the Metallica shirt stopped and gestured to one of the other men. He crossed the room to Grady and patted him down, checking for weapons. When he was satisfied Grady wasn't carrying, he stepped back and nodded at Mr. Metallica, who nodded at the man in the black trench coat.

"Mr. McCarthy?" he said.

"Yes."

"I'm Dmitry Sokolov." He tipped his chin in Caitlin's direction. "Ms. O'Reilly?"

Grady nodded.

"Francine said you wanted to ask me about my cousin Lev Chertok," Sokolov continued. "She did not go into detail."

"We need to speak to your cousin," Grady said. "It's of vital importance."

Dmitry shook his head. "I have not seen him in quite a while."

"Can you help us locate him?" Grady asked.

"Why do you need to find Lev so badly, Mr. McCarthy? I'm sure whatever you think he did, you are mistaken."

"We are not mistaken," Caitlin interjected. "Please, just tell us where he is."

The Russian scowled at her. "I told you I have not seen him. I cannot help you." He turned back to Grady. "If there is nothing else?"

It was an obvious dismissal. Before Dmitry could walk away, Caitlin stepped forward. Grady shot a glare in her direction, but she ignored him. He clenched his fists, waiting to see what happened.

"You don't understand," she said. "Your cousin had my boyfriend murdered."

Dmitry raised an eyebrow. "Oh?" He appeared indifferent.

Caitlin looked over her shoulder at Grady, cleared her throat, and continued. "Yes. Not only did he have him killed, but he tried to place the blame on me. He wanted to start a war between my family and the Morettis."

"What are you talking about?" Dmitry asked. "Who was your boyfriend?"

"The son of Aldo Moretti. His illegitimate son," she replied. "Lev had him killed and tried to frame me for the murder."

Dmitry muttered something in Russian, then Mr. Metallica darted forward and grabbed Caitlin by the hair. Grady moved but froze when three guns turned on him. The man yanked her head back and pushed his gun against the underside of her chin. He dragged her over the dirty floor until she stood in front of Dmitry.

"If you are lying, Misha will kill you, Ms. O'Reilly," he said. "Now tell me, how do you know Lev is responsible for the death of Moretti's son?"

Grady saw Caitlin's throat move as she swallowed. "He told me," she whispered, wincing as Misha dug the barrel of his gun into her chin.

"He told you?" Dmitry snorted. "Do you have proof?"

"I swear it's true," Caitlin continued. A tear leaked from the corner of her eye. "He … he wanted to start a war between my family and the Morettis so he could take over—"

Dmitry's shoulders stiffened. "Take over? Take over what?"

"I don't know," she cried. "The drug business, smuggling, prostitution? I don't know. I'm not involved in my father's business. I only know what Lev told me."

Dmitry stepped forward and, with one finger, pushed the gun away from her chin. Misha moved it to her temple. "Why would my cousin tell you anything, little girl? You are nothing."

"I was supposed to die. Fredo Russo was supposed to kill me. But I escaped. Maybe he thought he could tell me because I wouldn't be able to talk."

Caitlin trembled from head to toe. Grady itched to tear apart the man with the gun at her head. His fingers tingled to get a hold of him.

Dmitry snapped his fingers, and Misha released her. Not expecting him to let go, she fell to her knees.

Dmitry snorted, stepping away from her. "Misha, find my cousin. Now." He looked at Grady for a moment, then at Caitlin. "Wait here." He turned and walked away, surrounded by his men. They walked up a set of stairs and entered an office. The door slammed closed behind them.

Grady went at once to Caitlin's side, wrapped his arms around her, and helped her to her feet. He held her close and kissed her temple.

"Are you okay?" he murmured.

Caitlin nodded, but she didn't speak. Instead, she rested her cheek on his shoulder and sighed loudly.

"The Bratva aren't someone you should mess with, princess. They don't play games. Jesus Christ, you're lucky he didn't kill you."

"I know." A hiccupping sob escaped her before she buried her face against his chest.

Grady looked around until he spotted a stack of metal crates against the wall. He led her across the room, flipped over one of them, and eased her onto it. He crouched in front of her.

"Breathe, baby," he whispered.

Caitlin closed her eyes, sucked in two quick breaths, then slowly exhaled. She did it two more times until she was calm. On the second exhale, she opened her eyes and stared into his. He put his hand on her knee and squeezed.

"Better?" he asked.

She shrugged. "A little, I guess." She swiped her hands over her face. "He could have killed me."

Grady nodded. "Yes. You're lucky he didn't. The Bratva take familial relationships seriously, just like your father and the Morettis. You accused his cousin of murder *and* attempted murder with no proof, only your word. They don't take things like that lightly."

Her eyes narrowed, and she scowled. "What was I supposed to do? We need to find Lev, and Dmitry wouldn't tell us where he is. I didn't have a choice, did I?"

"You could have let me do the talking," he replied.

"It wasn't getting us anywhere," she snapped. "You weren't asking the right questions or getting the answers we need. I thought if I said something, he might talk."

"You were wrong. A lot of the Russians have no respect for women, especially ones they don't know. At first, Dmitry probably found you annoying. After your accusation, you became something else to him. You never, ever accuse one of their family members of murder without proof. You pissed him off."

"I hate these stupid, archaic rules you people have," she muttered. "They are so fucking dumb."

Grady rolled his eyes. "It's hard to break years of tradition. The old ways worked, and we're not in any hurry to change. I know you don't like it, but it is what it is. You accept it and move on."

Caitlin put her hands in her hair and pushed it away from her face. "What do you think they're doing?" she asked.

Grady sat on the other metal crate beside her. "I don't know. It could be anything."

"Plotting to kill us?" She sighed and shook her head. "I wish that was a joke."

"So do I."

Thirty minutes later, the door upstairs opened, and Dmitry emerged. He walked down the stairs with his men behind him and headed straight for them.

Grady got to his feet and stood in front of Caitlin with his arms crossed.

Dmitry stopped a foot from him. "I will help you find Lev. But you must understand, he is my family. If I am going to betray him, I expect something in return."

"What do you want?" Grady asked.

"A favor."

Grady raised an eyebrow. "What kind of favor?"

"A favor that is to be determined at a later time," Dmitry replied. "The O'Reilly family will be in my debt."

Grady rubbed the back of his neck. There was no way he could put the O'Reillys in this man's debt. He glanced over his shoulder. There wasn't a choice, though, not when Caitlin's life was on the line. They had to take Lev to Moretti, or Caitlin would suffer the consequences.

He closed his eyes and took a deep breath. "Okay. You have my word. The O'Reillys are in your debt."

Dmitry held out a folded piece of paper. "This is Lev's private residence in Smithtown. It's a substantially sized, secluded estate. He is there now; I can assure you of this. You are not to tell him I sent you. Understood?"

Grady took the paper and shoved it in his front pocket. "Understood."

The Russian turned to leave, hesitated, then looked back over his shoulder. "I *am* sorry for your troubles, Ms. O'Reilly. But I ask that you do not darken my doorstep again." With that, he swung around and walked out of the warehouse.

Once they were gone, Grady held his hand out to Caitlin. "Come on. We need to go to Smithtown."

Chapter 23
Caitlin

They were on the road. Again. How many hours had she spent in the car over the last six days, staring out the window? Had it really been less than a week since Bobby died? Everything was a blur, the days bleeding into each other. Exhaustion colored her view of the world, turning it soft and fuzzy around the edges. The fatigue was a dull throb in the center of her brain, making it hard to think, while the rhythmic hum of the tires and the neon lights flashing by lulled her into a hypnotic state. She rested her head against the glass with her eyes closed, wondering how many more sleepless nights she would be forced to endure.

Caitlin wanted her life back—her stupid, boring, going-to-law-school life. If she could go back in time, she'd walk away from Bobby. Maybe she'd even run in the other direction. If they had never dated, none of this would have happened.

"Would have, could have, should have," she mumbled under her breath.

"What?" Grady asked.

She shook her head. "Nothing. Talking to myself. The 'what-if?' game. What if I hadn't dated Bobby? What if I had been inside the apartment? What if, what if, what if?" She pressed two fingers into the center of her forehead. "I'm tired, Grady."

He reached over and took her hand. "I know, princess. Hopefully, it will be over soon."

The weight of Grady's hand on hers was a minor comfort, as well as a reminder of what they faced once this was over. They had two choices—a life together or a life apart. The first choice subjected them to the wrath of Sean O'Reilly. The second choice was not one Caitlin wanted to think about it. Everything about her was inexplicably connected to Grady, and she couldn't picture herself living without him.

Unfortunately, it might not matter whether she pictured herself with Grady or not. His promise to "figure something out" was empty at best. Caitlin suspected her future meant a life with no Grady. She pushed the thought away, afraid if she lingered too long on the possibility of a future without Grady, she'd cry.

She glanced at the clock on the dashboard. It wouldn't be long before they were in Smithtown where they would face Lev. They had to get him to Moretti; her life depended on it.

The thought made her stomach churn. Undoubtedly, getting Lev to Moretti was an impossible task. He'd put up a fight and if he had Joey LaGuardia and Gino Russo by his side, it would be anything but easy. She'd seen enough violence in the last week to know how quickly things could spiral out of control. Fear snaked up her spine, sending a chill racing through her.

The headlights of a passing vehicle illuminated Grady's face for a moment. His jaw was set, determined, his eyes narrowed, and his brow furrowed. Caitlin was sure he had a plan—he always did. He was sharp, intuitive, used to dangerous situations. He wouldn't walk into the lion's den without an idea of how to proceed.

She fought to keep her breathing steady. If only this was a nightmare she could wake up from instead of her new reality. Deep down, she knew things would only get worse before they got better.

The car slowed as they approached a turnoff on the outskirts of Smithtown. Grady drove a short distance down the road, pulled onto the shoulder, and shut off the car. When the lights went out, the dark encompassed them completely. It took a few minutes for Caitlin's eyes to adjust to the darkness.

"We're close to the house," Grady said, drawing her out of her musings. He opened his phone, pulling up a map of the property. "According to Dmitry, no one else should be in there except for Lev, Joey, and Gino. If we're lucky, they won't be worried someone will show up, so they'll be inside." He enlarged the map and pointed at it. "There is no road leading to the back of this place; it butts up against the river. I'm going to go in the back door. Hopefully, the assholes won't know what hit them."

"What do you want me to do?" she asked.

"You are staying here."

"No, I'm not," Caitlin snapped.

Grady reached into the back seat and grabbed a duffle bag, dragging it onto the seat between them. He opened it and took out a gun. He checked the magazine, cocked it, then he tucked the gun in his waistband.

"Yes, you are. I cannot have you in there, distracting me. I need you to stay here. You can lie low until I get Chertok out of there." He put his phone in the front pocket of his jeans. "I'll call you when I've got him. Drive up to the house, I'll throw Lev in the trunk, and we go." He took hold of her chin, forcing her to look at him. "Do as you are told for once, okay? None of your bullshit."

Caitlin winced at the harshness of his words, but she nodded, her throat too tight to speak. It was useless to argue with him, as she wouldn't win. She could only watch as he kissed her forehead, shoved open the door, got out, and started up the road.

"Bastard," she muttered under her breath.

Grady was almost out of sight. Caitlin could let him go and stay in the car like a good girl, or she could follow him. It took her less than ten seconds to decide.

She reached into the duffle bag, grabbed a gun, and tucked it in her waistband. Then she slid to the driver's side, removed the keys from the ignition, and shoved them in her coat pocket. When she got out of the car, she was careful to close the door as quietly as possible before she walked up the road after Grady with the gun in her hand. The last time she'd held a gun, she'd killed a man. Her hands shook, and another wave of fear crashed over her. She closed her eyes, willing it away.

Her pulse pounded in her ears, drowning out all other sounds. Caitlin stayed back, following Grady from a hundred yards away. When he reached the driveway, he slipped into the trees on the side of the narrow road leading to the house.

Caitlin followed him, sticking to the fence line on the east side. It took her a minute to realize it had gotten easier to see the closer she got to the house. Every light in the place shone brightly. Upstairs, downstairs, even the lights outside were ablaze.

Grady paused, and she ducked behind a tree. She watched him cut across the lawn and pause next to a large bush before he darted through an unlocked door.

Caitlin's hand tightened around her gun, her fingers aching. This was the moment she'd both waited for and dreaded, so she couldn't back down now. She checked to make sure no one was nearby, then she hurriedly crossed the grass to the same door Grady had entered, turned the knob, and pushed it open.

It opened to a mudroom off the kitchen. It was dimly lit, the only light coming from a bulb above the sink. She inched forward, pausing at the end of the counter to listen. Voices came from somewhere to her left. One of them was loud, gruff, and abrasive, while the other was calm with a Russian accent.

Lev.

Caitlin moved through the house, out of the kitchen, and through a dining room that came out into a long hallway. Grady stood outside a room, his back against the wall. She ducked into an open doorway and waited a few seconds to make sure he hadn't seen her, then she peered around the corner. He was crouched beside the entrance to the room, head down, body tense.

Caitlin ran along the hall on her tiptoes, staying close to the wall, eyes on Grady. Before she could reach him, he stood up and walked into the room.

"Good evening, gentlemen," she heard him say calmly.

She took the spot where he stood seconds earlier, crouched, and looked around the corner. If the situation hadn't been one fraught with danger, Caitlin would have laughed at the shocked looks on the men's faces.

Everything happened at once.

Lev's hand opened, his drink tumbling to the floor. The thick glass bounced once on the carpet, hit him in the knee, and rolled to a stop a foot away from him. Lev shouted something unintelligible as he dove behind a small leather couch. Joey and Gino reached for their guns, but Grady fired first, the shot deafening in the confined space.

Joey dropped to the floor as blood flowed from his shoulder, immediately staining his cream-colored shirt crimson red. He dragged himself behind the couch with Lev. Gino darted behind a pillar in the center of the room.

Grady aimed his gun in Gino's direction and pulled the trigger three times. Wood splintered off the pillar.

The mobster screamed, "Fuck!"

Joey popped up from behind the couch, a sadistic smile on his face, blood running down his left arm, his gun pointed directly at Grady. Everything slowed to a snail's pace as Joey's finger tightened on the trigger.

Without thinking, Caitlin got to her feet, lunged forward, and slammed into Grady from behind, knocking him to the ground as the shot rang out. The bullet whizzed past them, hitting a painting of a serene lake on the wall behind them.

"God dammit!" Grady raged, his eyes alight with fury. He scrambled to his feet. "Stay down!"

Lev jumped up and backed away, headed for a door on the left side of the room, Joey in front of him, moving with his boss. She didn't see Gino anywhere.

Another shot rang out, grazing a table near Grady. Grady fired back, hitting Joey right in the center of his chest. He collapsed to the floor in front of Lev, dead.

For a moment, Lev was exposed. Caitlin didn't hesitate. She got to her knees, raised her gun, and fired.

To her surprise, the shot hit its mark. Lev grunted in pain and stumbled forward, his leg buckling beneath him. He dropped to one knee, clutching his thigh as blood gushed from the wound.

Grady was on him in an instant, Caitlin right behind him, her body still humming with adrenaline. Lev locked eyes with her as she stood over him, pain and rage warring on his face.

"You *сука*," Lev muttered. "This isn't over."

Grady leaned over him. "Trust me, it is." He loosened his belt, yanked it out of his jeans, and held it out to her. "Put this around his leg before he bleeds out."

She stepped forward to do as he asked. As she moved to secure the belt around Lev's leg, his expression shifted. His eyes flicked past her and focused on something over her shoulder. Before she could react, she heard a low growl of anger.

Gino.

Caitlin barely had time to turn before Gino, bloodied but still on his feet, rushed at her with a knife in his hand. Grady shouted her name, but she was already moving, instinct taking over. She fell to the side, narrowly avoiding the slash of the blade.

The next few seconds were a blur. Grady darted forward and hit Gino with enough force to send them both crashing to the floor. The knife flew out of Gino's hand as the two men struggled. Grady punched Gino in the jaw, but Gino fought back, hitting Grady in the kidneys, his fists flying, pummeling Grady as his bloodied face twisted in anger.

Caitlin dropped Grady's belt and scrambled across the floor to grab the knife. Her fingers closed around the cold metal handle as Gino shoved Grady off, pounced on him, and wrapped his hands around his throat. Panic rushed through her at the thought of losing the man she loved. She jumped on Gino's back, screaming as she plunged the knife into the side of his neck.

His grip on Grady loosened, and he fell over, blood spurting from his neck like a broken dam. He grunted, flailing wildly as he struggled to contain the crimson tide pouring out of him. A strange gurgle came out of him. Then nothing.

Grady gasped for air, coughing as he sat up. He stared at Caitlin, eyes wide with both shock and relief.

"Thank you," he rasped.

Caitlin dropped the knife from her shaking hands. She trembled from head to toe from the fear that had clung so tightly to her just moments earlier.

But it was over. At least part of it. Joey and Gino were dead, and they had Lev. Now they had to get him to Moretti.

"I thought I told you to stay in the car," Grady muttered.

"I didn't listen," she mumbled.

"No shit." He got to his feet and hurried to Lev's side.

The Russian appeared to have passed out. Grady kneeled beside him and checked his pulse. "He's still alive. Give me the belt."

Caitlin reached for it, freezing when she saw her hand completely covered in blood. A choked wheeze came out of her. She snatched the belt and tossed it at Grady.

"I … I need to wash my hands." She sprinted out of the room, down the hall to the kitchen. She turned on the water, dumped soap on her bloody hands, and scrubbed until they were raw.

"Are you okay?"

Startled, she squeaked, bumping her elbow on the faucet as she swung to face him. Grady stood in the doorway, his arm around Lev, holding the man upright.

"Um … yeah, sorry." She wiped her wet hands on her jeans. "Can we get out of here?"

Grady tossed her a set of keys. "I took those from Gino. I think they're for the SUV out front. We'll take that."

Caitlin followed him out the door they'd come through and around the side of the house. The black Escalade, likely the same one they'd thrown her into, was parked next to a closed garage. She hit the button on the remote and the lights flashed.

Grady opened the back of the vehicle, angling Lev inside while she got in the driver's seat. Once Grady was seated beside her, she looked at him, grim and determined.

"Let's get this asshole to Moretti," she said.

Chapter 24
Grady

Grady sat in the passenger seat, fuming and biting his tongue. It took all his self-control not to yell at Caitlin for being so stupid. He told her to stay in the car for a reason. She could have been killed. It was bad enough that he'd let her come with him to find Chertok, but he would not consider taking her into the line of fire. Of course, she didn't listen to him.

When they reached the Mercedes, Grady asked her to pull over. She parked the SUV on the side of the road and shut down the engine.

"Follow me in the Mercedes," he said. "There's a rest area not far from here. We'll stop there, clean Chertok up, contact Moretti, and arrange a time to meet him."

Caitlin nodded. She climbed out of the Escalade without a word and got into the car. He slid into the driver's seat, adjusted it, and started the vehicle. He watched in the rearview mirror as she pulled out behind him.

Twenty minutes later, he pulled into the rest area and drove to the darkest part of the parking lot. A few minutes later, she parked beside him and got out.

"It looks like we lucked out. Nobody's here," she said.

"Let's get Lev out of the car and see if we can find a first-aid kit." Grady opened the back of the SUV.

Lev squinted as the overhead light hit his face. He was deathly pale; even Grady could see that in the dim light. He grunted in pain as Grady put his hands under his arms and dragged him out of the back.

"*мудак*," Lev muttered. "You and that little *сука* are going to regret this. Do you know who I am? Who my cousin is? The Bratva does not take things like this lightly."

Grady snorted. He itched to tell Chertok his cousin Dmitry was the one who told them where he was, but he remembered his promise. He wouldn't tell the Russian anything.

"I'm going inside to see if I can find a first-aid kit," Caitlin said. "There must be something somewhere." She stopped at the back of the Mercedes, opened the trunk, and grabbed her tote bag. Then she jogged across the grass and into the building.

"Did you hear what I said? My cousin will kill you," Chertok repeated. "It will not be pleasant."

"Dying never is," Grady retorted.

"What are you going to do to me?" Chertok asked.

Grady propped Chertok against the back of the SUV and kneeled in front of him. He ripped the Russian's pant leg until he could see the wound on his leg.

"We're taking you to Aldo Moretti," he said.

If it was possible, Lev paled more. "You ... you can't do that."

The wound wasn't as bad as Grady feared. The bullet hadn't hit a major artery; it had hit the meaty part of Chertok's thigh, passing straight through it. If Caitlin could find medical supplies, they could wrap it up, give him pain medication, and hand him off to the Italians.

Grady checked his watch. They had eighteen hours until Moretti's timeline expired. Plenty of time to get Chertok to them.

"You are not listening to me," Chertok snapped. "You cannot turn me over to Moretti."

Grady grabbed Chertok's collar, yanking him forward. "I don't give a shit what you want. You fucked with the wrong family and the wrong girl. You are going to stand in front of Aldo Moretti, and you will tell him what you did, just like you told Caitlin what you did. After you do that, I hope Moretti serves you to his attack dogs for breakfast."

Chertok entire body trembled. "I … I have information. If you let me go, I can tell you things."

"I don't want to hear what you have to say," Grady snarled.

"You will want to hear this." He glanced around, as if afraid someone might overhear him, before he looked back at Grady. "There is a traitor in the O'Reilly family. I know who it is."

Grady crossed his arms over his chest and glared at Chertok. "You're lying."

The Russian shook his head. "How do you think my men found you in Connecticut? I had this person follow your every movement, using the GPS in your Bronco and reporting it to me."

Intense fiery anger turned Grady's vision red. He reached out, wrapped his hand around Chertok's throat, and squeezed. "Listen, you piece of shit, tell me who it is or so help me, I will take your *dead* body to Moretti."

Grady released him. Chertok sucked in a desperate, gasping breath, then he coughed, his face purple. Once he could breathe, he stared at Grady for a few seconds before he spoke.

"His name is Angus Hayes."

Out of the corner of his eyes, Grady saw Caitlin jogging across the grass. She had a blue box clutched in her hands. She had changed her shirt, and her jacket was gone. He clenched his fists, stepping away from Chertok. He intercepted her at the back of the Mercedes.

"Do you have a gun?" he asked.

She nodded. "Yeah, it's on the seat."

"Grab it," he ordered. "Give him the first-aid kit. Let him fix his leg. You keep an eye on him and keep your gun ready. I'm going to call your father."

Caitlin's shoulders stiffened at his words. "Why are you calling Daddy?" she asked.

"Because I have information for him," Grady replied. "Important information about someone who works for him."

"It can't wait?"

"No." He nodded his head in Chertok's direction. "Don't take your eyes off him, Cait. I'll be right back."

Sean screamed at him for the first five minutes of the phone call, using every foul word he could think of. Some Grady hadn't heard since his Irish grandfather passed away. Once he calmed down, Grady filled him in on their apprehension of Lev Chertok—leaving out the fact that Caitlin had been in the room with bullets flying— then he told his boss what Chertok said about a traitor in the family.

When Grady was done speaking, Sean was quiet for so long that Grady checked his phone to see if they'd gotten disconnected.

"Are you positive?" Sean asked.

"I only have Chertok's word," he replied. "But he is desperate to keep himself out of Moretti's hands. He could be lying. But it needs to be checked out. Talk to Declan or Finn. They'll be able to find out if Angus tracked my Bronco using the GPS."

Sean sighed. "Did you set the meeting with Moretti yet?"

"No. He's the next phone call."

"I want to be there," Sean said. "Once you have the details, let me know. If I'm there, maybe he won't hurt my daughter."

"Yes, sir."

He was about to disconnect when Sean added, "One more thing?"

"Yeah."

"When this is over, you and I are going to have a long talk," Sean continued. "I've known you for years, which means I know there are things you aren't telling me, things about you and my daughter."

Grady cleared his throat. "I'm not sure what you mean, sir."

"Cut the shit, McCarthy," Sean muttered. "Stop hiding behind your job as my second. We're friends and that is important to me. I hope you feel the same. I'm trusting you to take care of my little girl. Do you understand me?"

He knew. Grady didn't know how he'd found out, but he knew. This wasn't a boss asking his employee to take care of his kid; this was a father asking the man who loved his daughter to take care of her.

He pinched the bridge of his nose and closed his eyes. "I'll protect her with my life, Sean."

"I know you will."

The line went dead.

"Grady!" Caitlin called.

He shoved the phone in his pocket and hurried to the vehicles. Chertok was stretched out in the back of the SUV with his eyes closed and a coat thrown over his shoulders.

"Is he okay?" Grady asked.

"I think so," she said. "He's cold. By the way, he said he told you who betrayed us. It's someone in the family?"

Grady nodded. "Yes." He pointed at the car. "Pop the trunk."

Caitlin hit the button on the remote to open the trunk. "Is that what you needed to tell my father? That someone betrayed him?"

"Yes. It needs to be investigated and handled."

"Who is it?"

He sighed. "You don't know him, so it doesn't matter." He took a package of zip ties out of the trunk, slammed it closed, and returned to the SUV. He grabbed Chertok's ankle and secured a zip tie around it, then he did the other ankle before he connected them together with a third zip tie. Then he did the same with Chertok's wrists.

Caitlin ran her fingers through her hair and stared at the ground. "I'm sick of the secrets. It's such bullshit."

Grady ignored her grumblings. Her frustrations came from the goddamn shitty situation. Nothing he said would make her feel any better. Not right now, anyway. He needed to get her mind off it, so he held out his phone.

"Call Moretti, tell him we have Chertok and we're ready to meet."

Caitlin's eyebrows shot up. "You want *me* to call him?"

"He doesn't want to talk to me," Grady said. "He wants to talk to you. You saw how he reacted when I said something at the meeting. Unfortunately, this is about you, not me. Set up the meeting. Tell him you're bringing your father."

"What?"

"Sean insisted, and I will not argue with him." He wiggled the phone back and forth. "The number to the strip club is in the phone."

Caitlin plucked it out of his hands, pulled up the number, and hit send. She walked a few feet away, far enough that Grady couldn't hear what she was saying.

He leaned against the side of the SUV, crossed his arms, and waited. He watched her face, but it was emotionless. To his surprise, she didn't roll her eyes once. Once she'd disconnected the call, she came and stood in front of him.

"He wants us there at midnight. When I told him Daddy wanted to be there, he acted like he'd expected me to say that. He said, 'He'll be here, trust me.' Then he hung up on me." She looked up at him. The exhaustion was clear on her face. "It's almost over, right? I want it to be over."

Grady held out his hand. "Come here."

She took his outstretched hand and let him pull her into his arms. Her head fell against his chest, and she sighed. He hugged her close, his lips pressed to her temple.

"I'm sorry," she whispered.

"What? Why are you apologizing?"

"Because this is my fault," she mumbled. "If I hadn't been so determined to defy my father at every turn, I never would have dated Bobby. I was only with him because I thought it would piss off Daddy. Look what that got me."

"This isn't your fault," he said. "I think Chertok would have figured out a way to fuck with the families no matter what. If he hadn't used you, he would have used someone else. If anything, you're unlucky."

A sardonic laugh sputtered out of her, and she shook her head. "That's me, unlucky." She dropped her hands to her side and stepped back. "In love, life, and everything in between." She dug the keys out of her pocket and wiggled them. "We should go. I don't want to be late." She turned her back on him and got into the Mercedes.

He went around to the driver's side of the SUV, got in, started it, and pulled out of the parking lot, checking the rearview to see if Caitlin was behind him.

An ache had settled in his gut. Grady wanted to tell her the truth about his feelings for her, but now wasn't the time. They had to stay focused, keep the end goal in mind, and make sure nobody ended up dead.

He'd tell her he loved her once he was sure she was out of harm's way.

Chapter 25
Caitlin

Her life was a mess.

Caitlin didn't know what was the truth, a lie, or an omission. She was sick of everyone keeping things from her. No one trusted her. She hated it. They treated her like a child, unable to handle the truth. But she had seen it firsthand, and it was ugly. She'd been thrust into this world unwillingly, a product of her upbringing. An awful world where nothing was fair.

But what if she could change things for the better?

It was long past time for a change. For years, she had avoided her father's world out of fear. Now that she was smack in the middle of it, her fear had dissipated, though it had thrown her into a tailspin. She used to know what she wanted to do with her life—finish school and get away. Far away, out of the world of mobsters. But since all of this had started, things changed. What she thought she wanted changed. Her eyes had been opened.

Maybe those damn mobsters weren't so bad after all.

She still wanted to be a lawyer, but her thoughts had shifted. She wasn't sure she wanted to be an environmental lawyer, fighting the good fight, but likely never winning. That had always been for show anyway, one of those "look at me, I'm doing good" degrees. Even before her life turned into a mob movie, Caitlin had found herself drawn to the criminal side of the law, the nitty-gritty, down-and-dirty shit that made other people balk. An idea had taken hold of her, tightening its grip on her over the past six days, leaving her paralyzed with fear. Maybe she could help her family. Somebody needed to confront the constant prejudices that came with the O'Reilly name. Who better than someone who had dealt with those issues her entire life?

Bright lights hit her face, and Caitlin blinked. She'd zoned out, her mind wandering, and somehow, she drove thirty miles without realizing it. She forced herself to focus. It wouldn't be a good idea to drive herself into a ditch before she met with Moretti.

Her hands tightened on the steering wheel, squeezing it until they hurt. How the hell could she possibly think about her future when she wasn't even sure she'd live to see the sun rise?

She turned up the radio and stared at the back of the SUV. An hour later, they were driving down narrow, dimly lit streets, headed for Fred's Sin Bin. Every turn brought them closer to Moretti and the moment she dreaded.

Her pulse thudded in her ears as the weight of what she was about to do pressed down on her. Moretti wanted blood for his son; the only thing that would save her was the truth.

In the distance, the strip club's neon lights flickered, the woman standing tall, then bent over, up and down until her head spun. Caitlin's hands were clammy and sweat dripped down the middle of her back. God, she didn't want to do this. She wanted to go home.

Caitlin followed the SUV into the strip club lot. Since the last time she was here, one of the overhead lights had started to flicker, casting weird shadows over the few parked cars. Grady parked at the end of the lot, so she drove past him and pulled in next to the entrance. Her heart raced when she spotted her father and Declan standing near the door. Sean's expression was unreadable. Two men stood behind them, arms crossed menacingly.

Caitlin killed the engine. This was a family affair now. She shoved open the door and stepped out. Her father was at her side almost instantly, his arms going around her, hugging her tight. Declan hung back, silent but watchful.

"Are you okay?" Sean asked, looking her up and down.

She nodded. "I'm sorry about all of this, Daddy. It's all my fault."

Her father shook his head. "No, it isn't. You got dragged into something that has nothing to do with you. At least, it shouldn't have anything to do with you. Once again, being my daughter only causes problems."

Caitlin looked up at him. "I love you. And I love being your daughter *and* being part of this family."

Sean raised an eyebrow. "Really?"

Before she could answer, Grady appeared, pushing Chertok in front of him. His hands were still bound, but his ankles were free so he could walk. The bruises on his face stood out sharply under the flickering lights. To her surprise, a defiant gleam flickered in his eyes. Chertok smirked, his split lip bleeding. He wasn't scared—he seemed like he was waiting for something.

"Let's get this over with," Grady said.

Sean tipped his head in Chertok's direction. "He give you any trouble?" He seemed calm, but Caitlin sensed the underlying tension in his voice.

"Nothing I couldn't handle," Grady replied, tightening his grip on the Russian's arm until he winced.

Chertok chuckled, low and bitter. "What a sweet little family reunion. We are only missing Mrs. O'Reilly and the lovely Olivia."

At the mention of his wife's name, Declan stiffened. A menacing scowl marred his handsome face. "Get her name out of your mouth."

Chertok's smile only widened.

Sean glanced at her, then at his son-in-law. "Let's go inside. It's almost midnight. We don't want to keep Moretti waiting."

Declan clenched his fists at his side, spun around, and yanked open the door. He went in, Caitlin right behind him, followed by Grady with Chertok, her father, and his bodyguards bringing up the rear.

Caitlin's jaw ached from clenching it. She kept her eyes on Declan's back, resisting the urge to look over her shoulder at the Russian.

The strip club was mostly empty except for a few people sitting at the bar. A lone woman danced on the stage, her expression blank as she stared off into space and wiggled her hips in time to the music. The door they'd gone through earlier opened, and the same two men ushered them into the back room.

They stepped into the room, once again face to face with Aldo Moretti. He sat at the same table, a glass of amber liquid in his hand, his expression grim. He looked up when they entered, taking in everyone one by one until they finally settled on Chertok. The tension in the air, the sense that something was about to happen, was so thick, so dense, Caitlin tasted it on the tip of her tongue.

Moretti set his glass on the table and wiped his mouth with the back of his hand. "You brought him," he said.

Grady shoved Chertok into a chair across from Moretti. The Russian's lips curled in a sneer, opening his cut and sending blood running down his chin. He didn't move but stayed seated, his bound hands in his lap.

"Just like I said I would," Caitlin said.

"Do you really think he's going to tell me the truth?" the Italian asked.

Her shoulders sagged. She didn't know if Chertok would admit what he'd done. "I had to try," she replied.

"My son is dead. Nothing changes that."

Caitlin's throat tightened. "I know. For that, I am unbelievably sorry. But I told you, I didn't kill him. He did." She pointed at the man in the chair.

The silence in the room was suffocating. Until Chertok laughed—a loud, bitter sound echoing off the walls. "I don't think he cares, Ms. O'Reilly. Moretti wants someone to bleed. Me. You. It doesn't matter."

Moretti's face darkened. He rested his hands flat on the table and glared at Chertok. "Start talking. Before I lose patience with you."

"Why should I tell you anything?" the Russian sneered. "No matter what I do, you are going to kill me. It is better to keep my mouth shut."

The mobster slammed his hand down so hard everyone in the room jumped. "Tell me what happened to my son, or I swear I will remove your limbs, followed by your eyeballs, the tip of your nose, and your fucking dick. Talk."

Chertok leaned back, a twisted grin on his face. "You are bluffing."

Moretti raised a hand and gestured to one of his men. The man walked to the table, yanked a knife from his pocket, grabbed Chertok's bound hands, and placed them on the tabletop. He cut the zip ties, then he held the Russian's wrists against the table.

Caitlin watched in horror as the man pushed the knife against Chertok's pinky finger and began sawing back and forth. When Chertok screamed and tried to jerk his hand away, two more of Moretti's men stepped forward, one of them holding his hand on the table, while his friend held the other behind his back. Lev screamed so loud it made Caitlin's ears ring as Moretti's man removed his finger, chopping, and pulling until it was on the table, a single bloody digit.

Chertok's screams faded into a choked cry. He yanked his wounded hand into his lap, cradling it against his chest. The men holding him moved away.

"Talk," Moretti said.

"Fine!" Chertok cried, tears and snot mixing with the blood on his chin. "You want the truth? I had your son killed and framed Caitlin for the murder."

"Why?" Moretti asked.

"To start a war between your family and the O'Reilly's." He sucked in a shaky breath. His dark eyes were wide in his pale face. "If your families were fighting one another, I could take what I wanted from both of you."

Morett's knuckles whitened as he gripped the table, his jaw clenched in fury. Caitlin exhaled. She couldn't believe Chertok confessed. She had hoped he would, but deep inside, she hadn't believed it would happen.

"Oh, thank God," she whispered. She had to force herself to stay upright when all she wanted to do was sag in relief.

She saw it coming a split second before it happened. Chertok lunged, pushing himself to the left, slamming into the man who cut off his finger. He stumbled back, and the knife slipped from his hand as he fell. Chertok dropped to one knee, snatched the gun from the man's waistband, scrambled to his feet, and aimed it at Caitlin.

Grady moved so fast it took her a second to realize it was him darting across the room. He tackled Chertok to the ground, the two of them landing in a heap at her feet. The gun went off, the sound exploding through the room, deafening, deadly. She dropped to her knees as Grady grunted and Chertok howled in triumph. Her heart lurched in her chest. Declan appeared, pulling Chertok away from them and shoving him against the nearest wall. Chertok's head slammed into the bricks, and he crumpled to the floor, his eyes glazed.

"Stay down," Declan muttered.

Caitlin rushed to Grady's side. His breathing was shallow, and blood soaked his shirt. He looked up at her, grinning weakly.

"You idiot," she whispered. "How bad is it?"

"Bad," he grunted.

She bolted to her feet. "Daddy! Grady needs an ambulance."

Sean stalked across the room and kneeled by his friend. He checked the wound, then he got to his feet. "Aldo, he needs medical attention. Let my people take him to the hospital."

Moretti nodded.

"Thank you." Her father gestured to his men, who hurried to Grady's side. They picked him up and carried him from the room. When Caitlin tried to follow, Sean grabbed her arm, holding her in place.

"Wait," her father said. "Not yet."

She balked and attempted to pull away. Sean's grip on her tightened. He shook his head and mouthed, "No." She folded her hands in front of her and bit her lip. She wanted to be with Grady, to make sure he was going to be okay.

Chertok struggled to sit up. He rubbed his head, his missing finger smearing blood across his forehead.

Moretti gestured to his men. "Take him out of here," he ordered.

Moretti's men dragged the Russian from the room. His blatant defiance had vanished, replaced by fear over the realization that his end had arrived. His eyes were wide as he stared back at Caitlin.

Moretti's gaze fell on her. "You brought him to me, and now I will deal with him."

"Does that mean I'm free to go?" she asked shakily.

Moretti crossed his arms over his chest. "I don't suppose you would reconsider marrying my son, Massimo? It could reestablish peace between our families."

Before she could speak, her father said, "No. Absolutely not."

The Italian shot a dirty look at Sean. "I'd like to hear Caitlin's answer."

Keep the peace.

"I appreciate the offer, Mr. Moretti," she replied humbly. "But I could not marry somebody I don't love. Especially when I'm in love with someone else."

Beside her, Sean sucked in a deep breath, but he didn't speak. Out of the corner of her eye, she saw him clench his fists.

"Your honesty is ... enlightening." Moretti straightened his jacket. "Now, if you'll excuse me, I need to speak with our Russian friend. Sean, will you join me?"

"Yes," her father replied. He turned around, kissed her on the cheek, then he called Declan's name. Her brother-in-law hustled to Sean's side.

"Take Caitlin to her car. Wait out front for me. If I'm not out in thirty minutes, you come back in here and raise a stink."

Declan shook his head. "I don't think this is a good idea. I should stay with you."

"No." Sean made eye contact with Caitlin. "I can handle this. Find out where Grady is so she can go see him. Understood?"

"Daddy?" she whispered.

"Go check on Grady, sweetheart," her father said. "Make sure my friend is doing okay."

"Yes, sir." She hugged him before she followed Declan from the room.

Once they were outside, Declan pulled his phone from his pocket. He hit a button, held it to his ear, and waited.

"Conor? Where'd you guys take him?" Declan listened, nodded, then he disconnected the call. "Conor is texting me the address. I'll send it to you."

"Thank you," Caitlin mumbled. She took the keys out of her pocket to unlock the Mercedes. "Take care of my dad, okay?"

"Trust me, I will. The last thing I need is you and Olivia angry with me." He winked, then checked his phone. "I got the name of the hospital. I'll forward it to you. Promise me you'll be careful."

She nodded. "I promise. I just want to see Grady, make sure he is all right."

"I know." Declan tucked his phone in his suit jacket. "Let me know if you need anything. My friend Conor will stay with you and drive you back to the Ritz."

She was only half-listening, her mind already on Grady. She gave Declan a quick hug before she got in the car. She wouldn't feel right until she was with Grady.

Chapter 26
Grady

Grady couldn't remember how he ended up on the floor with blood seeping from his side, with the sharp sting of pain radiating through him. It was immediate, excruciating, and intense. He remembered seeing Chertok turn toward Caitlin, the overhead lights reflecting off the gun in his hand. Everything after that was a blur of burning heat and darkness.

The next thing he knew, he was being lifted. Sean's voice was nearby, giving orders, though he couldn't make out the words. The room spun, the floor tilted at a crazy angle, and the pain sharpened deep in his side. He clenched his teeth, but it didn't help.

"Caitlin," he mumbled.

"She's okay." The voice belonged to Declan's friend and *leascheannasaí*, Conor.

Grady glimpsed Calvin, a young recruit who worked for Declan, walking on the other side of Conor. He was green to the world of mobsters and getting a crash course in the lifestyle.

"Let's put him in the car," Conor grunted. "Grab towels from the bartender. We need to put pressure on the wound."

When Calvin released Grady, he slumped against Conor. He dragged Grady out the front door of the strip club to the car and lowered him into the back seat.

He groaned, every movement sending white-hot pain shooting through his body. The darkness relentlessly pursued him, even though he tried to focus and keep his eyes open.

The car door slammed, then a few seconds later, it jolted forward, his head rolling on his neck as they moved. Something ripped in his chest, fresh blood oozing from his wound. Conor cursed under his breath and pressed the towels against his side. Grady attempted to breathe, each lungful a struggle and insanely painful. Black dots filled his vision before he slipped into silence.

He woke to the sterile smell of antiseptic and the steady beep of a heart monitor. The white light above his head was harsh, too bright, making him squint. Everything around him—walls, floor, linens on the bed—was stark white. His throat ached as if he'd swallowed gravel, and his mouth was dry. He tried to move, but his body was heavy, like an anchor sat on his chest. The pain was gone, replaced by a floating, serene feeling.

It took a minute for his memory to come back and everything to click into place—the trip to the strip club, Chertok going after Caitlin, the bullet slamming into him. He groaned and pressed his hand to his bandaged side.

"Grady?"

He turned his head slowly to find Conor sitting in a chair by the bed, deep circles under his eyes. Calvin stood in the corner with his arms crossed and a grim expression.

"You're awake," Conor said.

"What ... what happened?" he asked. His voice was weak and raspy.

Calvin pushed himself away from the wall. "Chertok shot you. You're lucky it wasn't worse than it was."

Grady grimaced and shifted on the bed. "How bad is it?"

Conor chuckled. "You'll live. The doctor said the bullet missed your lung by millimeters. If it had been a little higher, you wouldn't be talking to me right now. As it is, you might be sore for a while, but it shouldn't be long before you're back on your feet."

"What did you tell the doc?" he asked. "About what happened?" He cleared his throat.

Conor got up, poured water in the small plastic cup, and handed it to Grady, who drank it with shaking hands.

"I told him you were mugged," Conor explained. "I pulled your wallet and cash, made sure you didn't have any weapons on you before we brought you in. They bought it with no arguments. We gave the cops a statement, invented an assailant, gave them a shitty description. I don't think they'll look too hard for anybody."

Grady nodded, the movement sending a wave of dizziness through him. "How long have I been out?"

"Almost twelve hours. Including the surgery," Conor said. "The doctor wants to keep you for a couple of days, make sure you don't have a concussion, and the bullet didn't nick the lung. It was too close for his liking."

"What about Caitlin?" Grady asked in a tight voice.

Conor glanced at Calvin, who tipped his head in a slight nod before he left the room.

"She's fine," Conor said. "Walked out of Fred's unscathed. She wants to see you."

"Where is she?"

"Downstairs. Calvin went to get her," Conor explained. "She'll be here soon."

He nodded, too tired to respond. The exhaustion pulled at him, dragging him back into unconsciousness. He closed his eyes and dozed.

When Grady woke up again, the room was dimmer; the lights had been turned down, and the beeping heart monitor was quieter. He blinked a few times, adjusting to the light. Then he saw her.

Caitlin sat in a chair beside the bed in a too-large sweatshirt with her legs drawn up, her eyes locked on him. He shifted uncomfortably under her scrutiny.

"Hey," he croaked.

Her lips twitched, and she managed a small, relieved smile. "Hey, yourself."

She reached for his hand. Grady squeezed her fingers.

"You know, that was stupid, what you did." Her grip tightened, and a single tear slipped down her cheek. "You scared me."

"I didn't mean to, but I couldn't let him hurt you."

"You cannot do that again," she muttered.

Grady snorted. He hated that she worried, but they both knew the life he lived. As much as he wanted to tell her he wouldn't, there was no way he could make that promise.

"You can't ask me not to protect you," he whispered. "That's not even an option."

Caitlin rolled her eyes. "You're so damn stubborn."

"Not a secret," he retorted.

She leaned forward and propped her elbows on the bed. "The doctors said you were lucky."

He nodded. "I heard."

"They also said you'll have to take it easy for a while." She raised one eyebrow, challenging him to disagree with her.

"That's not really my thing."

"Well, it is now. Doctor's orders."

He sighed, closed his eyes, and let his head sink into the pillow. He was too tired to argue with her. "Fine, but once I'm out of here, it's business as usual."

"Back to work for my dad?" she asked.

"Yes," he replied, drawing out the word.

Caitlin nodded, but her lips were pursed, and she wouldn't meet his eyes.

"Hey?" He grabbed her upper arm, despite the ache radiating from his side—the damn pain meds must have worn off—and tried to drag her closer. She got out of the chair and perched on the edge of the bed beside him.

"This is my life, Cait," he said. "This is who I am. It's not the first time I've been shot. It probably won't be the last. Nothing will change. Once I'm healed, I'll get up and keep going. It's who I am."

Caitlin sighed. "I know, but I don't have to like it."

"No, you don't." He cleared his throat. "Tell me what happened after I left."

She told him everything, including how Moretti asked her to reconsider marrying his son. Grady's eyes widened, and his hand clamped down on her wrist.

"I said no," she said.

"Hmm," Grady grunted.

"Do you know why?"

He raised an eyebrow and shook his head.

"Because I'm in love with another man," she whispered. "A stubborn, grumpy, older man who I can never be with because he works for my father *and* he's my father's best friend. It's a big, complicated mess."

"Big mess," he muttered. God, he hoped that the pain in his chest was from his bullet wound and not something else. He didn't want to think about the alternative.

"What are we going to do about it?"

Grady closed his eyes. He couldn't look at her. "Nothing."

She tensed, her shoulders straightening. "What do you mean, nothing?"

"We won't do anything about it, Cait. We're from different worlds—"

"We're from the *same* world," she snapped.

He sighed and shook his head. "You don't want to be with me, and you know it. Not only am I older than you, but I'm stubborn. I'm a fucking asshole. I live a hard life. A life I'm not willing to give up. You're on the fringe, and it should stay that way."

"You son of a bitch." She jumped to her feet and backed away from him. "After everything we've gone through, after the shit we endured."

"You know as well as I do this can't happen. Whether or not you believe it, we *are* from different worlds."

"Bull. Shit." She clenched her fists and glared at him. "That isn't true. The problem is, nobody trusted me to be part of our world until I was thrust into it, kicking and screaming. Things have changed. I'm not naïve little Caitlin anymore. Shit, I *never* was."

Grady tried to sit up, but intense pain washed over him. He grunted and fell back against the bed. "I don't think you're naïve. I never have. And yes, I realize things have changed."

"Then why don't you—"

"*But* not everything has changed. I'm still twenty-one years older than you and you're *still* my boss's daughter. Those are two obstacles I don't think we can overcome."

Caitlin bit her lip and stared at the ceiling. "Jesus Christ." When she looked back at him, he saw fresh tears on her cheeks. "Do you love me?"

"That doesn't matter."

"It matters to me!" she shouted. "Answer the question. Do you love me?"

"I care about you. A lot."

"That is not an answer, you … you fucking asshole!" She crossed her arms over her chest. "Are you really going to do this? Push me away, pretend you don't love me because of my *father*?"

Grady raised his voice. "Jesus Christ! Why can't you understand this will not work? Our lives are too different." He winced as a sharp pain barreled through him.

The door to his room burst open, and a nurse stepped in. "Is everything alright in here?"

Caitlin snatched her backpack off the floor. "Yeah, everything is great." She shoved past the nurse, bumping into her hard enough to push her against the door jamb. She paused, looked back at him, shook her head, and walked away.

Two days later, the doctor released him from the hospital, even though Grady was covered in bruises from not only the events at the strip club but those at Chertok's house. His side ached with every step, the medication made him nauseous, and he was dizzy. He'd never been much for pills; liquor was his preferred painkiller. As soon as he got home, he planned on drinking an entire bottle of scotch.

Conor picked him up. For a split second, he wondered if it would be Caitlin. Not that she'd want to see him after what happened. He doubted she'd ever want to see him again. He bit his tongue to keep from asking where she was.

All the way to the airport, Conor cracked jokes, giving Grady a hard time, asking him if he'd gone soft after being cooped up in a hospital bed for two days. He took it in stride, though every laugh pulled at the stitches in his side.

The O'Reilly's private jet sat on the tarmac, waiting to take him home. He couldn't wait to crawl into his own bed and sleep for a week.

Sean and Declan were waiting for him when he walked through the plane's open door. His boss pulled him into a tight bear hug, holding him until Grady grunted in pain.

"Sorry," Sean mumbled. He took a step back as he looked Grady up and down. "How are you?"

"Still standing," he replied.

"Thank God." Sean sat down and gestured for him to do the same.

"You look like hell," Declan interjected as Grady eased into an open seat.

"Feel like it, too," he said.

Sean poured four glasses of Glen Livet scotch and passed them around. "You know, that's two members of the O'Reilly family you've saved. I owe you a debt."

Grady shook his head. "It's been repaid a thousand times over."

"No. This was … above and beyond the call of duty. Not only did you keep my daughter safe from harm, but you took a bullet for her. I don't know how to thank you for what you did. For Caitlin. It's not something I'm going to forget."

"I didn't do it for you," Grady murmured. "I did it for her."

"I know," his boss replied.

Grady stiffened, and his gaze locked with Sean's. This could go so many ways—Sean could kill him, banish him from the family, demote him, or a million other things. He had no way of knowing how the man would react to the knowledge that his best friend had sex with his daughter.

"And?"

Sean downed the liquor in his glass. His expression didn't change, but there was a flicker of something in his eyes that Grady couldn't make out. "We'll discuss it later."

After nearly a minute of the two men staring at each other, Declan cleared his throat, breaking the awkward silence stretching out between them. "How long are you going to be down?" he asked.

"As long as he needs," Sean said.

"There's still work to do," Declan continued. "Chertok is gone, but the fallout from what he did will be around for a while. The Bratva is watching and waiting to see how this plays out."

"Speaking of the Bratva," Grady interjected. "I had to, uh, make certain promises to Dmitry Sokolov so he would tell us where Chertok was."

Sean's fists clenched. "What promises?"

"One that is yet to be determined," he explained. "I don't know what he wants, but I'm sure it won't be good."

"Shit," Declan muttered.

His boss rubbed the center of his forehead. "We'll deal with it when it happens. For now, I'm just grateful Caitlin is safe."

Grady had another question. "What about Angus? Have we dealt with that situation yet?"

Sean smiled. "I thought you might want to take care of him."

"God, yes." Grady chuckled. "Can I take care of it like *I* want to?"

Sean leaned forward. "As long as you make that little shit suffer, yes, you can do whatever the hell you want."

"Good." He shifted uneasily in his seat. The pain had escalated from a slight annoyance to a deep ache in his side. "By the way, where is Caitlin?"

"At home," Sean replied. "She needs time to recover after everything she's been through. So do you. Everything else can wait until you are back on your feet. Including Angus Hayes."

The pilot came on and asked everyone to fasten their seatbelts. Grady rested his head against the back of the seat and closed his eyes as the plane lifted into the air.

Almost home.

He couldn't wait.

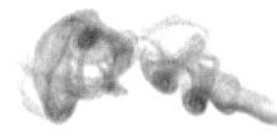

When they rose from their seats to disembark, Sean grabbed Grady's arm, leaned close, and whispered, "You're riding with me."

Grady nodded and mumbled, "Sure, boss."

It wasn't until they were in Sean's limo, seated across from each other, that Grady's nerves got the best of him. His hands shook, and his heart thumped wildly in his chest. This man was his best friend, had been since they were kids. Their lives were inexplicably intertwined, in ways most people couldn't fathom.

"Tell me about your relationship with my daughter."

Grady sighed. "Are you sure you want to hear this?"

Sean scowled. "I wouldn't ask if I didn't."

"Okay." He cleared his throat and picked at the seam of his jeans. He couldn't look his friend in the eye. "I, uh, well … I slept with her."

Sean was silent, his only reaction a tightening of his fists.

"I don't know how it happened," Grady continued. "One minute she's fucking annoying the shit out of me, the next I can't keep my hands off her." He snapped his mouth shut. Not what Sean wanted to hear. He tried again.

"Caitlin drives me out of my fucking mind, but that's part of her appeal. She challenges me, makes me rethink everything about myself. She … when I'm with her, I can believe I'm not the bad guy I always thought I was."

Sean sighed. "You are not a bad guy."

Grady snorted. "You don't know what I am."

Sean tapped his fingers on his legs. "Tell me about Oona."

"What?"

His friend glared at him. "You heard me. Oona. Your former girlfriend. I want the truth."

"I don't know what you're—"

"Yes, you do. And it's time you got it off your chest."

Grady exhaled, staring at the ceiling for almost a minute before he spoke. "Oona helped put the bomb in the cafe."

Sean was silent, waiting for him to continue.

"She … she was a set-up. A plant."

"The Muldoons?" Sean asked.

Grady nodded. "Oona got comfy with me so she could learn your patterns, schedule, shit like that. Donovan

Muldoon wanted to take you out, and he used her to do it. She told him we were supposed to be at the cafe that day. They planted the bomb. When she went to the bathroom, she called and gave them the go-ahead to detonate it." He swallowed. "When it didn't kill you, her job was to shoot you. I got in the way."

Sean's hands fisted in his lap. "What did Dante have to do with the bombing?"

"Nothing. He took the blame when he didn't have to because I let Oona run."

"Dante's a good friend," Sean said.

"Yeah, he is." He cleared his throat. "Two years after the attack at Foley's, Oona showed up on my doorstep. She told me she still loved me, and she wanted us to disappear together."

"Obviously, you didn't."

Grady shrugged. "Obviously."

Sean shifted in his seat and straightened his pant leg. "What happened?"

He shrugged. "She's gone and she won't come around again. Do you understand what I'm trying to say?"

"I do." Sean cleared his throat. "Does Caitlin know about Oona?"

"No."

His boss looked out the car window and rubbed his chin. Grady knew that look. The contemplation, the concentration, all of it. He braced himself.

"I don't like it," Sean sneered, his voice low, menacing. "She's twenty-one years younger than you."

"I know. That's one reason I ended things with her."

"What?"

"I told her it won't work," Grady continued.

Sean raised an eyebrow. "How did she take it?"

"How do you *think* she took it?"

"If I know my daughter, she was pissed. And she made sure you knew it."

"Yeah." He nodded. "Yeah, she did."

Sean chuckled low in the back of his throat. "That's my girl."

Grady laughed, too. "She is definitely your daughter. Tough as fucking nails. She's strong, resilient, intelligent. One in a million."

His boss leaned forward, his elbows on his knees. "You care about her, don't you?"

"Do you really want me to answer that?" he asked.

Sean grinned. "Yeah, I do."

He took a deep breath. "I could fall in love with her. She … she makes me whole. It's been a long time since somebody made getting out of bed in the morning worthwhile." Grady closed his eyes and pinched the bridge of his nose. "You know what? It doesn't matter. I'll be fine."

"Grady?"

He glowered at his friend. "I said I'll be fine."

Sean put his hands up and shrugged. "Okay, okay. But if you want to talk, I'm here."

A loud guffaw burst out of him. "Yeah, that's not gonna happen. Ever."

Chapter 27
Caitlin

As she stepped through the imposing double doors into the foyer, the familiar scent of leather and polished wood surrounded her, a smell that always reminded her of home. Understated luxury was the only way to describe this part of her family home. Deep chestnut floors buffed to a rich, glossy finish reflected the warm glow of the massive crystal chandelier hanging from the vaulted ceiling. To her left was what her mother referred to as the library, a formal space hosting a pair of oversized black leather armchairs and a solid mahogany table. On it was a brass lamp with an elaborately designed base and volumes of books lined the bookshelves in the room. None of them were meant to be read; they were aesthetically pleasing.

Framed family photos and artwork selected by her mother hung at carefully chosen intervals, so it was visually appealing. Along the walls on either side of the foyer, benches upholstered in dark leather offered a space to sit, though Caitlin had never seen anyone use them.

She stopped at the bottom of the grand staircase. Her eyes danced over the banister carved from darkish wood up the wide steps covered in a plush carpet in a deep shade of maroon. It wasn't the same, not like it had been when she was an innocent girl, unaware of what her father did for a living or what the "family business" really was. Back then, she didn't know how they got their money. Oh, to be that innocent again.

In one short week, her life had been cracked open and completely rearranged. She wasn't sure if she could put it back together or if she even wanted it the way it had been.

Everything she'd endured with Moretti and Chertok hung over her like a dark storm cloud. The relief she should have felt at having her name cleared was muted by all that happened. Bobby was dead. Lev Chertok was most likely dead. The tenuous hold the Moretti and O'Reilly families had on the peace they'd fought for was fractured. Chertok's trail of destruction had left a mess that would take months—maybe years—to clean up. Enemies of both families circled like vultures, waiting for any sign of weakness.

Caitlin brushed her fingers along the banister, rubbing the grain of wood under her fingertips. After fighting for so long to get out of her father's house, she was back under his roof. But not as the woman she'd once been, but someone hardened by betrayal and loss. She sat on the bottom step with her head in her hands, the weight of her choices sitting heavy on her chest.

"Caitlin?" Her father's voice pulled her out of her thoughts.

Sean O'Reilly stood in front of the double doors. His piercing blue eyes, the same ones she'd inherited, were softer than usual, laced with concern. He rarely showed his emotions, keeping a tight rein on them. He'd obviously been shaken by what happened to her.

"Hi, Daddy. How was your meeting?"

"It was okay," he replied. He crossed the space between them in a few brief steps and sat next to her on the step. He bumped his shoulder against hers. "How are you doing?"

"I'm fine." The words were hollow. She wasn't, and they both knew it.

Her father put his arm around her, hugged her close. "You don't have to pretend with me. What you went through—no one should have to go through that."

Caitlin forced a smile. "I'll get over it. That's what's important, right?"

He studied her for a minute, his expression unreadable. "I don't think it is, do you?"

She shrugged. "I guess. I don't know."

"You survived something awful. I don't expect you to get over it. In fact, take as much time as you need. This is your home. Your mother and I want you here. We want to help you."

Caitlin swallowed back the sob threatening to escape her throat. She nodded and rested her head on her father's shoulder.

"Thank you," she whispered hoarsely.

They sat in comfortable silence for a few minutes until Sean cleared his throat.

"So, have you thought about what comes next, what you want to do now?" he asked.

"I *have* considered that," she replied. She glanced up at her father, who watched her intently and waited. His silence encouraged her to continue.

"I'm going to finish law school."

Sean smiled. "Good."

Caitlin sat up straight and looked her father in the eye. "But I'm not going into environmental law anymore.

I plan to study criminal law. After I graduate, I want to join the family business."

There it was. The truth laid bare between them.

Sean's eyebrow arched, surprise flickering across his face. "You're serious?"

"I've never been more serious about anything in my life," she replied. "I always thought I could stay out of it, that I could somehow live in two worlds—one foot in the family and one in the outside world. But after everything that's happened, I can't pretend that's the case anymore. I belong here with my family."

Sean's lips pursed into a thin line. Caitlin thought he'd fight her or insist she finish what she started. But to her surprise, he nodded slowly, a grin spreading across his face.

"I can't believe it. I always hoped one of my daughters would follow in my footsteps, maybe even take over for me someday. I'm not surprised it's you. You're strong-willed, determined, and you've got a good head on your shoulders."

"Think so?" she whispered.

"You've been through hell, sweetheart, but you came out stronger. I won't lie to you. This won't be easy. This life, it comes with a price, which you saw firsthand. But if this is what you want, I'll support you and help anyway I can."

Caitlin nodded, her resolve hardening. It was her choice to commit to this way of life and come hell or high water, she planned to own it.

"There's something else," she said, her voice barely above a whisper. "Something you need to know."

Her father's eyes narrowed slightly, as if he sensed the shift in her tone. "What?"

"Grady."

Sean didn't move, though his shoulders stiffened enough for Caitlin to notice.

"We, I mean he and I, we uh, kind of had a thing…" She peeked at her father out of the corner of her eye. She couldn't tell what he was thinking. Sean O'Reilly had perfected the stoic expression, making his face unreadable. Her heart pounded in her chest as she waited for his reaction.

"I know," he said. "I spoke to Grady."

"He told you?" she asked.

"He did. I mean, he didn't go into detail—"

"Thank God," she muttered.

Sean chuckled. "I agree. Thank God. But we talked. He also said he broke things off with you. Is that true?"

"Yes," she murmured.

"How do you feel about that?"

Caitlin squared her shoulders and turned to her father. No sense lying to him. If they were going to work together, they needed honesty between them. "I don't like it. I think … well, I'm pretty sure I'm falling in love with him."

"Does he love you?" her father asked quietly.

"I thought he did." She sighed. "But all he'll say is he cares for me. He won't say the words."

Sean rested his elbows on his upper thighs and took a deep breath. "Have you ever heard the name Oona?"

Caitlin shook her head. "No. Who is that?"

"She was Grady's fiancée."

Caitlin's stomach dropped, and her jaw clenched. Grady had been engaged. Had he ever been married? Divorced? Why hadn't he told her?

"I… He was engaged?"

"It didn't last," Sean explained. "It was only for a short time. I'd never seen him like that. He was head over heels for this woman."

She shifted on the step, suddenly uncomfortable. "What happened?"

"She betrayed him. Us." Her father rubbed the back of his neck. "The Foley cafe thing; it was because of her." He swallowed. "Oona told them I would be there and when the bomb didn't kill me, she was going to shoot me. Grady jumped in front of the bullet. Oona vanished." He took Caitlin's hand. "That … it destroyed him. For the first time in his life, he allowed someone to get close, and she deceived him. He swore he'd never let it happen again."

By the time her father finished speaking, Caitlin had her hand over her mouth and a knot in her stomach. "I had no idea," she whispered.

"Few people do," Sean continued. "He doesn't talk about it. Hell, I just got him to tell me." He got to his feet, pacing back and forth in front of her. "I won't lie to you, Cait. The idea of you and Grady together? I hate it. But it's not for me to decide who somebody loves. Especially after what happened to Liv."

"What are you saying?"

"I'm saying I won't put my foot down or be a hard ass. He feels *something* for you. I can tell by the way he looks at you, talks about you, all of it. And you said you love him. Nothing I say will change your mind or keep you away from him if you two are determined to be together." He walked halfway done the hall, stopped, and turned around. "You have always been stubborn. I respect that. If this is the path you choose, you need to understand that it won't be easy."

"I know," Caitlin replied.

"It could turn your entire world upside down."

"My world has already been turned upside down," she retorted. "Grady grounds me. He keeps me sane."

Sean crossed his arms over his chest and stared at the ceiling. "You'll have to give me time to get used to the idea."

"Do you hate me?" she asked.

Her father hurried back down the hall and crouched in front of her. "Jesus Christ, Caitlin, how could you think that? You're my daughter. I love you. Am I happy that you're sleeping with a man old enough to be your father? No. But if there is anybody in this world who will do right by you and protect you, it's Grady. But you need to understand something. It's been a long, long time since he cared for somebody. I remember how he was when he was in love with Oona. She was his universe. That man loves fiercely, so intently it is almost frightening. It's going to be different from anything you've ever experienced. I hope you're ready for it."

"I am," she murmured. "I'm ready for whatever the future holds for us."

Later that night, Caitlin pulled into the driveway of a modest home on a quiet, tree-lined street in Waltham. She put the car in park and turned it off, but she didn't get out. She stayed where she was, staring at the front of the house, unable to believe this place belonged to Grady.

It was a classic New England-style colonial, crisp white with blue trim. A welcoming porch stretched from one end of the house to the other. On one side was a swing, painted the same color as the house, along with two wicker chairs and a table. The yard was small, but well-kept, with a neatly trimmed lawn and a brick walkway that led to the door. Tall, leafy trees blocked anyone from seeing the house from the street, and a wooden fence deterred visitors. At the top of the driveway sat a detached garage. The door was open and pulled halfway out was a gray Mustang that looked like the one from the movie *Gone in Sixty Seconds.* Its hood was up, and the driver's side door was open.

Grady stepped out of the Mustang, wiping his hands on a rag. Her breath caught in her throat. Only he could pull off looking as if he'd sauntered off the cover of *GQ Magazine* in jeans and a too tight T-shirt with a streak of oil across the chest. He watched her as she got out of the car.

"How did you find me?" he asked.

"Daddy gave me the address." Caitlin shut the door and inched forward a few steps, stopping by the hood.

Grady raised an eyebrow. "Is nothing sacred in your family?"

"In my experience, no." She crossed her arms over her chest and leaned against the car. "How are you?"

"Still sore. Stiff. But I'm healing. I'll get there." He tucked the rag into his back pocket. "What are you doing here?"

"I wanted to see you. Talk to you." Caitlin followed him as he walked up the driveway to the Mustang.

"We said everything we had to say at the hospital," he mumbled. "Or did you want to yell at me some more?" He slammed the hood shut before he turned to look at her.

She rolled her eyes, and his shoulders stiffened, but he didn't speak. She moved closer to him.

"I wanted to see you," she murmured.

An awkward silence spread between them. God, she wanted to throw herself into his arms, kiss him, touch him, feel the hard length of his body against hers. She wanted to make love until the sun came up. Except first, they had to get past the bullshit.

"That's not a good idea," he said. "Your father—"

Caitlin shook her head. "My father isn't part of the equation. This is between us."

Grady laughed. "Princess, your father and your family are always part of any equation, especially with us."

"He told me about Oona," she said.

His eyes widened. "He did what?"

"Daddy told me about Oona," she repeated. "How you loved her, and she betrayed you."

He sighed. "He had no right to do that."

"Daddy meant no harm. He was trying to help me understand."

He snorted. "Nobody understands. There is no way anyone can fathom what it is like to love someone with every fiber of your being, and they betray you. Oona took what I gave her and threw it back in my face."

Caitlin moved closer. "I'm so sorry."

"Great, thanks for the sympathy." He crossed his arms over his chest. "You should go."

"Don't push me away, Grady," she whispered.

"We resolved this at the hospital."

She stopped moving toward him and crossed her arms over her chest, mirroring his stance. "No, we didn't resolve anything. We argued. I yelled, and you yelled, which is what we always do."

"So, why are you here? To continue the argument? Because if you are, you might as well leave now. I won't change my mind."

"I don't want to argue with you," Caitlin mumbled, defeated. "That's not why I came. I hoped we could talk."

Grady dropped his hands to his side and sighed heavily. "Let's go inside. I'll make coffee." He pushed the Mustang's door shut, then he tipped his head toward the house. "Come on."

She followed him across the yard through the back door into a tidy, unadorned kitchen. Dark granite countertops and smooth white cabinets contrasted nicely with stainless steel appliances. Everything was so neatly organized it looked like it was barely used on a day-to-day basis. A single bowl was upside down in a rack next to the deep sink. The hardwood floors were spotless, and under-cabinet lights cast a soft glow over the counters. In the corner was a small, round table with two chairs. A newspaper was folded on top of a placemat.

Caitlin bit her tongue so she wouldn't laugh. It didn't surprise her that Grady still got the newspaper instead of going online to read it.

"Have a seat." He pointed at the table, then he took a can of coffee out of the cabinet.

She watched him as he made the coffee. He was quick, efficient, and neat, cleaning up after himself as he worked. They were silent until he'd finished and set her cup in front of her. He eased into the other chair and pushed the newspaper out of the way.

Caitlin sipped her coffee. "I talked to my father. About us."

"I gathered as much since he talked to you about Oona. What did you tell him?"

"That I'm falling in love with you." She traced the rim of her cup, looking anywhere but at him. "But I couldn't tell him how you feel."

Grady sighed. "Cait."

"Don't you want to know what he said?"

He raised an eyebrow. "Does it involve me losing my life?"

She laughed. "No. In fact, Daddy was quite accommodating. He probably won't try to kill you." She grabbed his hand and held it tight. "If my father being against us had been holding you back, you don't have to worry. He won't fight it."

"What about the age difference?" Grady asked.

Her shoulders slumped; it was always something. "What about it?"

"Twenty-one years, princess. I'm past my prime. You need somebody who can keep up with you, give you the life you deserve for as long as you're alive. Why would you want a guy who's going to get old before you, die before you? Nobody wants that."

"I don't care," she whispered. "I love you. I want to be with you. The age difference doesn't bother me."

"Caitlin—"

She slammed her hand on the table. "I'm not done. Age is a number. All it means is you've lived longer than me and seen more things. But it also shows you know what matters. You can't be bothered by the stupid games that guys my age usually play. You don't have time for shit like that. The years between us aren't important. What is important is that you understand I want to spend the time we have left together. I'm begging you not to push me away because some woman broke your heart. I'm not her. Give me a chance to prove it."

Grady stared at her without speaking. It went on so long she fidgeted in her seat. He looked at their clasped hands, then back up at her. "Come here," he murmured, tugging on her hand.

Caitlin got to her feet and let him pull her into his lap. He grunted when she bumped into his side where the bandage was. She wrapped her arms around his neck and rested her head on his shoulder.

"You're damn stubborn, you know that, right?" she asked.

"Always have been, probably always will be. It's what keeps me alive." He kissed her temple. "I'm sorry. You're right, by the way. I pushed you away because of what happened with Oona. I have spent the last eight years of my life regretting every minute of my time with her. She destroyed me. I swore I would never go through that again. That's why I fought so hard to keep myself from falling for you. It didn't work."

She looked up at him. "So, you love me?"

"Yeah, princess, I love you."

Chapter 28
Caitlin

Caitlin walked across the foyer into the library, a room she rarely, if ever, entered. The big house was silent around her, lulling her into an odd sense of calm. She turned on the brass lamp, casting a yellow glow over the dark room. She glanced at the clock beside the lamp, surprised to see it was almost midnight.

Through the window facing the back of the house, she could see the pool. As she crossed the room to look outside, she noticed steam rising off the water—it was heated—and the moon reflecting off the still surface. It was always weird looking at it through the frosted glass, knowing it was near or below freezing, but it was in the mid-seventies. A chill raced through her, so she pulled her cardigan tight around herself before she sat in one of the overstuffed leather chairs, wishing she'd changed out of her dress when she got home. She exhaled and rested her head against the thick headrest of the chair.

Caitlin had the mansion to herself, for the first time in six months. Her father was on his way to New York with Declan while her mother had gone to stay with Olivia and Caitlin's newborn nephew. She was alone.

The last six months had been insane, a whirlwind of activity that exhausted her. Instead of returning to NYU, she had transferred to a school in Boston. It was an adjustment learning to live at home again, especially after living away for so long. Fortunately, school kept her busy—classes, homework, lectures, plus an internship three days a week at a top law firm in Boston, not to mention the time she spent with Grady—making her time in the family's mansion limited.

They had gone all in on the relationship shit, and they were doing everything they could to make it work. While she hadn't moved in with him, not yet anyway, Caitlin tried to spend a couple of nights a week at his place in Waltham. She'd do homework while he read a book or watched TV. It was unnervingly domestic.

She had also gotten used to having security following her around when she was away from home. After the events in New York, her father insisted she have at least two armed guards and a driver. Caitlin hated the idea of being watched all the time, but things had changed. She had to change with them. Especially now that she was joining the family business.

"The family business," she muttered out loud. "Face it, Caitlin. You're a mobster's daughter."

"You're just realizing that?" a voice asked from the foyer.

Startled, she jumped to her feet as Grady stepped into the light cast by the lamp.

"Hi," he said.

Caitlin smiled at him. "Hi. What are you doing here?"

"I heard a rumor you were home alone."

"Oh? Where did you hear that?"

"Declan," he replied. "I took them to the airport, along with ten of your father's best men."

"I thought you were going?" she asked.

Grady chuckled and shook his head. "Moretti doesn't care for me. He requested that *I* not be there. Besides, Conor and I had something we had to take care of tonight."

She smiled. "Okay, why wasn't I invited? Moretti seems to like me."

"Because you haven't started your official duties with the family yet."

Caitlin laughed. "I don't even know what my official duties are. I think Daddy is going to figure it out once I finish law school."

Grady sat on the other leather chair next to hers. "He might figure it out sooner. Your father is good at keeping his emotions in check, but he's excited that you want to learn the ropes."

"How do you feel about it?"

He shrugged. "I'm not sure yet. I guess we'll see." He pushed a hand through his hair. "I worry about you. I want to protect you, but being in the business makes it harder."

Caitlin sighed. "We've talked about this."

"I know," Grady replied. "That doesn't mean I have to like it." His eyes darted around the room before settling back on her. "I haven't been in here in ages. Your father doesn't use it much; he says it's stuffy and reminds him of *his* father."

She nodded as a memory came to her. "Grandpa called it his receiving room. He used to put people he didn't like in here to make them wait for him. Sometimes for hours. I got stuck hiding under that highboy when I was a little girl. Liv and I were playing. I hid in here. Somebody visited Grandpa, and they had to wait in here. We were forbidden to be downstairs when he did business. I couldn't get out, and Liv couldn't come in. I'm not sure how long I was in here before I escaped." She laughed. "I forgot about that. It must be why I don't like this room."

"Fear of getting stuck?"

She nodded. "My grandfather was a formidable man. He scared me."

Grady snorted. "I was terrified of him, even after I came to work for him. That man intimidated people."

Caitlin laughed again. "So, you learned everything you know from him?"

"Possibly."

After a few minutes of comfortable silence, she got up from her chair, kneeled on the floor between his legs, and rested her hands on his thighs. "So, we have the whole place to ourselves."

"Isn't your mother here?" He smirked at her.

She took his hands, noting the knuckles on his right hand were bruised and bloody. She brushed her lips across them, then shook her head. "No, she's with Olivia, helping with the baby."

"Hmm," he hummed. "Is that so?"

Caitlin placed his hand on her chest. She stared up at him, her hand on his wrist, as he slid it up her neck and around her throat. He leaned over and kissed her. When they broke apart, he kept his hand on her throat and rested his forehead against hers.

"What are we going to do about it?" he asked.

"Tell me what you want," she whispered.

Grady released her, and she sat back on the floor. He got to his feet, stripped off his jacket, strode across the room, and shut the sliding doors before he returned to the overstuffed leather chair.

"Stand up," he ordered.

Caitlin did as she was told. She took off her cardigan and slid her hands to her hips. She pulled up her dress, but Grady reached up and grabbed her hand.

"Leave it on."

She nodded, unable to disobey him. He tugged her forward until she was in his lap, her knees on either side of him, her dress pushed up to the middle of her thighs. He took her hands and placed them on the arms of the chair.

"Keep your hands right there," he said. "Do not move them unless I tell you."

"Whatever you want," she whispered.

Grady gripped her waist, holding her in place as he leaned forward and caught her bottom lip between his teeth, nipping it lightly. He unbuttoned each of the delicate pearl buttons on the front of her dress until the peach-colored bra covering her breasts was exposed. He yanked the cups down and fondled her, his thumbs circling the nipples. He kissed a line along her jaw to her ear, biting at the lobe.

A loud groan escaped her. Grady pulled back and looked at her, one eyebrow raised.

"I want you to be quiet," he murmured. "You are not to make a sound. Do you understand me?"

Holy shit, he loved to torture her. This was his favorite game, asking her to be quiet while he did things to her that made her want to scream his name.

Caitlin nodded. She closed her eyes as his hand slid under her dress and between her legs. His sinful lips kissed a hot, wet trail from her neck to her breast while his fingers drifted over the bare skin of her thighs, his touch arousing her instantly.

"No underwear?" he asked.

She shook her head.

"I love how you're always ready for me, always anticipating what I want from you." His finger slipped between the lips of her pussy, and he smiled against her neck. "I feel how much you want me, how wet you are for me." A second finger joined the first, caressing her, his thumb brushing her clit, making it pulse with need as he teased her.

Caitlin whimpered, the sound echoing through the room. Grady stopped, his hand still between her legs, not moving, but oh God, it was there and if he wanted to, he could make her cum in only a matter of seconds with those two fingers and his thumb. His eyes were dark and hooded as he stared at her. One hand moved up her back and into her hair, holding her head in place, forcing her to look at him.

"I told you to be quiet. Didn't I?"

She gasped as his fingers twitched. "Y-yes."

He barely touched her, but that didn't matter because heat exploded through her and she wanted to move, wanted to grind herself against his hand until those fingers of his were deep inside her, fucking her senseless. Her hips moved on their own, flexing toward him.

Somehow, he knew what she was thinking, because the grin on his face grew wider as he looked at her. He smirked. "Do it."

Caitlin didn't have to be told twice. Her hips shot forward, seeking the friction she desperately desired. Grady cupped her, the palm of his hand pressed against her clit, his fingers thrusting deep inside her, twisting to graze against her sweet spot. She gasped, pleasure overwhelming her as she rutted against him, writhing in his lap, her knuckles white as she gripped the arms of the chair.

With his other hand, he held the back of her head so he could suck and bite at her neck, marking her with deep, purple bruises she wouldn't be able to hide. Not that she wanted to. She gnawed on her lower lip, holding back her screams of pleasure, her body wound so tight she could barely breathe. Grady pressed his mouth to her ear.

"Let me hear you, princess," he rasped, his fingers twisting in a come-hither motion, a low chuckle rumbling from his chest as she came undone. He watched her orgasm, her walls clenching around him as she climaxed, screaming his name.

Grady opened his jeans and pulled his hard length free, stroking himself as he fucked her with his fingers, the head of his cock rubbing against her inner thighs, smearing cum all over her. He eased his fingers out of her, slid his hands under her, lifted her up, and lowered her onto his throbbing shaft. He buried himself inside her, filling her completely.

"Hold on, baby," he growled.

Caitlin wrapped her arms around him while he grabbed her waist and yanked her forward, flexing his hips at the same time. She dug her fingers into his shoulders and held tight as he pulled her down to meet him, pumping wildly into her. She rode him hard as he urged her on, enticing her to move faster, to ride him harder, to *fuck* him harder.

Grady's face was between her breasts, biting, licking, and sucking every inch of her skin he could reach. He squeezed her ass while his cock was so deep inside her that his pelvic bone pressed against her clit. It didn't take long before she came unglued for the second time, plunging over the edge, the orgasm pulsating through her, the slick of her juices covering him.

Caitlin was ready to collapse, but Grady was insatiable, slamming into her repeatedly, his feet braced against the floor as his hips snapped up to meet hers, obscene moans falling from his lips. She felt another orgasm coming, right on the heels of the last one. A high keening noise escaped her as he fucked her into oblivion.

Grady's hips jerked several times, then he came, his body tensing as a shudder ran through him. He loosened the tight grip he had on her, pulling her against his chest to kiss her, his fingers tangled in her hair.

She fell into his arms with her head on his shoulder. He rubbed her back, his touch gentle, his lips on her jaw. Caitlin could have fallen asleep right there.

Grady kissed her temple and hugged her close. "Too much?"

"Hell, no." She giggled. "That was freaking amazing." She sat up and looked at him. "Why don't you come upstairs? Stay the night."

"Hm, are you sure?"

She nodded. "Yeah, I'm sure. My father isn't here to have a heart attack if he sees you coming out of my room in the morning."

Grady chuckled. "Which is why you usually stay at my place." He kissed her. "Yeah, I'll spend the night."

She wrapped her arms around his neck and gazed up at him. "I love you."

He grinned. "I know." His nose brushed against hers as his hands plunged into her hair. "You know, I've been thinking. Maybe you should think about staying at my house on a more permanent basis."

She sat up straight. "Grady McCarthy, are you asking me to move in with you?"

"Yes, Caitlin O'Reilly, that is exactly what I am asking. Will you live with me?"

"You bet your ass I will!" She giggled. "Took you long enough."

Grady stood up with her in his arms. "You're a pain in my ass, you know that, right?"

"Yeah, but that's why you love me."

He helped her straighten her clothes, then he buttoned his pants. When he was done, he grabbed her, hugged her close, and whispered in her ear.

"That's why I'm going to marry you."

Epilogue
Angus Hayes

Six Hours Earlier

Angus's footsteps echoed in the vast, cold, empty space of the hangar. His heart pounded so hard his chest ached. Or maybe that was the fear consuming him.

He told himself that there was a chance he could talk his way out of this—that Grady might listen to reason.

"Walk," Conor growled behind him.

Angus hadn't realized he'd stopped. Every instinct screamed at him to run. Not that there was anywhere for him to go. The exits were likely cut off by Grady's men.

He was alone. Cornered.

He clenched his fists and walked into the deep recesses of the hangar. This wasn't supposed to be how his life ended. He was supposed to be somewhere far away with the money the Russians gave him. He'd planned everything to the last detail—he'd take a midnight flight to the Caymans, withdraw his cash, and disappear. His bags were packed, sitting on the floor by his front door. His passport was in his jacket pocket, waiting for him to take it out and show it to someone in customs. He was hours from freedom.

Then Conor Sullivan showed up at his apartment just after dark and changed everything.

Twenty feet in front of him, Grady stood still, silent, and scowling under the harsh, white lights in the middle of the hangar. Angus never saw him smile, not even after he got home safely and ended up living happily ever after with Sean O'Reilly's daughter.

Angus froze again, tripping over his own feet as a shiver ran down his spine and his gut churned. His hand went to his throat, and he had to resist the urge to claw at it until he could catch his breath.

Grady's eyes were unreadable, his face unrelentingly composed as he watched Angus walk toward him, tracking him like a predator studying his prey, his gaze hard, appraising.

This wasn't a conversation; they hadn't brought him here to talk. This was retribution.

"Mr. McCarthy," he murmured, his hollow voice barely cutting through the suffocating silence of the immense hangar. He stopped in front of the elder mobster.

Grady tilted his head, one eyebrow raised. He glanced over Angus's shoulder at the man standing behind him.

"Thank you, Conor," Grady said. "Wait outside for me."

Angus didn't take his eyes off Grady as Conor's footsteps receded, and a door closed somewhere off to his left. Sweat dripped down the middle of his back, and his hands were clammy. He cleared his throat, opened his mouth, then snapped it shut again.

"Are you ready to explain yourself, Angus?" Grady asked. The sound was so low, so menacing, Angus's blood ran cold.

He swallowed past the lump rising in his throat. The sharp, metallic taste of fear filled his mouth. Grady knew. He'd always known. Angus had suspected the family knew what he had done, but those seven words sealed his fate. For the last six months, Grady had watched Angus, letting him sweat, dragging him along, keeping him hanging by a thread. Toying with him, playing with him. Psychological warfare.

There was no point in lying, no reason to try to weasel his way out of any repercussions. Every scenario Angus had rehearsed in his head, every justification for his actions, crumbled under Grady's scrutiny. The weight of what he'd done pressed on him, tightening like a noose around his neck. If he confessed, admitted his mistake, maybe he could walk away from this.

"I'm sorry, Mr. McCarthy," Angus said. "Please try to understand." He tried to keep the tremor out of his voice as he spoke, but he knew he still sounded pathetic and whiny as he begged for his life.

Grady snorted and his scowl deepened. "Understand? Tell me what I'm supposed to understand."

Angus shook his head. "I had to do it. Once the Russians had a hold of me, I couldn't break free. They … they wouldn't take no for an answer. The money was good, more than I'd ever seen in a lifetime. Especially if I stayed where I was, some guy behind a desk. No respect, no future. Nothing but small-time stuff. I was destined for mediocrity. I wanted more. When the Russians offered to give it to me, I took it. You would have done the same thing."

Grady shifted, his muscles tensing. Angus braced himself for a blow, but nothing came. When Grady tipped his head to the side, Angus heard the distinctive crack of his neck popping.

"I would never betray my family. You betrayed us for *money*," he spat. "Caitlin almost died because you wanted cash?"

A flash of anger bubbled up. "What the hell do you know? You're the best friend, the one who has been by Sean O'Reilly's side his whole life. And Declan is the anointed one, guaranteed to take over the business when his father-in-law is gone. Me, I'm nothing. I deserved more. So, I went out and got it. No one can blame me for that." As soon as the words left his mouth, he wished he could take them back.

Grady didn't respond, didn't blink. He let the silence stretch between them, drawing it out until Angus was suffocating under the weight of what he said. He tried to fill the void, words rushing out of him in an effort to bring Grady around to his side.

"I did everything O'Reilly asked of me. The stupid errands, the meaningless jobs, while you—" He gasped, desperate for air. "You got respect. I got scraps."

Grady took a measured step closer, his arms crossed over his chest, his face set in that infamous, perpetual scowl.

"How?"

Angus shook his head. "What do you mean, how?"

"How did you find us?" Grady snapped. "We switched the phones; we stayed off the grid. You didn't know about the safe house. How did you find it? How did you know Caitlin was at Finn's club?"

"Jesus Christ," Angus muttered. "You're so fucking stupid. It was the GPS in your Bronco. I've tracked the family vehicles for years. All of them. Whenever the

Bronco moved, I knew where it was. It was easy. All I had to do was call the Russians and tell them where to find you."

"How much did they give you?"

Angus shrugged. "It wasn't much."

"Don't fucking lie to me." He was so calm that he didn't raise his voice. "How much?"

Angus looked at the ground and stammered, "T-two million."

"So, your loyalty has a price tag?" Grady asked.

"You don't get it," Angus grumbled. Anger mixed with fear surged through him, and tears filled his eyes. He was justified in what he did. He was. If he could make Grady see that, maybe he could walk away unscathed. "I finally mattered to someone. The Russians *needed* me. I earned their respect."

"You think that was respect?" Grady shook his head. "You think they needed you? Bullshit. You were a pawn. They used you, and then they threw you away. Do you think if you called Sokolov right now, he'd save you? Come to your rescue? If you do, you're delusional."

Angus groaned. "You're wrong."

Grady laughed, a full-throated, deep laugh. "It was nothing more than a business transaction to the Russians. A paltry amount paid for information. They won't even bat an eye when they find out you're dead."

A bead of sweat trickled down Angus's temple. His anger gave way to raw, desperate fear. Dead. Jesus Christ, he was going to die. He glanced behind him at the towering metal doors at the end of the hangar, doors that had been opened a few minutes ago. There was nowhere to go if he ran.

The scrape of a shoe on the floor drew his attention back to Grady. He had inched a few steps closer, so close to Angus he could smell his cologne.

Angus raised his hands and stumbled back a step, the words spilling out of him in a desperate rush. "Grady, please. I … I made a mistake. I see that now. Let me … let me fix it. Give me a chance to make things right."

"You're right, you made a mistake," the elder mobster said, so matter-of-factly, one would have thought he was reciting a grocery list. "You traded family loyalty for money. You sold us out because your pride was wounded." The corner of his mouth twitched up in an evil smirk. "There is no going back from betrayal."

It happened so quickly that Angus didn't see it coming. Grady swung, his fist connecting with Angus's jaw, the crack of the punch reverberating through his whole body. He dropped to his hands and knees, his ears ringing, his face aching. When he looked up, Grady hit him again, splitting his lip. Another punch and his eye closed. He fell over with a groan, his blood dripping on the floor.

His heart hammered in his chest, and his last remnant of courage dissipated as Grady put his hand inside his jacket and drew his gun.

"Wait! Please, Grady, wait!" Angus struggled to sit up, scooting backward as he did. "I'll do anything you ask." He hated to beg, but he had no choice. "You don't … you don't have to do this. I was wrong. Let me prove my loyalty to you. I swear I won't mess up again."

Grady's expression didn't change. He stared at Angus, his eyes as cold as steel as he spoke. "It's too late."

"I'm sorry," Angus whispered.

"Sorry doesn't fix the betrayal." His finger tightened on the trigger. "You earned this, Angus. And now, you'll get what's coming to you."

The gunshot ripped the empty hangar, a brutal, deafening sound that echoed off the walls. The pain hit the center of his chest, a white-hot, searing shock of intense agony spreading through him as Angus toppled over. His last thoughts were a chaotic whirlwind of regret, sorrow, and bitterness. The world around him dimmed, the air sucked into a vacuum of silence.

The last thing he saw was Grady turning and walking away without a backward glance, leaving him to die on the floor of the empty hangar.

The End

Book Club Questions

1. How does Caitlin's upbringing as a mobster's daughter shape her actions and outlook on life? Do you think her desire to stay out of the family business was realistic, given her circumstances?

2. How does the forbidden nature of Caitlin and Grady's relationship intensify the stakes in the story? Does the age gap and their backgrounds add depth to their connection or create more challenges?

3. Grady is loyal to Caitlin's father and the family business. At what point do you think Grady's duty to protect Caitlin became something deeper, and what risks did he face in choosing her over his obligations?

4. Trust is a key element in Caitlin and Grady's journey. How do the betrayals by family members and rival mobsters affect Caitlin and Grady's relationship?

5. How does the tension between the O'Reillys and the rival mob family impact the story's plot and the characters' choices?

6. How do Caitlin and Grady change throughout the novel? Do you think they became stronger and more united because of the challenges, or did the danger expose cracks in their resolve?

7. How do power dynamics play out in Caitlin and Grady's relationship and within the mob families? Do you think either Caitlin or Grady is truly free to make their own decisions, or are they influenced by forces beyond their control?

8. Without revealing the end of the book, what did you think of the final decisions Caitlin and Grady made? Can you imagine a future for them, given the risks of their world?

Author Bio

Mimi Francis is a sassy and confident romance writer known for her steamy tales of passion that leave readers breathless. Mimi's love for writing began when she was a teenager, and she honed her craft by penning countless short stories and journaling. As an adult, she turned to fan fiction as an outlet for her need to write. But it wasn't until she started writing romance novels that Mimi truly found her niche. Her books are filled with sizzling chemistry, well-developed characters, and laugh-out-loud humor.

When she's not busy crafting her latest heart-stopping romance, Mimi can be found sipping margaritas and indulging in her favorite Marvel movies. She's a self-proclaimed fangirl who can't get enough of superheroes and epic battles. But her true obsession lies with the TV show *Supernatural*, which she has watched from beginning to end more times than she cares to admit.

Mimi is also a wife, mother, and grandmother, as well as a loving dog mom to four adorable Shih Tzus named Sebastian, Sadie, Sasha, and Sophie. Her furry companions keep her company while she writes. They provide endless entertainment with their playful antics.

Connect with Mimi on Instagram, Threads, and Facebook at @author.mimi.francis, on TikTok at @authormimifrancis, or on her website mimifrancis.com.

**Discover more at
4HorsemenPublications.com**

10% off using HORSEMEN10

www.ingramcontent.com/pod-product-compliance
Lightning Source LLC
Chambersburg PA
CBHW021038310726
48969CB00006B/1716